No Time for Goodbye

By Marion Myles

* * *

Copyright © June 2018 Marion Myles

All rights reserved.

This is a work of fiction. Any resemblance to actual events or any persons, living or dead, is entirely coincidental.

* * *

Edited by Kathy Case

Cover by Robin Ludwig Design Inc.

Copywriting by Carol Eastman

* * *

Join the [Marion Myles VIP Reader List](#) and be the first to hear about new releases and special offers!

* * *

Dedication

To RDM – first reader, biggest supporter, finder of book titles.

Prologue

He hadn't planned to kill her.

He stared down into her blank eyes, and a thrill tickled his belly when he realized the last thing she'd seen before dying had been him. Only him. For a few glorious moments, he had been the most important person in her life.

Now she could never leave him. Would never leave him. She belonged to him and he to her. An eternal bond.

Yes, yes, yes. This was how it was meant to be. If only she'd understood. If only she'd listened. The ugly scene from before was already fading from his mind. He'd come to save her in her hour of need, offering a way out and a path to true happiness. She'd told him no. Told him he was sick and needed help.

Gently, so gently, he brushed a few strands of hair from her face and traced a fingertip across her cheekbone. Her beauty was breathtaking. Sometimes it hurt just to look at her, but not now. Not when she was finally his.

He pulled her skirt down and twisted it back into place and straightened her blouse. Where the buttons had been ripped away, he settled the fabric together as best he could. Then he took her hand in his, turned her wrist, bent down, and kissed her palm.

Struck by a sudden idea, he crawled around the area on his hands and knees searching for the red velvet box. Very little moonlight filtered through the leaves and he was deep enough into the woods that none of the lights from the park reached the clearing. *It has to be here,* he thought with mounting panic as he moved farther away from where his beloved lay.

At last his knee struck the small solid object, and he clutched it to his chest for a moment before standing and walking back to the girl. While kneeling down, he flipped open the lid of the box and pulled out the emerald ring.

"My gift to you, my love," he said softly. "This time you won't get angry, will you? You won't tell me I'm delusional. This time you'll finally understand we are meant to be together."

Lifting her left hand, he slid the jewel onto her ring finger. He'd imagined this moment so many times. Not like this, of course. Yet somehow, even in his darkest hours, he'd absolutely believed she would wear his ring. Be his wife. His heart burst with love. Tears poured down his cheeks.

"I'm going to take good care of you, my darling," he murmured.

He bent at the knees and gathered her up, grunting with the effort, and eventually settled her over his shoulder in a fireman's lift.

Slowly, careful not to jostle her, he made his way out of the forest.

Chapter One

After twenty-eight years of bouncing from institution to institution and place to place, Mia Reeves had unexpectedly found home.

She'd moved to the town of Dalton eight months earlier thinking it would be nothing more than another short stop before wanderlust sent her back out on the road again. But she'd settled in so quickly, and with such ease, she could no longer imagine living anywhere else. In fact, before the end of the second month, she'd approached the owner of her rental property and negotiated a deal to buy it outright. It seemed she was finally throwing down roots and couldn't have been happier about it.

Now, though, as she drove slowly down Main Street, her stomach clenched to the point of pain. Even though she consciously tried to control her breathing, it came out in short, shallow gasps.

What she was contemplating was insane. Seriously and utterly insane.

The best case scenario was ridicule and being forever branded as a crazy woman. Of course, she didn't actually know very many people. There was Sherri, who occasionally worked for her and had helped man the jewelry booth this past weekend at the annual spring fair. Gabriel owned the local diner, and they sometimes exchanged small talk while she waited for her take-out once or twice a month when she treated herself to a night off from cooking. Plus, there was sweet Mrs. Bird who ran the post office and always asked Mia how she was. Not exactly a bustling group of friends but a girl had to start somewhere, didn't she?

To Mia's mind, it would be bad enough losing even these tenuous relationships, but oh, it could be so much worse. She was potentially opening herself up to charges or fines. If they were really vindictive, the threat of six months in jail.

Still, she had to do it.

The police station was only a block away now. It was early enough that hardly any of the stores were open, and the sidewalks had very little foot traffic. Gabe's Diner was doing their usual brisk business, and she'd seen more than a few heads in the window when she rolled by Bean Time café; otherwise, she was virtually alone.

Mia's hands tightened on the steering wheel. It wasn't too late to turn back.

She shook her head. No. The decision was already made. For whatever reason, this echo had reached out from the past and chosen her. Now she felt compelled to do what she could for the young woman. A stranger, yes, but also someone through whom she'd experienced first-hand the worst kind of pain and terror.

Besides, this was her town now and she, Mia Reeves, was a brand new person. The kind of person who walked the straight and narrow, and lived the life of a good upstanding citizen. The girl from the vision may be years dead, but she deserved justice and Mia might be the only person who could get it for her.

Flicking on her indicator, she made the turn into the parking lot and cruised up to the police station. The front of the building was surprisingly modern wood and glass. Two black and white cruisers sat parked in the first row of spaces, along with three civilian cars. She steered her SUV into the empty slot closest to the front door and turned off the engine.

Closing her eyes, she took a final, bracing breath. Mia reassured herself that even if she was detained for some time, her dogs would be fine. The doggie door was open, the food bowls full, and plenty of water bowls were scattered about the place. They had a large, fenced yard and enough provisions to see them through several days without her. In case worst came to worst, she'd left a key hidden beneath the pot of azaleas by the side door. Surely, Sherri wouldn't mind going over and checking on the pack for her.

It was still a mystery how she'd ended up with four dogs. She'd never wanted a pet. Well, maybe for about five minutes when she was a little kid, but she'd soon learned they needed a dependable, trustworthy person. Mia surely wasn't that. At least she hadn't been.

But then along came Mac. She'd found him on the side of the road. A tall, skinny Doberman covered in scabs and frightened out of his mind. Somehow she couldn't say no.

That had been back in Altoona. By the time she'd hit the highway four months later, hip bones and vertebrae were no longer prominent features along Mac's back, and his coat was coming in shiny as a seal's. He loved her with an unconditional and unstinting loyalty that took her breath away. She'd sooner die than be parted from him.

It was Mac who'd found Layla near their new accommodations in Savannah, Georgia. She was young, barely more than a puppy, and part of a local animal shelter adoption program being staged one weekend in a nearby park. Mac had dragged Mia over to the portable pen and pushed his nose through the gap in the wire to lick Layla's golden muzzle before swiveling his head up and gazing questioningly at Mia. She cursed under her breath as she looked into those soft brown eyes. Next thing Mia knew, she was signing on the dotted line and bringing the yellow lab mix home with them.

For the following six months, Mia had settled into being the parent of two large dogs. Where Mac was serious, the self-appointed head of security and always on guard, Layla was really only looking for a good time. She loved to play fetch, pull the rope, and wrestle for hours without tiring. With her, Mac, at first befuddled by the foreign activities, soon started to romp and frolic like a young pup. It brought a lump to Mia's throat seeing the lanky Doberman letting go and enjoying life to such an extent.

It seemed they were complete. A family. The first proper one of Mia's life.

But then Mac went and did it again. Shortly after they'd moved to Unionville, he disappeared from the back yard. Mia was frantic. In the time since she'd rescued him, the dog had barely ever been more than jumping distance from her, and suddenly he was gone. Over the fence, no less.

Taking Layla, she walked the streets calling his name for hours on end with a ball of dread in her gut and tears in her eyes. Layla, in her typically happy-go-lucky way, sniffed at the grass, bounced at passers-by, and generally behaved as though she hadn't a care in the world. When darkness fell, Mia finally turned for home. Refusing to let loose the tears, she swiped angrily at her eyes.

She'd go out again in a few hours, she told herself. She'd make up flyers and paper the town with his picture. She'd call around to all the vets and animal shelters. He had to be somewhere. This was not how their story would end.

Turning up the path to her rental unit, Layla tugged on the leash and let out a victorious bark. There, sitting on the dark front porch, was Mac. Sprinting to him, Mia dropped to her knees and threw her arms around his neck.

"Don't ever do that again," she hiccupped while fighting down a sob.

Lifting her face, she let him lick at a wayward tear. It was only then she felt a small furry body pressed in by her thigh. Looking down, she saw the long nose and floppy ears of a miniature dachshund. He crawled into her lap and with a surprisingly deep sigh, melted against her.

Once inside the house, Mia found a name tag, Tucker, and a phone number on the frayed nylon collar.

The owner lived several miles away on the other side of town and hadn't even noticed he was missing. Fighting off Mac's bitter recriminations, she drove the little dog home and placed him in the hands of an unpleasant middle-aged woman whose four rambunctious boys apparently laid waste to the house behind her.

"Shut the hell up," the woman bellowed over her shoulder while the dachshund trembled and looked beseechingly up at Mia. "Danny, if I go in there and find you flicking lit matches at your brothers, you're dead meat. I mean it. Colt, get out here. Your stupid rat dog ran away again. I told you he can't be left loose in the yard. Put him on the chain next time."

She practically threw the dog at a boy of about ten and slammed the door in Mia's face without so much as a thank you or a goodbye. *You're welcome,* Mia mumbled under her breath while trudging back to the car and wondering if she'd just made a colossal mistake. What kind of life did that poor little dog have in that Godforsaken house?

Two days later, Mac went on another rescue mission, bringing the tiny sausage dog home in the late afternoon. This time when Mia phoned, she asked the woman point blank if she wanted Tucker back.

"Hell, no," she answered. "I never wanted that thing in the first place. Colt's bastard of a father got him without asking me. Can't manage to pay child support most months, but somehow comes up with the fifteen hundred to buy the yappy little dirtbag. I looked it up online. That's how much they cost. I hate dogs. Nothing but trouble. You keep him. I doubt the kids will even notice he's gone." She slammed the phone down, and that was that.

When Layla and Tucker paired up like long-lost soulmates, Mia was initially concerned for Mac, hating for him to feel left out. But Mac, far from being hurt, seemed to find the situation very much to his liking. He now had a small pack to rule and keep safe and was content in his role as guardian of the dogs. He played with them from time to time. Mostly, though, he stayed glued to Mia's side during the long hours she crafted her crystal jewelry.

It wasn't until a year later, when Mia and the pack were moving to Dalton, that Mac brought another dog into the fold. It happened at a truck stop on I75 about fifty miles outside Knoxville. Mia was fueling up, and the dogs, anxious to stretch their legs, leapt about inside the Ford Escape. All of a sudden, Mac stood stock still staring out the driver's side window past Mia. She thought maybe he'd seen a man with a mustache. The reminder of his former abusive owner always sent poor

Mac into a tailspin. Mia mentally geared up to soothe the big guy.

But there was no man. No mustache. What she saw was a tiny Pomeranian tied to the edge of the gas station booth with what appeared to be bungee cords.

"No, Mac," she sighed. "No more dogs."

The animal probably belonged to the attendant anyway. And so what if the dog's fur was dingy gray and matted into dreadlocks in places. She couldn't save every damned animal on the planet.

She purposely kept her eyes adverted when she got back in the truck and parked on the opposite side of the large parking area before allowing the dogs to jump out for a quick walk. But Mac was apparently part mule, for no sooner had his feet hit the asphalt than he was dragging Mia and the other two dogs straight back to the gas pumps.

Layla and Tucker soon got in on the act, and even though Mia strained against them with all her might, there was nothing she could do but half run along behind while they towed her straight over to the tiny dog. In an uncharacteristic display of submission that had Mia's mouth gaping open, Mac dropped to the ground. Head bowed, he bellied over to the sad little creature. He sniffed her delicately then licked her all over while she squirmed with delight.

The bored teenage girl behind the counter managed to look up from her iPhone long enough to tell Mia the dog had been abandoned four days ago. Someone was supposed to have called animal services, but so far no one had come along to take her away. There was no collar. No name tag. No way to know where she'd come from.

During the exchange with the attendant, Mac hadn't left the Pom's side. Mia came out, letting the door slam shut behind her and rubbed a weary hand across her face. It was obvious she had to take her. What else could she do? Unclamping the bungee from around the fragile little neck, she scooped up the almost weightless dog and stomped back to her vehicle while the rest of her pack followed along as docile as lambs.

In the end, it had been no trouble. Little No Name had slurped up a huge amount of water, enough to make her tummy swell like a balloon, before collapsing onto the back seat and closing her eyes. She didn't move until Mia pulled into a Motel 6 later that night. Even then, she sat quietly waiting to be told what to do as if fearing any wrong move could see her abandoned again.

Mia shut herself in the bathroom with the newest addition, and taking a pair of scissors, she ruthlessly hacked away all the dirty, tangled hair. A shampoo and conditioning treatment later, the dog was closer to snowy white. Although the haircut was hardly flattering, her little coal black eyes seemed to shine with relief. She licked Mia's hand once as if in thanks then sat quietly awaiting her fate.

"Okay, I guess you're going to need a name," Mia said. "Got any ideas?"

Fifi came to mind, clear as a bell, and so it was she opened the door to the bedroom and introduced the rest of her family to the new version of Fifi the Pomeranian. Mac was immediately and absolutely smitten. From that moment on, the huge lanky Doberman and the seven-pound snowflake dog were inseparable. It was stupid to feel jealous, but when Mia was especially tired or beaten down, she sometimes did anyway.

Once they'd settled in at home, Mia had taken Mac outside, leaving Fifi and the others behind. In the woods at the back of her property, she sat on a stump and waited until Mac stopped sniffing something fascinating on the ground and came to sit beside her. Then, in no uncertain terms, she laid down the law. No more dogs. Four was beyond too many. He stared at her, eyes intent on her face and brought his nose down as if in a slow nod of assent. She could only trust he understood how serious she was, but part of her still worried.

* * *

That meeting of the minds had been eight months ago. So far so good. Mia wished the four of them could be with her right now. She always felt stronger when surrounded by her pack.

Okay, no more stalling. She could and would do this.

Inside the police station, the main lobby was bright and spacious. Every wall was painted a Mediterranean blue, and a fountain bubbled soothingly in the corner surrounded by half a dozen lush, potted plants. Mismatched furniture, the color of sand, and the table appeared to be a piece of reclaimed driftwood. A reception area counter resembled a beautifully tiered pile of wood fashioned to look like a retaining wall at a beach. The whole space gave the impression of a spa or a meditation center and was unlike any government office Mia had ever seen.

Setting her jaw, she walked straight up to the counter and waited while the woman there finished speaking into her headset.

"How can I help you today?" Her voice was pleasant and managed to convey an absolute interest in whatever Mia might have to say.

Looking the receptionist straight in the eye and pushing aside all thoughts of her dogs and the home she loved, Mia gathered every available ounce of courage.

"I have information about a murder," she said.

Chapter Two

Detective Roman Mancini stood sipping a mug of truly awful coffee and staring through the one-way glass at the woman in the interrogation room.

His partner, Kevin Latterly, walked over and joined him. "So that's her, huh? She looks damned calm for someone who says they have information on a murder."

Roman snorted. "Yeah. Makes you wonder, don't it?

"At least she's easy on the eyes," Kevin commented.

"Sometimes the lookers turn out to be the craziest." His brow furrowed, and he turned to stare at his partner. "Whoa, back it up. I thought you were soft in the head over Lisa. She know you're still out window shopping?"

Kevin blushed to the roots of his hair. "Not me, you asshole. I was thinking of you. It's been a while. Too long. Time you got back in the saddle. Or if not in the saddle, at least threw your leg over the horse. Celibacy is not a good look for you. Plus, it makes you mean as a snake. Consider hooking up as a public service and a much-needed gift for your partner."

"Bite me." Roman glanced back at the woman. "Even if I was interested in…mounting up…I'm not so desperate I'd be plucking from the dregs of the lost and found at the police station. Besides, she's not my type."

"I'd wager redheads built like her and biting their sexy pillow lips are the type of every man on the planet."

"You know what? Sometimes you're a total dickwad."

Kevin punched his arm. "Aw, come on. You know you love me."

"Like a venereal disease, that's how I love you." Roman tipped his head toward the interrogation room. "So, you gonna take the lead with her?"

Kevin sighed. "Let me guess, you want me to go in all soft and understanding, right?" He shook his head sorrowfully. "Why do I always have to be the good cop?"

"Because you've been blessed with that wholesome, sweet-as-apple-pie face that makes women, especially, want to spill their guts on the floor for you. You've got to play to your strengths, buddy."

"You do know good cop, bad cop is the worst kind of cliché?"

"Clichés are clichés for a reason. No point in going against a hundred years of cop history. Okay, give me a smile." Kevin curled back his lips in a vicious snarl, snapping his teeth together, and Roman clapped a hand on his shoulder. "Good, all warmed up and ready to go. Let's get this over with and get back to doing the real police work."

Kevin smiled. "Man, I love my job."

* * *

Mia sensed someone watching her. Make that two someones. She worked hard to stay calm and steady and give the impression of being a credible witness, but it wasn't easy. The serenity of the main lobby had given away to the more familiar drab and depressing interior of the police station. She hated cop shops. They reminded her of every child services office she'd been in, and even worse, the hospitals.

So many hospitals.

This interrogation room was as grim as it got. The walls were painted an unfortunate vomit green, and the linoleum floor was a tired grey with a ragged line of rips by the door. In several places, it had worn through and showed the concrete beneath. On her right the wall sported a large, asymmetrical stain. She imagined it might be anything from water damage to coffee to blood. *Probably blood,* she thought, suppressing a shudder.

Purposely, Mia didn't let her eyes stray to the video camera mounted on the tripod. It was trained at the metal table where she sat on an unbelievably uncomfortable wooden chair. Mia doubted the camera was recording, but it made her nervous anyway.

She'd been stuck in the room forever. It was a tactic. She knew damned well there was nothing she could do except wait it out, but she didn't have to like it.

Finally, the door opened, and she glanced at the two men as they entered. The first, blond and blue-eyed with a handsome, friendly face. His counterpart was taller, broader, and all kinds of dark and broody.

The dark-haired man stepped forward. "Ms. Reeves, I'm Detective Mancini. This is my partner, Detective Latterly. We understand you have information about a murder?"

"Well, maybe…I mean, it might not be a murder, but it's to do with a girl who went missing a while ago." The two men slid onto chairs opposite her.

"Okay, why don't you tell us what you know."

Mia swallowed once. *Stay cool,* she coached herself. "I found this bracelet."

Reaching into her purse, she pulled out a swath of bubble wrap and placed it on the table. She unrolled it to reveal a delicate piece of jewelry. Silver and designed as a series of interconnected hearts, the tiny solid silver heart hung down at the midpoint with initials A R inscribed inside the tracing of yet another heart.

Detective Mancini was a smooth one, all right. If she hadn't been studying him so closely, she might have missed the expression of horrified shock flick over his face or the way his hands clenched into fists on the table. His knuckles showed bone white against his tanned skin.

Detective Latterly merely looked down at the bracelet with a measure of curiosity before glancing back at Mia. "I'm afraid I don't understand. How do you think this connects to a murder?"

"Well, I've heard the stories about a girl who—"

"Where did you get this?" Detective Mancini cut her off.

"I found it in the woods at the edge of Carlton Park."

"It was just lying there?" he pressed. "Where exactly? Be specific."

Her eyes flicked to Detective Latterly who watched his partner in surprise. "It was pretty far in…maybe a hundred feet or so from the parking lot. I could show you."

"You came in here to tell us you found a bracelet deep in the woods by the park? No offense, Miss, but maybe some kid lost it. Why didn't you put an ad in the local paper?" Detective Latterly asked.

Before Mia could answer, Detective Mancini cleared his throat. "Could you excuse us?"

He jerked his head at Detective Latterly and sprang to his feet. When the door slammed behind them, Mia was once again alone in the room. She released a slow, steady breath. It was going to be fine. Detective Mancini was taking the bait. All she had to do was stay true to her story. She'd show them the spot in the woods, and then she'd be out of it, free and clear.

After a further hour of questioning, during which Mia stuck stubbornly to her story, it was decided that the detectives would follow her out to Carlton Park. Mia pulled into a parking spot beside the walking trail and braced herself for the final step of her plan. She got out of the SUV. The men, both wearing serious, grim faces, joined her near the edge of the forest.

"In through here," Mia said, pointing straight into the heavily treed area.

"What made you go into the woods?" Detective Mancini asked.

"Um…well…I was a vendor at the fair, and it was a long, tiring weekend. Lots of people. After we packed up on Sunday night, I guess I felt like going for a walk to clear my head before heading home."

"But it was dark by then," Detective Latterly said, sounding doubtful.

"I'm a big girl, Detective. I'm not afraid of the dark." Her tone came across as amused.

She led them deep into the woods, ducking below branches and weaving between the trees as though guided by a homing beacon. Finally, she stopped beside a felled tree.

"I found it right here," she said, pointing to the ground beside the rotting wood.

"Let me make sure I've got this straight," Detective Mancini said. "You've been working all weekend at the fair. It's dark. You're all packed up ready to go home, and you suddenly decide to go for a walk in the woods where you happen to find a bracelet beside an old log." Skepticism dripped from every word while his eyes stayed steady on her face.

Squaring her shoulders, she defiantly held his gaze. "I tripped," she shot back. "On the log. Went right down on my hands and knees. That's when I found it."

"And it was sitting there on top of the ground in plain sight?"

"No, of course not. When I dug into the earth to get up, I could feel something bumpy under the rotten leaves, so I scraped the dirt back and there it was."

Detectives Mancini and Latterly shared a long look. She knew her story sounded hinky, but what other option did she have? There was no way in hell she was telling them the truth, and this was all she could think of to get them looking for Anita. Mia stood silently watching while they explored the area. Once the detectives had satisfied themselves there was nothing else to see, they all returned to the parking lot.

After pulling the keys out of her back pocket, she clicked the lock on her Escape. "Maybe I shouldn't have wasted your time with this, but I figure if it helps bring answers for a missing girl, it would be worth it," she said.

"If you think of anything else, no matter how small it seems, make sure to call. Here's my card," Detective Latterly said, extending a hand her direction.

Detective Mancini stepped forward, and opened the car door, gesturing her into the driver's seat. He pulled the seatbelt loose and passed it to her. "You buckle up now and make sure to drive safe." His eyes locked with hers as he leaned just enough to crowd into her personal space. "We may have some follow-up questions. Please let us know if you're leaving town for any reason. You have a nice day now."

His words were all Southern softness, but they came out like a warning. She stared back boldly, not blinking, before closing her door and starting the engine. As she drove slowly away, she watched in the rearview as the two men continued to stand like sentinels at the edge of the parking lot.

"You believe her?" Roman asked.

"Not for a second. She must think we're morons. No way someone goes walking through a pitch black forest and trips over a piece of jewelry."

"Then how the hell did she get my sister's bracelet?" Roman's voice was laced with anguish. "Anita was wearing it the day she disappeared. That was one of the details the police held back. No one knows other than family and close friends and whoever helped her disappear. Now, ten years later, this woman turns up pretending she found it. She has to be involved somehow or know someone who was. "

"And how come today she asked to speak to us specifically? She knew damned well it was your sister," Kevin said.

"Word's gonna spread faster than wildfire." Roman sighed. "This will kill my mama. It's not like it ever went away but, shit, something like this opens up the wound all over again."

"I'm sorry, man. This sucks large and wide." Keven glanced back toward the forest. "Still, maybe it is something. Wouldn't you rather have answers?"

Roman shook his head. "I don't know. Sometimes I imagine Anita's somewhere else, living a great life. She'd be turning thirty this year. Hard to believe she's been gone all this time."

"One thing's for sure, we're going to be looking at Mia Reeves and looking at her hard," Kevin said. The grim tone of his voice matched the expression on his face.

"Oh, hell yeah. You drive, okay? I'm going to start running her right now. If she's got so much as an overdue parking ticket, I'll have her back in the interrogation room so fast her head will spin."

Chapter Three

Not until Mia turned onto her gravel driveway and her house came into view did the knots of tension in her shoulders and neck finally loosen their grip. It had only been five hours since she'd left, but it might as well have been five days and nights without sleep based on how drained she felt.

The dogs ran the fence line in the side yard, leaping and barking in joyous welcome, and she couldn't remember ever seeing a more beautiful sight. When she got out of the car, they arrowed toward the doggie door and inside, throwing themselves at her en masse the minute she stepped in the house. She stumbled back against the wall and sank to the floor letting them crawl over her, lick her, bump against her.

This was where she truly belonged. This was her heart. She'd done what she'd had to do at the police station, what her brand new conscience insisted was the right thing. Now she could let it go and relax back into her happy, quiet, peaceful life.

"I think it's about time we went for a walk," she announced. "Come on boys and girls. Let's go clear our heads."

The dogs ran out ahead of her, jostling each other gleefully while they galloped across the lawn. Mia sighed, took a deep breath, and raised her face to the sky. The hot rays of the afternoon sun warmed her inside and out.

She wandered along the gardens, deadheading flowers, pulling the odd rogue weed, and checking the perimeter of the vegetable patch. This spring she'd fought a bitter war with the rabbits. When she saw the fence was still intact, she couldn't help smiling. Yes, the little victories in life made it all worthwhile.

Mia had plans to expand her gardening and was in the process of ordering equipment for the small greenhouse. The idea was to experiment with aeroponic growing. The technology excited her with its highly efficient methods that didn't require soil and only used a fraction of the water when compared with traditional gardening.

Looking back at her house, she sighed happily. She'd loved this place from the first moment she'd set eyes on it, and now it was all hers. The property was large. Not farm large, but fifteen acres was the perfect size for her and the dogs. Most of the land was open except a small grouping of trees at the back of the property through which a lazy stream wound its way. The dogs loved it back there, so she made a point to walk her land every day.

Mia's log house was set so far back from the road, she had the sense of living in the remote wilderness. Yet, the property was still only a couple miles out of town. When she'd first moved to Dalton, weeks had passed with her only human contact being the UPS and FedEx delivery drivers who arrived on her doorstep on an almost daily basis.

Lately, though, she'd started venturing into town once or twice a week to personally pick up groceries and other supplies rather than ordering everything online. People were friendly here. It was the South, after all. At first, Mia had been annoyed by the questions, the casual interest, but gradually she'd learned the art of small talk. Now she could manage conversations about the weather or complain about the potholes like any of the natural-born townsfolk.

"Layla, Tucker, get over here right now," she shouted, catching sight of them digging by the hostas. "I mean it. If you harm so much as a one petal on a single plant, you guys are in the dog house. Overnight. With no food or water. Because that's how much I love my plants."

The pair ran back to her with muddy paws and guilty expressions, like teenagers caught smoking under the bleachers at the back of the school. Mac pushed in at Mia's side, claiming his place of dominance, and they returned to the house a touch more soberly than they'd burst out of it moments ago.

"Okay, guys, it's about time I got to work. I'm so behind it's not funny."

The dogs arranged themselves around Mia's workroom off the kitchen, stretching out in slivers of afternoon sun and luxuriating in the added warmth. It took almost an hour to unpack from the weekend trade fair, a job she'd neglected last night while researching the disappearance of Anita Mancini and preparing her story for the police, complete with prop.

When her workspace was finally set to rights, she booted up her laptop and opened the orders file. In anticipation of how tired she'd be after working the spring fair, she'd thankfully scheduled a light day for today. Even still she was dangerously behind. Six items were in the queue, which meant they had to be completed, packed, and ready for pickup by nine o'clock tomorrow morning.

Yawning, she stretched her arms overhead and cleared her mind. The first order was for Coral. Mia remembered the conversation she'd had with the client in need of inner peace after going through a difficult divorce. She swiveled in the chair and reached into the appropriate tray. Closing her eyes, she let her hand wander over and among the stones.

It took longer than usual, probably due to lingering stress from the questioning at the police station. Finally, one of the stones made itself known, warming under her fingers and vibrating ever so slightly. She closed her hand over it and held it against her chest. Oh, yes, this one would do nicely for sad Mrs. Brooks.

Mia worked on into the night, taking breaks after finishing each piece to clear her mind and emotions. She fed the dogs, brewed cups of tea, and even took another short walk right after moonrise. Each diversion served to separate her from the previous crystal so she could start open and fresh for the next client. By two o'clock the final necklace was nestled in bubble wrap and ready to be sent to its new owner.

At last, she crawled into bed. Despite sheer and utter exhaustion, she was unable to sleep. Her mind tumbled and twirled like a gymnast. She turned to her tried and true technique of directing thoughts to quietly babbling brooks, fields of wildflowers blowing gently in the breeze, the calm surface of a mountain lake. Yet, somehow it was Detective Roman Mancini who pushed his way front and center in her mind's eye.

She knew well the tidal wave of emotions he'd been riding ever since her arrival with the bracelet. After the initial shock, he'd kept himself in tightly controlled check, but no matter how flat and detached he came off, his eyes showed the toll of a decade's worth of rage and grief. Mia had to remind herself it wasn't her fault. She'd only done what she had to do both for herself and for Anita Mancini.

* * *

Roman stood by the yellow police tape, overseeing the technicians sweeping the area in the woods where Mia Reeves had brought them two days ago. He didn't expect they'd find anything. Mostly because every cop instinct he had told him Ms. Reeves was full of shit.

What he couldn't figure was why she was doing it. What could she possibly have to gain by coming in with this cockamamie story about finding Anita's bracelet? The only thing that made sense was she was somehow involved in whatever had happened to his sister.

In his experience, guilt was the wild card. The random factor. Lord knew it didn't seem to affect the hardened criminals, but for the average Joe who'd done something stupid, made a single, fatal mistake, it could nibble away at them until they broke.

If this Mia woman was trying to atone for her sins, it was admirable all right, but he'd still nail her ass to the wall and make her pay to the full extent of the law, for whatever part she'd had in ripping his family and his world to pieces.

He sighed heavily when he saw his mother stepping through the woods toward him. She was bound to find out sooner or later, but he'd been fervently hoping for later, like next month later, after he'd closed the file on this stupid woman and her false claims.

"You know you can't go in there," he said in a resigned sort of voice.

Molly Mancini, all four feet, eleven and three-quarter inches of her, stopped long enough to pin her son with a withering stare. "I'm a cop's mama, and I'm not stupid. Of course, I can't go tromping around contaminating a potential crime scene. But I can stand here and watch, can't I?" She continued the final few steps and stood beside him. "You should have told me," she said, poking him in the ribs.

"Why? So you and Dad could get upset over nothing. This is gonna turn out to be another false lead. And there's been too many of them over the years. We can't keep getting our hopes up because it kills us a little more each time."

"I don't care if we have a hundred more false leads. I want you to promise you won't keep anything from your papa and me. Anita was our baby girl. Our last child. We love you and Lina with all our hearts. Having only the two of you would have been enough, but there was once a third. I'll never have any peace until we find our missing girl. Now tell me why the police are looking here."

It wasn't strictly protocol, but Roman explained about Mia and the bracelet and how she supposedly came to find it.

"I know that bracelet," she said, eyes lighting with memory. "Your sister never took it off, not even to shower. Luke gave it to her not a month before…well, before. She was so happy when she showed me. He'd bought it at Tiffany's in the city. It came in one of those special turquoise boxes." When Roman looked blank, she tsk-tsked. "Every girl knows a Tiffany box. And you should, too, my boy. Between you and Lina, I'm never going to have any grandchildren to spoil."

"Mama, Anita could have lost it at the fair that year. Maybe some kid found it and kept it and, then, years later, lost it again. You need to be prepared. This is probably all there is to the story." He gestured with his arm to the two men and three women combing the small area. "Anyway, they're going to be here at least until end of day tomorrow. Then we'll see."

"And who is this Mia Reeves? I don't know her."

"She's the lady who bought old man Jasper's log house outside of town. Haven't seen much of her since she moved in last fall. She's quiet. Keeps to herself. Does something with crystals and sells them online. I'm working on tracing her. Seems to have moved around a lot. I've got feelers out, but so far she's coming up clean." He paused, rubbing his hand along his jaw. "I don't like her. There's something there. Something strange. Something she's not telling us."

"Hmm," was all his mother said, but he knew that expression.

"Don't you dare. You stay away from her. This is police business. And besides, you don't know any of this anyway, remember?"

"You're a good boy, Roman," she said, standing on tiptoes and kissing his cheek. "You come over for dinner tonight after you're done here. I'll make meatloaf and mashed potatoes."

"Maybe…I'll see what time we finish up and let you know."

"I'm going to stand here for a while longer. I won't be in the way," she said softly. "I need to be nearby…in case. You understand, right?"

"Sure, Mama. No problem. I'm here for a bit more myself before heading back to the station. I'll let you know about tonight."

He ducked under the tape and walked over to check in with Donna, one of the techs. Slowly, Roman perused the area, watching as they screened dirt and leaves and took pictures. When he next looked back, his mother was gone, and he let out a breath he didn't realize he'd been holding.

Oh, yeah. Mia Reeves was going to answer for this.

Chapter Four

Just as Roman had predicted, he spent two and a half days standing in the woods and found exactly nothing. Nada. Zippo. Zilch.

He hadn't wanted to admit it, especially to himself, but the whole time a flutter of hope had been swirling in his belly. When he finally walked away from the scene, there was a viscous throbbing behind his eyes. The hope in his stomach had given away to a grinding burn, and his mood was darker than the bottom of the ocean.

Upon arriving at the station, he immediately stomped down to the evidence room and signed out the bracelet. He wanted to look at it again. Back in his office, he unsealed the evidence bag and pulled the piece of jewelry free. The crime scene techs had already pulled prints, only Mia Reeves's, of course, so it was cleared to be handled. He traced the edges of the connecting hearts and opened and closed the clasp. Like his mother, he remembered how thrilled Anita had been when showing off the bracelet as though it was some rare and precious treasure, all the while telling them Luke was The One.

At the time, and through his jaded twenty-two-year-old eyes, he'd thought her unbearably juvenile. Just wait till she went to college, saw all the guys, experienced life a little. He'd doubted she'd still be so ready to settle down with her small town high school sweetheart.

His mind roamed to Luke McNally, now a doctor practicing right here in Dalton, shoulder to shoulder with his father. Maybe in the end, he and Anita would have married exactly as she'd planned. Maybe it would have been her walking two little boys to school every morning instead of Mandy Simmons, another local girl who'd wasted little time swooping in and providing comfort to a shocked and grieving Luke only months after Anita's disappearance.

Roman shook his head violently. Who the hell knew? Not him. Not anyone.

Picking up the bracelet again, he draped it over his palm, flipping it back and forth. The gesture made the little dangling heart dance. Tiffany's, huh? It probably cost a pretty penny for a kid barely out of high school even if he was a doctor's son.

Setting aside the jewelry, he swiveled to his computer and started a search. Yep, even ten years ago it would've set him back a chunk of change and then some. Roman didn't get it. The bracelet looked like any other out there. It could have come from one of those stalls at the local fair for all he knew. It was the same thing with all that high-end shit. Slap a Gucci or a Chanel label on it and people would hand over their first-born without so much as a whimper.

He glanced at the bracelet again. With eyes narrowed, he picked it up and held it to the light. Where was the maker's mark? He scanned each link and found nothing. Turning back to the computer, he did another search and discovered it was from a collection all branded with the words Tiffany and Co. Even using his magnifying glass, he found nothing other than the engraving of Anita's initials.

Interesting.

When the receptionist answered, he asked to be put through to Luke McNally.

"I'm sorry, Dr. McNally is with a patient. Is this a medical emergency?"

"No, not medical," Roman said. "Have him call me when he's free. It's Detective Mancini. Tell him it's important."

He waited, tapping his fingers on the desk and turning over the possibilities in his mind. When the phone rang, he all but sprang at it. "Mancini," he barked.

"Hey, Roman. It's Luke. Martha on the desk said it was urgent."

"Yeah. Thanks for getting back to me. I have a question about the bracelet you bought Anita the summer she disappeared. She told us it was from Tiffany's. Is that right?" Luke's intake of breath was audible, and then the silence hung heavy for several seconds. "Look, it doesn't matter if it was a fake. I couldn't care less, but something's come up, and I need to know."

"It was Tiffany's all right," Luke finally said. "I saved like a madman to buy it. My sister came with me to help pick it out."

"Okay. Good to know. Thanks, man."

"Wait. Why are you asking? Have you found something?" When Roman said nothing, Luke's voice hardened. "I have a right to know. She was my whole life back then. All I cared about was her and getting into med school. You'd better tell me what's going on."

Roman sighed. "Nothing's going on. Next to nothing, in fact. I swear to you."

Replacing the receiver, Roman leaned back in his chair and rubbed a hand along his jaw. So, little Ms. Reeves wasn't as smart as she thought. That Tiffany's slip was a big one. And now he had the perfect excuse to bring her back to the station and turn up the heat.

* * *

Mia was sweating which was completely stupid. For once in her life, she hadn't actually done anything wrong. Thin trickles of moisture rolled down from under her arms, and she fought an incredible urge to dab at her damp hairline. She was back in the interrogation room, and Detectives Latterly and Mancini had been hammering away at her for close to an hour.

"We know it's not Anita's bracelet," Detective Mancini said, as he'd been saying over and over again throughout the questioning. "We know you know more than you're telling us. We're giving you this chance to come clean. Right now. It's a one-time offer. If you don't tell and we find out later you purposely mislead us or held anything back, we'll charge you with PC Section one four eight point five. What is that you ask? Well, that, my lovely lying witness, is a misdemeanor for making a false statement to a police officer. We're talking a thousand dollar fine and up to six months in jail. Could be, depending on the judge, we'll get the green light on an obstruction charge as well. That'll be more fines. More time in a cage."

Mia swallowed and looked away. She wasn't going to tell them what they wanted no matter what they said. Besides, there was absolutely no way to prove otherwise.

"You can threaten me all you want," she said. "All I know is I found the bracelet and I thought it might be something to do with Anita Mancini's disappearance. I can't tell you anything else."

"I've been looking into you, Mia Reeves. It all seems kosher on the surface," Detective Mancini said.

"Yeah," Detective Latterly added. "No trouble. No police record. Parents died in a car crash when you were twenty-three. Good grades in college. Yada Yada Yada."

"But seeing as we both have suspicious minds," Detective Mancini continued, "we couldn't help noticing there was a pretty big space of time where nothing much happened. No address. No phone records. No employment record. No credit card purchases. It was like you dropped off the face of the earth. Poof. Then five years ago, it's whammo, and you're back. Getting yourself a VISA card. Taking driver's tests. Buying a cell phone and a car. Now this house in Dalton. All with cash. It's…curious…you might say."

"I was traveling. Backpacking around Europe. I took jobs under the table here and there to make ends meet. And then I got into making jewelry, and it took off from there. It's not a crime to see the world," she said, forcing herself to meet their accusing eyes.

Detective Mancini smiled wide causing her stomach to bottom out. "Right, jewelry. I'm so glad you brought that up because I almost forgot. See, me and my partner here, we were batting around some ideas about this bracelet when it occurred to us…wait, I should really let him tell this part. Go ahead, Detective Latterly. Tell Ms. Reeves what we were thinking this morning."

Detective Latterly chuckled. "He's right. I do love telling this part. So, it occurred to us what with your business and all, you'd have the materials and equipment right on hand to make this bracelet yourself, wouldn't you?"

Detective Mancini leaned forward in his chair and placed both palms on the top of the metal table until he was eye to eye with Mia. "Why'd you do it? Why'd you come in with this fake story? What the hell do you know about my sister's disappearance?"

The walls were closing in. If they kept poking around in her past, there was a remote chance they might find something. She'd just gone and handed Detective Mancini all the motivation in the world to do exactly that.

Her plan had seemed foolproof when she'd come up with the idea last weekend. Now, though, she was well and truly screwed. Closing her eyes, she exhaled long and slow, like a diver preparing to go under.

"I had a vision. I saw Anita being dragged into those woods where she was raped and strangled." She blinked once before looking straight back into Detective Mancini's bitter chocolate eyes. "I'm so sorry," she said after a pause.

Chapter Five

Her situation went downhill from there. Mia sensed that neither detective believed her story for even a single second. They pounded and pounded at her, determined to get at whatever truth they thought she knew.

It was no use. Her visions were unpredictable at best. She couldn't always see everything in the scene; unfortunately for her, she couldn't give them so much as a basic outline of the attacker other than the fact he was taller than Anita. Based on the skin tone of his hands and arms, the man was probably white.

"She knew him," Mia told Detective Mancini. "I could feel that much. And he called her Anita at one point when he was on top of her during the…well, during the attack."

"How can you be so sure she was dead?" he pressed.

"Because…It's hard to explain, but I felt her leave. One minute she was there, next the energy was gone, wrenched away like a leaf in a hurricane."

"She could've been unconscious," Detective Latterly said, his eyes flicking to his partner in sympathy.

Mia shook her head. "I wish I could say yes, but I know what I know. She was dead. I'm sorry. So sorry," she said again to Detective Mancini.

He scowled at her. "You actually want me to buy into the fact you know without a shadow of a doubt that my sister died, but you can't tell me what happened to her? Did the guy run away and leave her in the woods? Bury her? What the hell happened?" His voice rose to a shout and Mia shrank back when he slammed his fist down on the table in front of her. "This is bullshit like everything else about you. You'd better start packing your bags, lady because you're done in this town. I don't care if I lose my badge. I'm going to hound you day and night until your life is a living hell."

"Roman, chill, man," Detective Latterly said in an undertone while glancing meaningfully at the digital device recording the interview.

Mia was kept in a holding cell for the three hours it took to procure the loan of a sketch artist and have him travel in from a neighboring police station. Then back to the interrogation room she went for another tortuous hour of questions on face shape, bone structure, skin tone, and a million other details she couldn't answer because she'd never seen the face of the man in her vision.

"It might as well be a fucking cartoon character." Roman swore and threw the sketch down on the desk. He paced his office. Kevin wisely held his tongue. "We're going to have to let her go, aren't we?" he finally said, sinking into his chair and pinching the bridge of his nose between his thumb and forefinger.

"Yeah, we are," Kevin said. "But that doesn't mean this is the end of it. We'll keep pushing on her and see what we can dig up. She has to have some connection to either Anita or the killer. We're going to figure this out one way or another." He got to his feet and clapped a hand on Roman's shoulder. "It's time to call it a day. You go home. Hit the crap out of your punching bag and have a beer. Tomorrow we'll make a plan."

"Yeah. Maybe I will. Thanks, man."

But Roman didn't go home. He got in his car and drove out to old man Jasper's house. Weird that Mia would buy a place this remote and isolated. Hardly ideal for her fortune telling and incense and crystal crap. Didn't her kind of people usually set up shop on the main drag of the town and put out one of those signs on the sidewalk to snag any potentially weak-minded passerby into coming in and plunking down their cash?

As soon as he turned onto her driveway, he jammed the car into park and let it idle. He wanted to hurt her so badly the blood pounded in his ears like a drum beat, urging him to give life to his fantasy. But he was a cop, dammit. And more, he liked to think he was a decent human being. Decent people didn't show up at people's houses and mess them up.

He drummed fingers on the steering wheel. It didn't hurt to talk to her again, did it? A follow-up conversation to see if she'd thought of anything else. Cops did that all the time. It was part of the job. Besides, it wasn't likely she'd report him. Not with the threat of misdemeanor charges hanging over her head.

He was about to continue on up the driveway when the door to the house opened, and the woman herself stepped out. She was surrounded by dogs. A literal fucking pack of them. *Who owns four dogs and why,* he wondered? He watched while she and the dogs walked toward the back of the house and disappeared from view. Perfect. He'd cruise up closer and poke around before she came back.

Driving so slowly up the driveway he barely raised any dust, he parked by the front door. He noted the lawns were well tended, and all the shutters had a fresh coat of paint. A deep, forest green. He thought the color suited the house. There were even window boxes, for

Christ's sake, with bunches of pink and purple blooms spilling out.

The front sun porch was no longer shabby but sported new looking windows, and the screens were free of tears and gaping holes. It would be a nice spot to sit on a warm summer day, sipping a cool beer with the dogs stretched out at her feet.

Impatiently, he shook off the cozy image and stomped around the side of the house, stopping short when he caught sight of the gardens. They were extensive. Beds of shrubs and flowers had been planted close to the house. What Roman assumed must be vegetables occupied the two large plots near the end of the yard. There was even a greenhouse, he noted, though on closer inspection, it didn't seem to be in use. Still, it was neat as a pin inside. The floor swept, a tidy stack of clay pots organized in the corner, and the glass panels, catching the light of the low evening sun, shone like mirrors.

"What are you doing?"

Roman spun around, furious at being caught flatfooted. "Looking for you," he said smoothly.

"Well, I'm not in the greenhouse," she said, eyes hard on his face. "Though how could you possibly know. It's not like the walls are made of glass or anything."

He stepped back out through the door she held open. The dogs rushed him, and when he saw that one of them was a massive Doberman, he froze, keeping his eyes on Mia. "You want to call them off?"

"It's not nice, is it?" she said. "It's an awful feeling to be surrounded and ganged up on by hostile creatures. Sort of reminds me of the interrogation room in the police station and a couple of dickhead detectives."

The Doberman pinned him with eyes as cold and dead as a shark's. "Call them off. Now," he said, keeping his tone firm but entirely pleasant.

"Yeah, I could do that," she mused. "Or me and Mac here could escort you to your car, nice and slow. That way nobody gets hurt."

He could see she was amused, and he held her gaze for several beats. "Sure. Or we could have a nice friendly chat. I guess it's your call," he said, slowly raising his hands into the air like a perp caught by the police.

Her eyes flicked down to the dog's. "Mac, it's okay. Friend." Reaching up, she touched Roman's chest. "Friend," she repeated.

Although the dog didn't actually move away, the quality of focused stillness in the Doberman changed subtly, and Roman knew he was safe to resume normal movement. "Should we take this inside?"

She shook her head. "Nope. We talk out here. What do you want, Detective Mancini?"

"I want to know what happened to my sister."

"So do I, but like I told you, I don't know."

"Look, this is two people talking off the record. You can drop the I-had-a-vision charade and tell me the truth. Did you know Anita somehow? Or Luke? Is that it, you met Luke at college maybe? What is your connection to all this?"

She sighed and dropping her gaze, rested her hand on Mac's head. The large dog watched her like an overbearing parent. "I never met any of them. The first I knew of Anita's existence was when that echo came out and grabbed me Sunday night after the fair."

"What do you mean echo?"

"The vision. That's what I call the ones I get from physical places. It's as if the event leaves an echo and sometimes it hits my frequency. I see things from people and objects, too, but they're all a little different. It's hard to explain."

He stared at her. "You really believe your own bullshit, don't you? Okay, I came here in peace because I hoped you'd show some compassion. If not for me, think of my family. We all miss her. Our lives have never been the same since she disappeared. Finding her might help a little."

She reached out and placed her hand on his arm. Roman felt a jolt when her warm fingers curled around his elbow. For a split second, her eyes widened in shock, and then she hastily withdrew her hand. "I want to help. I do. Hopefully, more of it will come to me. It sometimes works that way. I promise you'll be the first to know."

The detective stepped back, eyes hardening. "Right after we lost Anita, there was a woman like you. She came to my mama and told her a bunch of crap about how Anita was fine, in Florida, on a beach. Said she could see a sign with pink flamingos in the background. On and on that woman went, but she could never actually tell us where my sister was. She just kept insisting she was alive."

Roman turned away from the gardens and the greenhouse and looked out over the field toward the far tree line. "My mama clung to her like a drowning woman grabs onto a life raft. My dad, too. They couldn't let go because the woman kept coming up with more crap. I found out later they'd paid her." His voice hitched, and he cleared his throat. "My parents paid that gypsy scam artist thousands of dollars. The whole time she never knew a single thing about what happened to my sister. When I became a police officer, the first thing I did was run a trace on her. Unfortunately, the evil witch was dead. Cancer. But I found out she'd run dozens of grifts. Her specialty target was families of missing kids."

"I don't want money," Mia said fiercely. "I don't want anything."

"That's fine. Good for you. Just make sure you stay the hell away from my family." He turned back to her, staring into her furious face. Her eyes were huge and greenish-gold against skin leached of all color. "Because let me assure you…every single move you make, every breath you take…I'll be right there watching you."

Chapter Six

And watch her, was exactly what Detective Mancini did. She caught sight of his car early the next morning lurking predator-like at the bottom of her driveway. Later that day, determined to keep going about life as normally as possible, she and the dogs drove into town to pick up food from Gabe's Diner. The detective appeared in the restaurant, standing by the counter and staring at her with a look of disapproval on his face. He exited the building alongside her before dropping several paces behind and trailing her to the car.

There he was again the next afternoon, loitering outside the grocery store. He didn't say a word, simply crossed his arms over his chest and leaned a hip against her SUV while she loaded the bags in the back. Then he gave her a mock, two-fingered salute and casually sauntered away. Later that night, he was back at the bottom of her driveway. He dug in and stayed a full two hours making her feel like a prisoner in her own home.

Mia had always thought of herself as even-tempered, but this constant and blatant surveillance was getting on her last nerve. And to make matters worse, small towns being what they were, word had spread about her story to the police. Now, where people had previously been blasé about her presence in town, they watched, and they whispered.

She was sick of it. The whole situation was too much for one person to bear. All she wanted was: to find a community, fit in, and pass as normal so she could live a quiet, contented life.

Well, she could always pack up and move on again. Sell her beloved log house, take the dogs, and locate some other perfect place. And from now on, no matter what came to her in a vision, she was going to ignore it, her conscience be damned.

The monitor on her counter pinged and the dogs came to attention. Someone was coming up the driveway. Since there were no scheduled pickups or deliveries, she could only imagine it was Detective Mancini again, determined to take another pound of flesh.

Enough was enough. Throwing back her shoulders, she strode out the front door, across the porch and down the steps to the lawn. The dogs were on alert, milling about and ready to spring the moment the visitor's car pulled into the parking area.

Except it wasn't the black Impala she'd been expecting but a cherry red Volvo with an older woman sitting behind the wheel. The flash came to her like it sometimes did. Molly Mancini, mother of Anita and Roman Mancini.

Seriously? And here she thought things couldn't possibly get any worse.

The woman stepped out of the car, heedless of the dogs, all of whom seemed to immediately accept her and give way, parting like the Red Sea. She marched straight up where Mia stood uncertainly at the bottom of the steps.

"Do you know who I am?" she asked. Mia nodded. "Good. I thought you would. And you're Mia Reeves. I've heard all about you from my son and others." She flicked her hand, indicating their opinions didn't necessarily hold weight with her. "It's about time we got acquainted. Shall I come in or do you have somewhere out here we can sit and chat?"

Like a cornered animal, Mia's eyes darted around, but there was no escape in sight. "Um…I guess we could sit in the porch," she said, gesturing to the door.

Molly Mancini strode up the stairs as if she owned the place and let herself into the screened porch. The dogs trooped in after her. Mac glanced back at Mia with a clear *come on* gesture.

"I like what you've done with the place," Molly announced, looking around approvingly. "Jasper Martin had it for a good twenty years, but I don't think he so much as changed a lightbulb the whole time he was here."

"Thanks," Mia managed. "Mrs. Mancini, you must know your son doesn't want—"

"Molly," she interrupted. "Do you mind if I call you Mia?"

Mia nodded weakly. "By all means."

"Good. Okay. First off, if my son gives you any trouble, you come straight to me. He may be a detective, but he still minds his mama. Secondly, I'm a grown woman and can talk to whomever I want. I assume it's the same for you?"

"Yes, but he's pretty steamed…"

"Mia, you've got to relax. A young thing like you shouldn't get all worked up over nothing. Now tell me, do you have the gift of sight?"

The question was asked casually, as if nothing more than a simple inquiry about how she took her coffee. Mia sat blinking at her. "Um…I…well, yes, I do," she finally said, meeting Molly's eyes straight on.

"Oh, child, it must have been a very hard way to live. People might say it's a gift, and Lord Almighty it surely is, but it's a terrible kind of responsibility as well. There was a girl back home in my village in Italy. Things came to her from time to time. The poor thing was crushed by it. Killed herself on her eighteenth birthday."

Tears sprang to Mia's eyes. She wiped them away, but they kept coming, faster and faster, backing up in her throat until she was sobbing. No one had ever looked at her situation in such a straight-forward manner and gotten to the heart of it like this tiny, dark-haired woman. "Yes, it was hard," she hiccupped.

Molly leaned forward and patted her arm. "I'm sorry, dear. I can't even imagine." She waited respectfully until Mia had dried her tears. "Now, I want you to tell me what you know about my Anita. Don't hold anything to yourself. The not knowing is so much worse than the cruelest truth could possibly be."

"Are you sure?" Mia asked. When Molly nodded, Mia took a deep breath, closed her eyes, and told her everything.

Molly sobbed. Moved by desperation, Mia knelt beside the woman and rubbed a hand up and down her arm. The dogs crowded in. Little Fifi especially seemed to absorb the woman's pain, whining piteously until Molly scooped her up into her lap.

"Thank you," she said at last. "No one would tell me. Roman thinks he needs to protect me. Protect me, for heaven's sake? I come from tough peasant stock. My Frank and I traveled to a new country with barely a hundred dollars in our pockets. No English, no family or friends. No jobs. We worked and learned, built businesses and raised three children. With God's help, I can stand anything that comes."

"I'm sorry for your loss," Mia said quietly. "And I want you to understand I didn't go to the police for any reason other than the hope they might find something in the woods and bring Anita's killer to justice."

"I know, sweet girl. Now, I have a favor to ask. If you could come to my house, meet my Frank, maybe go in Anita's room. I'm hoping something else might come to you. Something that will help us find our baby girl. We need to bring her home and bury her properly." Molly's voice hitched, and she covered her mouth and swallowed hard. "I'll pay you."

Mia sprang back so quickly Mac let out a startled yelp. "No. No money."

Molly nodded her head approvingly. "Food then. That's what we'll do. You come tonight. I'll make pot roast and vegetables and maybe pie." She clapped her hands together. "Seven o'clock. And you can bring this sweet little dog." She patted Fifi's head. "The others might give my old Sylvester a heart attack. He's our cat. Eighteen this year."

Mia's heart sank. Truly, it was about the last thing on earth she wanted to do, but somehow she was nodding and saying yes. She might have the power of sight, but Roman Mancini's mother had the power of persuasion.

* **

In the end, she left Fifi at home with her beloved Mac and headed out…alone…to face Molly and Frank. They lived in the town of Dalton proper on a lovely old tree-lined street. The house was yellow brick with white shutters and large white columns on either side of the front door stretching all the way up to the second floor.

It was Frank who opened the door and welcomed her in. *This is what Roman will look like in his later years,* Mia thought, smiling at the tall, muscular man with thick salt and pepper hair and the same deep, dark eyes he'd passed on to his son.

"Please, come in. Molly is in her usual controlled chaos on the final countdown to dinner. Can I get you a drink?" His accent was thicker than Molly's.

"Water, please," Mia said, stepping into a spacious foyer and following him through to a room on the right. He pointed her to an armchair and disappeared through the far doorway.

"You're here. I'm so glad you came." Molly leaned out through the same doorway, wearing a well-worn red and white checkered apron and a matching oven mitt on her hand. "I'll be right out."

She disappeared again only to be replaced by her husband, a tall glass of water in one hand and a highball glass in the other. When he settled on the seat opposite her, he swirled the amber liquid and took a sip, watching her over the rim.

"Mia, I'm happy to have you in my home, and I'm sure you're a wonderful young woman. I look forward to spending an enjoyable evening with you." He took another measured sip of his drink, this time putting it down on the side table. "But I do not share my wife's belief in this magic hooha. When we lost our girl, I was so full of grief I went along with whatever Molly wanted, but we've had enough."

"Frank Edward Mancini." Molly's sharp voice cut through his words. She stepped into the sitting room and planted both hands on her hips. "You make me want to scream sometimes. I told you, you don't have to be part of this. That's your right, but you will not make our guest feel uncomfortable in our home."

Mia cleared her throat, "I understand—"

"No, you don't understand," Frank said mildly. "We believed someone like you before, and I swear to our Lord above, she was an evil spirit praying on our weakness."

"Frank," Molly said again, "take Mia up to Anita's room. I'll join you as soon as the meat comes out to rest."

Mia decided she must have taken leave of her senses accepting Molly's invitation. Talk about a mistake. When Frank sighed, she sprang up from the chair.

"I'll say good night…tell Molly thanks…"

"No. We'll go up otherwise I'll never hear the end of it."

Frank got to his feet with a determined look on his face and gestured her out toward the front door and up the stairs. The upper hall was lined with family photos, and though she wanted to stop and study each one, Frank brushed by her and strode to the last room on the right, pushing open the door.

Once she'd stepped inside, she imagined it hadn't been touched in the ten years since Anita had disappeared. Posters of boy bands lined the wall and a student desk sat in the corner. Pictures had been taped to the large mirror above the dresser. A few contained images of the Mancini family, but the majority were of a cute teenage boy either posed with Anita or simply on his own. Mia reached out and slowly ran her fingertips along the edges of the photos.

The flashes came. Not every picture, but here and there. They gave her a sense of a normal and happy girl, confident, ambitious and excited about the future. Through it all, though, was the overwhelming theme of Anita's love for this boy, Luke. She saw them kissing, fleeting moments of hands twining, feet touching under tables. The sweetness of it was foreign to Mia.

She turned away from the mirror and roamed the room. Nothing else spoke to her until she opened the closet. Mia was immediately drawn to a blue and grey silk scarf hanging on the back of the door. When she touched it, the vision came strong and fast. She was in an old house filled with the enticing smell of garlic and basil and pasta sauce. Anita sat on the bed while Molly and another woman sorted through clothes in an ancient dresser.

Your grandmother had this since she was a young woman. When she was old enough for courting, her mother bought it for her. She told her as long as a lady wore a lovely scarf, she could go anywhere with pride.

You must have it now. The words echoed in Mia's head as if hearing them in present time. In the vision, Molly's eyes were filled with tears, and the other woman sobbed into a white handkerchief.

"Oh, it's so lovely," Mia said, coming back to herself and stroking a finger up and down the fine fabric. "What a wonderful item to pass down to a grandchild. Your wife should wear it or else maybe Lina could have it. I know she got the shawl and the pearl earrings, but it's a shame to keep this beautiful keepsake hidden away."

The gasping sound from behind startled her, and Mia whirled around to see Molly, face ashen, a hand clamped over her mouth. Frank frowned deeply and put an arm around his wife's shoulder, drawing her against him. His eyes fixed on Mia, coolly assessing. "How did you know those things?" he demanded.

Mia spread her hands. "It's…well…the scarf showed me the scene in the bedroom after the funeral."

"Yes, that's right. Exactly right," Molly said, turning away from the shelter of her husband's chest and wiping at her eyes. Frank continued to study Mia as though she were a particularly unappealing insect.

"Are you saying you can pick up anything in this room and tell me something about my daughter?" he asked.

Mia sighed. "Unfortunately, it's not nearly as precise as that. Sometimes I see things, but not always. I have no control over what comes to me. It's not as if I can set an intention of finding out where she is right now and get the answer." She paused, rubbing her damp palm on the front of her jeans. "It's sort of like a whole bunch of TV screens on a roulette wheel. They're all spinning around, flashing by me, and then all of sudden everything stops before my vision is filled with whatever picture happens to be directly in front of me. Eventually, it whisks away, and I'm back to the whirling."

Though Molly nodded enthusiastically, Mia could see Frank remained unconvinced. That was fine. She knew not everyone understood. She'd long since given up trying to convert those who were determined not to believe in what she saw.

"Mom, Dad, where are you?"

A man's voice floated up the stairs, and Molly stiffened and turned to face Frank, eyes narrowing. "Did you call him?"

"Yes, I did," he said, voice calm against her threatening tone. "He's part of this, too."

"Oh, Frank. I wish you hadn't."

Footfalls sounded on the stairs. "Mom, are you up here? I ran into Tony and brought him along, too. I know damned well she's here."

"We're in Anita's room," Frank called out.

Mia braced when Roman filled the doorway. His eyes raked over his mother's face before zeroing in on her. "I thought we were clear about you staying away from my family?" he said, jaw clenched.

"It's not…I didn't—"

"I made her come," Molly cut in. "And this has nothing to do with you."

Mother and son stared at one another while Mia squirmed and wished she could disappear. After what felt like an hour, Roman stepped into the room and bending down, hugged Molly. He said something in her ear, and she laughed softly. After releasing her, he turned to his father and clapped a hand on his shoulder.

"It's okay, Son. Your mother really did drag the girl over here. And though I'm struggling with the concept, I think maybe she can help us," Frank said, shocking Mia to the core.

Frank and Molly smiled sweetly at each other. Roman's eyes flashed between Mia and his father.

"Maybe you really are a witch," Roman said to her. "After what we went through with gypsy Cassandra, I'd have bet the bank my father would've spit in your eye and sent you packing."

Right at this moment, Mia fervently wished he had.

"Come, everyone, let's go down and have our meal," Molly said.

"Dinner smells great." Roman rubbed his hands together and wiggled his eyebrows at his mother.

"Maybe I didn't make enough for a busybody son and an ungrateful nephew who hardly ever come to visit anymore," she replied managing to stare down her nose at him.

Roman snorted. "Name me one time you didn't make enough to feed everyone three servings and still have leftovers," he pointed out.

Molly shrugged and marched past him, stopping to pat Mia's arm. "Come on, my sweet girl. Let's go downstairs. I promise my family will now start behaving like proper Christians and make you feel welcome." She cast a glance over her shoulder, aiming it at the two men in the room. "Isn't that right, you heathens?"

"Sure, Ma. No problem. As long as Ms. Reeves understands I'm here to protect this family. One wrong move and she'll have to deal with me. Okay, let's sit down and break bread together."

The blue-eyed blond man waiting downstairs in the kitchen was introduced as Tony, son of Frank's deceased brother Gino. He flashed a charming smile and shook her hand.

"So you're the one who's got my cousin's jockeys in a twist?"

Mia pulled her hand away and stepped back. Before she could so much as open her mouth to reply, Molly swatted Tony on the head. "Antonio, enough. If you can't behave then leave. This poor girl has had nothing but insults from my worthless family, and only moments ago I promised her a nice evening."

Tony rubbed his head and smiled at Mia, his eyes as clear and blue as a summer sky. "I'm sorry. It wasn't you I was getting at so much as my tightly wound cousin, the self-appointed protector of the entire Mancini family."

This time Roman was the one thumping Tony, although he chose the shoulder to inflict his injury. "Yeah, well, someone has to look after this sorry lot. Especially you."

"Um…wow…I just realized I have to get back," Mia said, easing away from the group of them. "I think I left something on the stove. I'm so sorry I can't stay. Maybe another time. Good night, Molly. Thanks for the invite. Good night everyone."

She turned and fled the kitchen and was almost clear of the house when Tony bounded down the porch stairs after her.

"Hold up. Wait. I'm sorry," he called. Mia didn't stop, but he caught up with her at her SUV, pushing the driver's door closed even as she struggled to open it. "I mean it. I am sorry. Please, stay. My aunt is very upset, and my uncle gets pretty testy when anyone makes Molly sad. If I could bring you back, I'd maybe get myself out of the dog house with them."

"It's nothing to do with you. Like I said, I forgot to turn a pot off on my stove."

For several seconds, Tony kept his weight pressed against the car door and smiled down at Mia. "What's in the pot?" he asked.

"Soup," she said smoothly, calling on years of experience talking her way out of tight spots. "Minestrone. I make the beans from scratch."

"Sounds good," he said in a soft voice, stepping back and pulling the car door open. "Before you go, tell me, can you really see things or read people or whatever?"

She sighed and slid in behind the wheel. "Yes, I can."

"Do me," he said.

"What?"

"Read my mind. What am I thinking right now?"

Leaning her head back against the seat she closed her eyes. "It doesn't work like that."

"Okay. How does it work?"

"It's better if I can touch the person or object, but even then I won't necessarily get anything."

"Try me then." When she glanced over, she saw he'd extended his hands toward her.

"Okay, fine."

She turned slightly against the seatbelt and grasped his hands. They were large and warm, and hers were completely engulfed in his palms. Clearing her mind, she reached out and immediately saw a vision of Tony putting is arm around—what the heck? —her shoulders and leaning in to nuzzle her neck. When she opened her eyes and glance over at him, he winked.

"I think we'd look good together," he said with a cheeky smile.

She pulled her hands back and broke the contact. "Ha ha. Very funny."

His eyes crinkled in amusement. "So, is that a no?" He put his hand over his heart and shook his head. "Woman, you wound me."

"Good night, Tony."

This time he stepped back and let her close the door. With the greatest relief, she fired up the engine and started backing out of the driveway. Tony raised his hand in a wave and she ground her teeth and punched the accelerator.

Mistake, mistake, mistake, she chanted in her head once she was finally on the road to home. But, now, at least, it was over. All of it. She still felt incredibly sorry about Anita Mancini, but she'd done all she could, and more than most people would do. It was now out of her hands.

Chapter Seven

By the end of shift the next day, Roman couldn't have been happier. In general, he loved his job—and even had plans to transfer out to a bigger city in another year or two—somewhere with more action of the criminal variety in a month than Dalton could offer in a year.

Still, it had been a long week with this Anita thing preying on him night and day. And this morning, he'd been trapped in Mrs. Pringle's house for almost an hour while she reported various so-called sinister behaviors of her neighbors.

He'd longed to be called out for something else: a cat up a tree, a lost purse, any fucking thing. Instead, the radio had been deadly silent while Mrs. Pringle forced tea and cookies on him. Once she'd run out of accusations about her neighbors, she'd none too subtly probed Roman for details related to his romantic life. God, she was worse than his mother.

When he finally got back to the station, his lieutenant dumped a stack of folders on his desk and ordered him to clear the paperwork by end of day tomorrow. And Kevin, the slippery son of a bitch, suddenly had a forgotten dentist appointment. Oh, it was real, all right. Roman had made damned sure of that by calling the dentist's office the minute his partner stepped out. But given the fact Kevin's girlfriend's sister worked there as a hygienist, it seemed awfully convenient timing to him.

He almost didn't answer the desk phone when it rang while he was pulling his car keys out of the drawer. With a sigh, he reached for the receiver. "Mancini," he said.

"Oh, good, you're still there. That's perfect timing. I'm right outside, so I'll wait for you in the reception area." Molly's voice had a cheerful lilt to it.

He could dodge her. Say he was working late or whatever, but given she'd been calling his cell all day, he knew she'd get to him eventually. He tried not to sigh. "Okay, I'll see you in two minutes."

Damn it all to hell. She must still be pissed off about last night. It wasn't his fault, was it? All he'd done was make his position clear like any good son would under the circumstances. For some reason, Mia had taken offense and walked out before dinner. Probably because she had a guilty conscience.

"There you are," Molly said as though they'd run into one another unexpectedly. She rose from a chair in the waiting area and approached him with a smile that made Roman distinctly queasy.

"Here I am. Look, Ma, I'm beat. I'll walk you home. Then I'm going to my place, grab a sandwich, and maybe watch the game."

She positively beamed at him. "I'm so glad you don't have plans. Your father is playing cards with Fred and William, which means I'm free to take you to Gabe's for dinner. My treat. Come on. You can tell me about your day."

Roman's shoulders slumped, and he turned and followed her out of the station. Why did he have to be such a good son?

They slid into a booth by the window and Gabriel himself took their order. "Drinks are coming right up, and the food will be out in five or so," he said. "And don't worry, Molly, I've taken care of that other thing for you." He winked at her, shoved the menus under his arm, and strode back to the cash register by the front door.

Roman lifted an eyebrow. "What other thing?"

"Oh, nothing for you to worry about."

They chatted for a few moments about inconsequential things, but when the drinks came,

Roman took a sip of his beer and squared his shoulders, deciding to cut to the chase. "Are you mad about last night?"

"No, it wasn't any worse than I expected once I realized your father had called in reinforcements. I know how close-minded you men are. I'm only sorry poor Mia felt so uncomfortable she had to leave. I like to think we're kind, hospitable people. The way you boys treated her doesn't speak well of our family, does it?"

Roman winced. "We didn't do anything all that bad though I don't guess we made her feel welcome."

"It's nice to see Tony around again. He was gone too long on his last job. Imagine him head-hunting for big companies and you a detective and Lina running a marketing division. All so grown up and successful. I can't help wondering what Anita would be doing now if she was still with us."

"Probably driving us crazy and popping a kid out every couple of years while she decorated the world." Roman took another sip of beer and rested his head back against the padded booth. "I still miss her too, Ma."

"Oh, baby, I know." Molly stroked her hand over his. "I wish we could bring her back home. It hurts my heart knowing she's out there somewhere, at the bottom of a lake or buried in some forgotten place. You may not be able to understand, but I need to know what happened to her."

"Why wouldn't I understand? I want to find her as much as you do. I promise I've gone over her file a million times. There's nothing there. It's like she finished her shift here at the diner and disappeared off the face of the earth."

"I remember how proud she was when Gabriel hired her in tenth grade. She worked at the diner all through high school then kept on going, saving up extra for college so she could really focus on her school work when she got there. We should never have let her walk home at night. It wasn't right."

"Come on. You can't say that, Ma. It's a safe town. Anita was twenty years old. Even back then she had a cell phone. She was getting ready to go and live in Memphis for Pete's sake."

Molly's sigh was tearful. "I know all these things but still…maybe if—"

"Maybe nothing," Roman shot back. "It had to have been some freaky, random thing. Dalton hasn't ever had a like crime before or since Anita." His eyes flickered to the front door and seeing Mia Reeves step up to the counter, narrowed on his mother. "What's she doing here?"

"Who, dear?"

"You know who. This is a setup, isn't it?"

Ignoring her son, Molly got to her feet and waved frantically. "Mia, hello. What a wonderful coincidence."

Hearing her name, Mia turned toward their table and jolted as though shot with a Taser. Her eyes darted to the door, and she took a hasty step back, but Molly was too quick for her. Hustling across the short distance, she was at Mia's side in the next second, hand on her arm.

"I'm so glad you're here," she gushed. "Roman and I are waiting for our food. You'll join us. It'll help make up for last night."

Roman watched in fascination as even more color leached from Mia's face, and she swallowed uneasily. "Oh, no, I don't want to impose. Besides, I'm getting take-out. My dogs are in the car."

"We won't be long, and it's a lovely night, I'm sure they'll be fine. Come over now and sit down. Gabriel will bring your food to the table with our order."

Gabriel, who stood watching the scene with a knowing smile on his lips, nodded. "Don't you worry, Mia. We'll plate it up for you and send it on out."

Hand tucked in at Mia's elbow, Molly towed her to the booth. "You sit right in here beside me," she said, gesturing Mia onto the bench seat but wasting no time sliding in next to her and effectively blocking her exit.

"Kinda feels like you've been run over by a bulldozer, don't it?" Roman said soberly. "Same thing happened to me. If I didn't know better, I'd say this was the damnedest thing us running into you here." He turned accusing eyes on his mother, but Molly simply smiled warmly at him as though unaware of his meaning.

"Now, Mia," she said. "I didn't get a chance to apologize for last night. My family…well, my men are very protective. After what happened before…I'm sure you understand?"

Mia's head snapped up. "I told you, I don't want anything from you or your family."

"I know, dear. And now my men know too, so we can put it behind us."

Mia's eyes radiated fury. Roman realized she wasn't putting anything behind her no matter what his mother said. Maybe it was a good thing. With that resentment burning in her gut, she wasn't likely to come sniffing around his folks any time soon.

The food arrived, killing the conversation for a few moments. Both Roman and his mother dug into their burgers. Mia picked lethargically through her side salad, finally fishing out a crouton and forking it up to her mouth.

"Now that we're all friends," Molly continued. "I have a favor to ask both of you—"

"No, Ma," Roman said instantly. "Whatever it is, definitely no."

For a split second, Mia caught his eyes and her lips curved into a smirking smile. She really was a looker. Even with face bare of makeup and a smudge of dirt on her cheek, she had a pure, wholesome beauty. Remembering Kevin's comment about pillow lips, his gaze rested on her generous mouth, and his heart did an ungainly leap in his chest and seemed to crash into his ribs.

"—and working together seems like the perfect solution," his mother finished, dabbing at the corner of her mouth with her napkin.

Mia shook her head abruptly. Roman blinked in confusion. "What did you say?"

"She wants us to join forces and figure out what happened to Anita," Mia said.

"Exactly. You have access to all the information from before." Molly turned to Roman. "Not to mention you're an excellent detective. Mia, here, will maybe be able to fill in the missing details. And I'll bet when she's not worried about you and the rest of the family running her off, things will come to her more freely."

"She's a civilian. I can't let her read confidential police records," Roman said. "And besides, I told you there's nothing there."

"Police hire consultants, don't they? That's what Mia will be." Molly brushed his objection off as if it was neither here nor there.

"Yeah, sure," Roman said slowly, a smile blooming on his face. "But consultants go through a rigorous screening process. If Mia's up for that, I'll start the background check first thing tomorrow."

"I'm not," Mia said. "I don't want any part of working with the police."

Molly slapped a hand on the table. The cutlery bounced off her plate and caused the family in the booth across from them to look over. "My baby girl is missing, and you two are going to find her. Roman, I don't care what you have to do to clear this at work, but you do it, and you do it tomorrow."

"And you, Missy." She turned to Mia. "You have a God-given gift. We're all here on earth for a purpose. This is yours, so stop skulking around pretending you can't do it. I know you can and you will. Life is short, and we only get one shot at it. Get on with living yours the best way you can."

Taking her napkin from her lap, Molly threw it over her plate and got to her feet in a move as smooth as any athlete. "I hope neither of you ever have to feel what it's like to lose a child and in the worst way imaginable with no time to even say goodbye. Now, at least, you can bring her back to me."

Molly marched out of the diner, shoulders stiff and head high. She didn't look back.

* * *

Mia wished she'd never had that stupid vision of Anita.

She wanted to cry. Or scream. Or better yet, pack up all her stuff and the dogs right now and hit the road, not stopping until she'd put some serious miles between herself and the Mancini family.

Roman sat, head bowed over his plate. "My mother has this irritating way of making me feel about ten years old again," he grumbled. "We're going to have to do it. Work together I mean. Once she has a bee in her bonnet, she won't let up. Trust me on this. I'm only sorry you're being dragged into it."

She sat quietly for a moment, worrying her fingers in her lap and biting her lip. "It's not that I don't want to help," she said at last. "But I'm afraid she's getting her hopes up for nothing. I can't promise anything. That echo in the woods may be all I ever see of what happened to your sister. Not that it matters what I say since you think I'm a big fat liar anyway."

His head shook slowly back and forth. "I'm not saying I don't believe, but being a police officer and all, I like proof. So far, you've cost the department a shit load of money on forensics and techs, and I still don't have anything to work with. On top of that, I know damned well there's something in your past you're not too happy about us knowing, so it doesn't make for a real buddy-buddy dynamic."

"You're right. You're absolutely right." She held out her hand. "If we really are going to work together, maybe we should call a truce?"

"Yeah. Okay, fine."

He joined her hand with his and gave it a quick squeeze, but she didn't let go when he released. Instead, she reached over with her left hand and sandwiched his in between her palms.

He looked down, amused. "Is this like high school? Are we supposed to be going steady now?"

"Something like that," she murmured, closing her eyes.

"No offense, Mia, but this is weird." Roman struggled against her grip.

"Shush," she hissed, refusing to let go. Then a smile burst across her face, and she opened her eyes to his. "You went steady with Carly Francis when you were in tenth grade. She was your first serious girlfriend. You bribed your sister, Lina, to make peanut butter cookies. They were Carly's favorite, and you told her you made them. You two went to the junior prom together. She wore a pink dress with puffy sleeves and sparkly silver sandals, and you bought her a wrist corsage with lilies of the valley and white carnations. She lived in a bungalow on Willow Street, and you used to climb up to the window and into her room to wait for her on nights she was working late. Oh…but…she left her diary out, and you read about the school camping trip the week before and…"

Now Mia was the one trying to wrench her hand away, but he held fast, refusing to let her break contact. "Go on. Finish it." Turning her gaze away, she shook her head. "Finish it," he said again, this time his voice no more than a whisper.

"Okay. Fine. On the camping trip, after everyone was asleep, she snuck off with Chris Monties and had sex with him in the forest. When you confronted her about it, she said she'd loved Chris for a long time. You were nothing more than a stand-in to make him jealous." Mia blinked at him, eyes filled with regret. "It hurt you. Deeply. Even more when later she told everyone you'd treated her badly and then dumped her. Pride kept you from denying it. For the rest of the school year, all her friends shunned you. Every time you passed Chris in the hall, he gave you this smirky grin that made you want to smash his face in."

Eyes wide, he snatched his hand away and cradled it against his chest as though it were an injured baby bird. His breath heaved in and out while he sat staring at her.

Mia shook her head. "I'm sorry. I thought it would be a happy memory. I didn't mean to make you feel bad."

Roman dropped his hands to the table and straightened in the seat. "Did my mother tell you that stuff about Carly?" he demanded, eyes hard.

"What? No, of course not. Because of all your sneering comments, I wanted to show you that…well, I can see things."

Roman shook his head. "I don't know what to think, but one thing's for sure, you're one scary lady."

She sighed. "I know. Story of my life. I won't do it again, at least not on purpose. But I can't promise details won't come to me anyway because you're very easy to read." She paused and glanced away from his wary eyes. "I'm not saying I'll help, but if I did, how would it work? Us looking for Anita, I mean."

"Um…" His fingers drummed on the table. "Let me think about it, okay? I'll call you tomorrow."

"Fine." Mia got to her feet and stared down at him. "I'd offer to shake hands but…" She gave the barest chuckle and lifted her shoulders in a shrug before turning and walking out of the diner.

When she strode down the sidewalk toward her SUV, she passed the window where Roman sat, gazing at his hands still lying flat on the table. She almost felt sorry for him.

Chapter Eight

When Roman didn't call the next day or the day after that, Mia figured he likely wasn't going to. That was fine as far as she was concerned. She may have a soft spot for Molly and understood her deep grief for Anita, but there was something about being in proximity to Roman that gave her the feeling she was being constantly hit with low doses of electrical currents.

And not in a good she'd-never-noticed-how-blue-the-sky-was kind of way. When he was around, she could almost believe she was coming down with the flu or some other debilitating illness. Her body seemed *off*, her mind mushy, and often times she had trouble catching her breath as if he was somehow stealing every last bit of air away from her. It was off-putting, to say the least. The thought of working with him for any length of time made her want to poke herself in the eye.

In the comforting quiet of her home, she worked steadily on jewelry orders, determined to catch up after the distraction of Anita. Returning to normal was a relief, and she sank into the intricate work, especially the piece she was currently making. The client had sent a picture of a necklace worn by a celebrity at some red carpet event and wanted it replicated using crystals in place of the diamonds and emeralds.

Mia had the framework set for the pyramid tier and had spent the last hour feeling her way through the stones, finding pieces that would fit in both size and shape, as well as on an energy level to suit the woman. It was demanding work. When the driveway monitor pinged on the kitchen counter, she leaned back in her chair and rubbed the knots from her hands.

Her heart sank when she saw Roman's black sedan turn into the parking area by the front door. If he'd made the effort to drive out, then he must actually be considering going through with this idea of them working together.

She slipped the jewelry cutters into her back pocket and strode across the sunroom to open the screen door before he had a chance to knock. "Don't worry about the dogs. They won't hurt you," she said when he paused on the threshold.

He followed her toward the main door of the house and into the workroom where she gestured to the extra chair beside her table.

"So," he said. "I guess we should do this. Are you up for it?"

Mia wanted to shake her head and send him on his way, but ever since the night at Gabe's diner she'd been hearing Molly's parting words in her head. And the truth was if she wanted to continue living the straight life and trying to establish herself in the community, these were the kinds of things she had to do.

"Yeah, I'm up for it. Except I don't want you running any background on me."

"What are you so afraid I'll find? Are you hiding a felony? A family connection to the mafia? You know being all secretive only makes me more curious."

"My past is my business," she said, staring him straight in the eye. "Tell you what, you don't do any more poking into my background, and I won't go poking into your mind. That seems fair."

He cocked his head. "You already promised you wouldn't, so you can't very well use it as a bargaining chip now."

"Yeah, well, things change. And when you consider it, I'm actually offering two things. To find your sister and to leave your private thoughts and memories private. Under the circumstances, I think I'm being pretty darned generous. Plus, I'd hate to imagine how mad your mother would be if I go to her and explain you were too much of a prick to work with." She paused a beat and smiled sweetly. "Of course, I wouldn't actually use the word prick, but she'd get the message all right."

"Wow, that's cold." When she only continued staring, he sighed. "Okay, I accept your terms. Now here's mine. I'm not going to do this officially, at least not initially. It'll be simpler if I don't have to go through all the politics and red tape. I'm not keen on being laughed off the force right now."

"Yeah, I get how embarrassing it is to associate with me," she said bitterly, all hint of teasing amusement gone from her voice.

"Hey, Miss Huffy, climb down off your high horse. Cops are cops. We're trained to work with facts—not feelings—and definitely not psychic visions or whatever you call what you do."

"Okay, I get it." Holding her temper close to her heart, she breathed deeply and let it out in a long, slow exhale. "What's the plan?"

"I thought I'd fill you in on what I know, and you can see if you get any…I don't know… inklings, or whatever. Unless you have a better idea?"

"No." She looked at her unfinished necklace and the dogs, shifting about uneasily, and then checked the time. "I suppose you mean now? It would've been nice if you'd called first. I'm kinda in the middle of things, and the dogs need a walk and their dinner."

"I know. I'm sorry. To tell you the truth, I wasn't totally sure I was going to go through with it until I got out of my car in front of your house. How about this? Let's walk the dogs. Once they're fed maybe we can go out and get some dinner, and I'll lay it out for you."

"Or," she countered. "I throw something together, and we eat here. I don't like leaving them, and this will be more private for talking."

He held up his hand. "Or you do your thing with the dogs, and I'll go into town and pick up food and bring it back here. That way you don't have to cook."

She studied his face for several seconds. "Is everything we do always going to involve a long, drawn-out negotiation?"

"Can't say for sure but it feels that way. Your pick. Pizza, Chinese, or something from Gabe's Diner?"

"Gabe's Diner. I never did finish my food when we were in there the other night. I want an artichoke and beet salad and a veggie burger."

He gauged her expression, trying to decide if she was joking or not. "I didn't even know he had that healthy crap on the menu."

Her smile was smug. "He doesn't. At least not yet, but when I first went in there and told him what I wanted, he was happy to make it for me. He's such a sweetie. I think he's going to add it in the fall. Change things up."

"Okay. You want it, you got it." He swung his keys around his thumb and smiled. "I'll be back before you know it."

An hour later, Roman and Mia sat at the bistro table in her kitchen nook with a mountain of food between them. "You got so much," she said, eyeing the garlic bread, onion rings, and double order of potato wedges in addition to her entrée. His plate was heaped with a bacon cheeseburger and Caesar salad.

"I felt a lot of pressure to make up for your dinner the other night, and we might be here awhile. Bon appetite." Holding the burger firmly with both hands, he took a massive bite.

They chewed in silence for several minutes. She noticed the dogs, even Mac, had accepted Roman's presence as though it was a routine occurrence. It was odd since she never had anyone in her house for any length of time, but more especially, as a dinner guest. Not only had the pack relaxed into lounge mode, but Layla, the traitor, was sitting pressed up against Roman's thigh.

"You can move her away if it bothers you," she said, pointing at the Labrador.

"What?" Roman paused and glanced down. "Nah, I love dogs. If I didn't work so much, I'd get one of my own. We always had them growing up." He patted Layla's head, and she positively preened under his hand as though receiving a great honor.

This was wrong. Having him here in her house. Everyone getting cozy.

"Should we get started?" she asked pointedly.

Roman swallowed and wiped his mouth. "Sure. If you want." He took a sip of beer. "Let's see. Anita disappeared the day after the Fourth of July Fair at Carlton Park. It always used to be held then but after she...well, after what happened, the town moved the fair to the spring. Everyone felt it was disrespectful to celebrate when it was essentially the anniversary of her disappearance."

Roman swallowed and glanced away briefly before seeming to gather himself.

"Anyway, Anita finished work at nine that night. She waitressed at Gabe's Diner." He looked over at Mia who nodded. "Gabriel said she talked to Mary, one of the other waitresses, for a couple of minutes then left sometime around nine fifteen on foot. A customer, Betty Warner, saw her walk by the window. It's only about a ten-minute hike from there to my parents' house. No one saw her after she went by the diner window."

"Were any of her personal items ever found?"

"Nope. No cell. No purse. No nothing. All her friends and family were interviewed. None of the records show a call to or from Anita's phone. Her credit card was never used again, and neither was her bank card."

"Where were you?"

He lifted an eyebrow. "Am I a suspect, Officer Reeves?"

She held his gaze. "All I'm doing is trying to get a feel for the situation like you said."

"I'm sorry. It's hard. Doing this again is harder than I thought it would be. I had a couple of days off from my summer construction job and went camping with friends at Lake Shadlock about an hour from here."

"You and your friend Jason took your girlfriends on a camping trip to get some alone time with the ladies since you were both living at home over the summer to save money. It was the first time you and Elyse…" Mia stopped, her face fire-engine red and slapped her palm against her forehead in frustration. "I'm so sorry. I didn't mean to look. It was right there. Please don't be mad."

Very deliberately, Roman set his burger down and stared into her stricken eyes. "I'm starting to realize there's no point in being pissed off about it. It'd be like blaming an eagle for flying too high. It's completely natural for you, isn't it?"

Letting out a held breath, she slowly nodded her head. "I am sorry, though."

He jerked his shoulders and picked up the burger again, taking another bite. Mia followed suit and forked up a large piece of artichoke. Once Roman had washed the food down with a swallow of beer, he eyed her.

"Was it always that way? Reading people, I mean. You must've killed it in high school. You'd have known the answers to the tests just by sitting next to the smartest kid in class. Not to mention all the secrets, and in that cutthroat teenage environment, knowledge is power."

"I didn't really go to high school much," she mumbled.

"Hey, I get it, high school was hard on a lot of people," he said, relieved to see her weak smile.

"Anyway, back to Anita. What about her boyfriend? Did you look into him?"

"Dr. Luke McNally? Sure, I checked him out same as the police did when it happened. He was a clean kid. Got good grades. In pre-med at Vanderbilt. He and

Anita had been dating since she was sixteen. You already know all the jazz about the bracelet, so you get they were a solid couple. No cheating on either side. He was wrecked when it happened."

"And now, you still think he's clear?"

"Seems to be. He's married with two kids. He and his father run one of the family doctor practices in town. He did hook up with Mandy kinda fast though. They were together by the end of the year Anita went missing. It was hard seeing that."

"I'll bet. What about her? Could she have done something to Anita to get her out of the way?" When Roman simply frowned at her, Mia shrugged. "What? People do crazy things for love…or so I hear. Could be she'd been dreaming about Luke for years and went a little nuts."

"I guess it wouldn't hurt to look into her some more."

"What about other guys who might have been seriously crushing on Anita and wanted her for themselves?"

"You'd have made a good cop," Roman said with a smile. "Yeah, I thought of other guys but couldn't come up with anything solid. Luke was literally her first boyfriend. None of her friends had stories of any guy hitting on her or anything. I guess we could look again."

"Do tourists normally come and stay during Fourth of July?"

"More like out-of-town family members and friends. I see you've moved on to the random stranger theory?"

"Not really. She knew him," Mia said, thinking of her vision. "There was a kind of shocked disbelief in her head the whole time." She shook herself as though coming out of a trance. "I'm sorry. I shouldn't have said that. You're so matter of fact about everything, for a moment I forgot she was your sister."

Roman sighed. "You can't be worrying about my feelings. Don't hold anything back. Not ever. I need to know what you know." He paused and raked his fingers through his dark hair. "What if we go back to the woods by the park. Do you think you'll see more?"

"I don't know. Maybe. Maybe not. When I took you and Detective Latterly there to show you the spot, I saw it again, same as the first time. That was weird for me because it's normally a once only kind of thing. It could be that'll happen again, and I might notice something I missed before or could be the vision will last longer. It's worth a shot, I guess."

"Okay. That's something. It's late now, so let's do it tomorrow. Unless I catch something hot, I'll be off shift at six. I'll meet you there."

She stared at him for a moment. "Or you could phrase it like this…Mia, would you be available to meet me at Carlton Park tomorrow at six?" she said in an overly sweet voice.

"Yeah, that," Roman said impatiently. "You'll be there?"

"I'll be there," she huffed. "You know something? You're really bossy, and I'm not so good with orders. I guess we're going to have to work on that."

"Sure, Sugar, anything you say." Roman rolled his eyes, but he was smiling, too. "Okay, given that it's almost nine o'clock, I'm going to call it. I'll see you tomorrow." He pushed back from the table and got to his feet. Layla was right beside him again, staring up in adoration.

"I think someone wants to say goodbye," Mia observed.

Roman crouched down and rubbed Layla's face. "She sure is an awesome dog. Good night, Layla. Thanks for hanging with me."

"Be careful, you'll make the others jealous."

"Not him." Roman pointed to Mac. "He's a mama's boy if I ever saw one. And the two little ones seem to be more attached to the big dogs than anyone, so I'm hardly causing any trouble here."

Mia stared at him and shook her head. "Wow, I'd say you pretty much nailed the dynamics of the pack in one go."

"That's why I'm a detective," he said, winking at her and giving Layla one last pat. "Okay, I'm out of here. Thanks for…well, thanks. I'll see you tomorrow."

Spending the evening with Mia hadn't been so bad, Roman thought on the drive back to town. Sure, she was sometimes as prickly as a cactus, but she was smart and compassionate, and it was refreshing to be with a woman who pushed back a little. Not that he was looking at her as dating material because it was so not happening, but still, she was intriguing.

And it didn't hurt she had those big, soft, hazel eyes and all that long, thick, auburn hair with hints of fire running through it. The way the shades of brown and gold and red mixed together reminded him of a deer pelt. Her body wasn't bad either. Inviting to look at and plenty of curves. Almost begging a man to imagine exploring all the peaks and valleys of her.

He made a scoffing noise in his throat. And that was enough of that, he decided. Roman liked women, and especially sex, as much as the next guy, but he wasn't into complications. The kind of relationships—he thought the term was really too formal for what was essentially a series of sex-based companions—that suited him best were loose and uncomplicated. He knew damned well Mia was the polar opposite of uncomplicated.

Starting with the fact she wasn't really Mia Reeves. Oh, yeah, he knew the real Mia had died eight years ago. He found the obit for her in a Cleveland newspaper. Except he couldn't find a record of her death certificate. He'd even called around to a few of her friends. They'd confirmed she OD'd a month after graduating college.

Then five years ago, the Mia he knew had obviously taken on her identity. It was good, solid, black-market work. No doubt she'd paid a premium for the papers. If he weren't a cop and hadn't been digging so hard, he'd never have found it.

So the question that circled his head like a merry-go-round remained to be solved. Who the hell was this woman before she became Mia Reeves, and what was she running from?

Chapter Nine

Mia stepped off the asphalt and onto the soft ground at the edge of the woods where Roman stood waiting for her. He turned to face her and smiled. She glanced over his shoulder toward the trees. The sun had started sinking, but it was still plenty bright out. The forest, however, was shrouded in dim light as though determined to hold onto its secrets. She shivered.

"You…um…seeing anything yet?" Roman studied her face.

"Nothing so far. Let's keep walking."

They pushed in between the branches with Mia taking the lead. She worked to keep her mind clear and open. As though understanding, Roman remained silent while they walked all the way back to the rotting log. Mia dropped to the ground and sat cross-legged beside it, closing her eyes and breathing deeply. Silent minutes ticked by.

"I'm not getting anything," she said with a sigh.

Roman crouched down beside her. "Well, it was a long shot at best. Still, we had to try."

"Why didn't he leave her here?" Mia asked. "It had to be risky moving her body." Reaching out, she touched his arm. "I still find it tough talking to you about this. You'll have to tell me if I'm being too blunt."

"You're not," he said, his voice clipped. "This is how we find her. And yeah, I agree with you. It takes balls to move her from here. Remember what she was wearing?"

"Yes, navy cotton skirt and a light blue blouse."

"Right. Back in those days, Gabriel didn't have uniforms for his wait staff. The clothes you described are what she was wearing when she worked her shift the night she disappeared. You said it was dark in your vision, right?" He waited for Mia to nod. "If we put it all together, it's likely she was killed sometime during the night after she left work."

Mia nodded again, eyes on Roman. "And since she was walking, how the heck did she get here? It's a long hike from Main Street."

"More likely someone picked her up. All the stores on the street were closed by then. The coffee shop and Pizza Hut were open, of course, but no one remembers seeing her."

"Meaning she probably got in the car or was forced into one close to the diner. Are there any alleys around there? I should walk the route myself," Mia decided.

"Let's go now." Noticing her posture stiffen, he paused. "What I mean to say is, do you have time to do it now?"

"Why yes, Roman, as a matter of fact, this time suits me perfectly." She smiled at him and got to her feet. "See, it's not so hard, is it?"

"Harder than you'll ever know," he grumbled, trailing along after her.

When they got back into their separate vehicles, Roman took the lead, accelerating away from the parking lot and down the side street out to the main road. Mia shook her head. *Boys will be boys.*

He was already parked in a spot in front of Gabe's Diner and standing on the sidewalk waiting for her by the time she turned onto Main Street. An elderly woman stopped to speak to him, and Roman nodded and smiled, but his eyes were on Mia as she approached.

"Absolutely, Mrs. Smithers. I'll look into it first thing tomorrow. You have a nice night now."

Mia arched a brow. "Trouble?"

"Big trouble," he said, eyes solemn. "Those dang neighborhood thugs keep ripping off the lids of her garbage cans and throwing her garbage out on the street." He paused. "And by thugs, I have to assume she means the Jenkins boys, who are all of eight and ten, and the neighbor's child across the street, Gavin, who's at the dangerous age of eleven. According to Mrs. Smithers, he's on the cusp of committing his first felony." Roman's lips quirked up into a genuine smile. "There's no way it could be raccoons because Mrs. Smithers swears up and down there hasn't been a raccoon spotted in Dalton since the eighties."

"I guess she hasn't been to the park or looked in a tree or read the newspaper since then?"

"Probably thinks it's propaganda spread by possum lovers or maybe something even more sinister."

"Looks like you're going to have a busy day tomorrow," Mia said.

"Yep. But don't worry about me. I've run up against Gavin and the Jenkins's before. They're not as dangerous as everyone thinks."

She was caught by surprise when the laugh fell out of her. "You're funny."

"Everyone says so." His smile was huge, and they stood there grinning at one another.

Mia had a sudden awareness of him. He was a seriously hot guy with a tough, athletic body and dark Italian looks. His rich chocolate eyes were so deep, they seemed bottomless, and his skin looked as though it had been kissed by the sun. Though his smile was a little crooked, it was seriously sexy, and the way the skin creased at the side of his mouth made it seem as though it was not used to being pressed into that position.

No, she warned herself, when the warm, melty feeling rose up from her core. No, no, no. She absolutely could not allow herself to fall for Roman Mancini. Looking quickly away, she glanced over at the diner.

"Okay, Anita came out the front door, walked by the window right here, and disappeared?"

"That about sums it up." His eyes had gone cop flat again. "She'd have either gone down to the light and crossed at the end of the street or jaywalked over at some point. Up Oak Street four blocks then probably onto Drury or maybe Rebecca and then back over."

"If she'd gone to the end of Main to the lights, wouldn't someone in Bean Time have seen her?"

"Maybe. Especially as it was busy that night. According to the manager at the time, the tables by the window were full. Officially, we lean toward Anita disappearing from right here or crossing around here and then…"

"There's a variety store over there. Mia pointed to the other side of the street. "Plus, people in the café could still have looked out and seen her. I know it was about dark by then, but the street is well lit."

"We also have a witness who went jogging down that side of Main Street about nine thirty. It was a little after Anita left, but he still could have seen her. He claimed the street was empty. Then there's Alan Peterson who owns the third house along on Oak. He was out with his dog around nine fifteen. Said he hung outside for a time because it was such a nice night and his beagle likes sniffing around. He didn't see anyone go by. Grace Anderson on the other side and down a bit was smoking on her porch and said she saw a lady walking two dogs, but no one who looked like Anita. I don't think my sister went down Oak."

"Okay. If she didn't go that way then she didn't make it off Main Street on foot, right? What about this side street up here?" Mia pointed. She and Roman walked half a block north, stopping at the corner to look down the narrow street.

"It's an access road. See, it feeds into this alley that runs along the back of all the buildings on Main then keeps going a bit until it tees into Wellington. The police searched back here. I saw it in the report, but they didn't find any trace of Anita."

"But that doesn't mean she didn't get into a car. Once she was in, the driver could have kept going out to

Wellington and then over and up a couple of blocks onto Cressley where it's a straight shot to the park."

"Yeah, I know. So the person calls out to her as she's walking along the sidewalk. She hops in the car and is gone in seconds."

"Or he grabs her and tosses her in the car and disappears in seconds."

Roman pointed his index finger at her. "Except you don't believe that."

"No, I don't."

"Hey, Cuz, what're you doing?"

They turned to find Tony Mancini on the sidewalk. He winked at Mia and smiled broadly. The man was such a contrast to Roman with his streaky blond hair and light blue eyes. She wondered, then, if maybe he'd been adopted. But, no, as she continued studying his face, she realized his mouth was exactly the same shape as Roman's, and they both had an unruly cowlick on their hairline slightly left of center.

"We're poking around," Roman said. "Mia and I are going over what might have happened after Anita left work the night she disappeared."

Tony shut his eyes and shook his head. "I hate thinking about that night."

"I forgot. You were in town, weren't you?" Roman said.

"Sort of. I'd gone up to the cottage that morning. At least I had cell service, unlike you on your wilderness camping trip. If I hadn't left my phone in the car, I'd have come back straight away. As it was, the minute I checked my messages the next morning, I was in Dalton within the hour. We walked the streets all that day looking for her." Tony shook his head again, his expression bleak. "Even though it wasn't the required twenty-four hours on a missing person, the police took it seriously right off, but she was gone."

"I shoulda been here," Roman mumbled, shoving his hands in his pockets.

"And what? You'd have come down to the diner to walk Anita home because you had some psychic flash and knew something bad was gonna happen to her? No offense," Tony said, turning to Mia.

"None taken," she said lightly.

Not true, thought Roman, seeing the tiny vertical crease that had dug in between Mia's brows and the way she fought to keep her mouth soft when it really wanted to tighten into a hard line over her teeth. It shocked him to realize he knew even this much about the woman after spending only a handful of hours in her company.

"Anyway, even if I couldn't have saved her, at least it would've been easier for my parents if I'd been around."

"They had Lina and me. And the whole town was out looking for her." He paused, and his eyes flicked between Roman and Mia. "You really doing this thing with her?" he asked Roman.

Roman shrugged. "Sort of. We're going over old ground to see if anything pops out. I figure it can't hurt and has the added benefit of making Ma feel better."

"I'm glad to hear it. I think Mia's the real deal except I'm guessing by the fact you're both standing in an alley looking frustrated that you haven't found anything?"

"Not so far, but early days yet," Roman said.

"You should talk to Luke," Tony said, turning to Mia. "I never liked the guy."

"What's wrong with Luke?" Roman asked before Mia had a chance to say anything.

"He was never good enough for Anita. And then to top it off, he was with Mandy months after Anita goes missing. It still seems off to me."

"But he's a doctor, and everyone in town has nothing but good things to say about him," Mia said.

"I didn't say he wasn't smart, but Anita was…special. She had this kind of light about her. You know what I mean?" Tony cocked his head at Roman who nodded in response.

"She sounds wonderful," Mia said.

"Yeah, she really was. I miss her like crazy."

Roman patted his shoulder. "I know, man. Me, too."

"Talking to Luke seems like a good idea," Mia said. "Are any of her other friends still around?"

"There's Brooke. She took over the dance studio on Wellington. Too bad Ashley doesn't live here anymore. After college, she got a job in Nashville. It's not that long of a hike to go see her," Tony said.

"I think we can start with Luke and Brooke before we go planning a road trip. How come you're on board with this all of a sudden?" Roman asked Tony.

"I don't know. It sounded crazy when Uncle Frank called us, but now I've met the psychic…" He flashed a thousand watt smile at Mia." I kinda like her."

"Gee, I hardly know what to do with all this flattery," Mia said fluttering her eyelashes at the two men.

Tony shifted to the side, glancing past Mia to the diner. "Okay, folks, I gotta eat. Either of you want to join me?"

"I'd better get home," Mia said.

"I'll walk you to your car. See ya, Tony."

"Sure. If there's anything I can do to help, just say the word. And Cuz, make sure to let me know if you two find anything."

"He seems really nice," Mia said as they walked along the sidewalk.

"Yeah, he's a good guy. His mom left when he was around twelve. Then his dad died, so he's been living with us ever since. I basically think of him as my brother."

"Where's his mom now?"

"I assume she's still in Beverly Hills with her second husband and their kids. Don't get me started on Candice. As far as I'm concerned she's a stone cold bitch."

"Oh, poor Tony. Being rejected like that by a parent can cut anyone off at the knees."

"You can say that again. The first few years with us were tough, but then he turned it around. Anita was the one he really bonded with. They were close. I was worried he'd go right off the rails when she disappeared. Don't get me wrong, he was a total wreck just like the rest of us, but he also found his focus. Started working hard in college, getting ahead. He told me once Anita was the reason. She would have wanted him to do well. It made me feel better when he said that."

"It sounds like he's had a tough life, and now with me bringing the Anita thing back, it can't be easy on him."

"It ain't easy on any of us, but it's better to know, I think." Roman shook his head. "Sorry for dumping all that on you. Has anyone ever told you you're real easy to talk to?"

She snorted. "Not exactly."

"Well, you are. Anyway. We should make a plan. Tony was right about you talking to the players involved. Would you be comfortable if I set something up with Luke and Brooke?"

She nodded slowly. "I guess so. But don't say anything about what I can do, okay? People tend to get pretty weirded out."

"There've been rumors all over town since we went searching in the woods last week."

"Yeah, but rumors are one thing. Coming out and announcing it to people is something else entirely. It doesn't usually go well. Trust me on this."

He searched her eyes. "I guess I can see that. Okay, I'll think of something that doesn't involve witches or voodoo or psychic visions."

"Gee, thanks. I feel so much better now."

He slapped a hand on her shoulder. "Anytime, my gypsy friend. Okay, my work here is done. I'll call you tomorrow. Give Layla a pat for me."

He opened her car door and waited until she buckled up before shutting it firmly and giving her a short wave. Then he turned back and strode down the sidewalk toward his car.

Chapter Ten

As a rule, Mia didn't answer her phone while she was creating jewelry. It was all too easy to lose the thread of contact between herself and whatever crystal she was working on. She knew the reason her business had become a success, beyond her wildest dreams, was because the customers, although they couldn't fully explain why, felt an immediate bond with the piece of jewelry she made for them.

It all came down to the fact that once Mia had a sense of the person, she could find the exact stone that would bring them what they most needed. Whether that was increased energy, serenity, creativity, fearlessness, or any other thing in an infinite number of possibilities, there was a perfect crystal for each person.

And sure, that might change over time because no one ever stayed the same, but the beauty of it was the customer would simply contact her again when they felt a new need bubbling to the surface. In the last year, her percentage of repeat business was well above what she'd projected.

The thing that ignited the sales in the first place had been phenomenal word of mouth. Customers told family and friends about her products, tweeted about them, or posted pictures to *Instagram*. Within the first six months, she was already at the point of breaking even. The growth would no doubt have continued at a steady climb from there, but then one of those serendipitous things happened to shoot her into the stratosphere.

Rising Hollywood A-lister Melinda Frost somehow heard about her products and contacted Mia to order one of the pendant designs. Shortly afterward, Melinda landed the biggest role of her career when she was cast as Rebecca in the Rebecca Jones movie franchise. When the first movie came out, it hit big and hit hard, smashing all box office records. The second one was due to be released in the fall, and everyone was predicting another home run.

While doing publicity for the first movie, Melinda had been a guest on *Girl Talk with Corrine,* the top-rated daytime talk show in North America. Not only did she wear the azurite necklace Mia made for her, but it caught the eye of Corrine herself. This sparked off a discussion of Melinda's belief in the spiritual power of crystals, and she gushed on and on about Mia's work.

Since then, Healing Crystals had been a non-stop, going concern.

Mia had grown up believing the straight life was for losers and suckers; yet here she was, a bona fide businesswoman and loving every minute of it. She'd never imagined she could get so much pleasure from creating something and putting it out in the world. And even now, more than two years later, she still loved the process of making jewelry and bringing joy to her customers while swelling her bank account.

She was concentrating on a bracelet of green aventurine and amethyst when her phone signaled. She was so used to ignoring it that several seconds went by before she registered the *Jaws* theme music she'd assigned to Roman Mancini. Sighing, she placed the amethyst down on the table and plucked up her cell.

"Hi, Roman."

"Hey, Mia. I know we talked about meeting up tonight. The thing is I caught a case. It's a messy domestic, and I'm going to be tied up for the rest of the day and then some. I'll touch base with you tomorrow when I know what's what."

"Oh, okay. Sure." She was hit with a sudden sense of pain. "You're all right? Not hurt?"

The background noise was overpowering, and at first, she wasn't sure he'd heard her, but then he chuckled. "I'm fine. Can't say the same for the husband who's in emergency getting his face stitched up. Okay. Gotta go. I'll call you."

She returned focus to the bracelet, but when thirty minutes had passed, and she still couldn't settle into her work, Mia put down the pliers and dropped the crystals into a temporary holding tray. It was no use pushing when what she obviously needed was to clear her head. Besides, it was already early afternoon. She'd missed lunch, and the dogs were more than ready to stretch their legs.

Mia and the pack wandered along by the stream at the back of her property. All the canines loved it, but Tucker found this especially thrilling and darted in and out of the stream like a deep sea diver. The happy Dachshund shook furiously, spraying Mia's shins and knees before turning with a bark and throwing himself in head-first once again.

This was good, Mia thought. Nothing beats walking her property with the dogs on a beautiful day. She'd grab a snack back at the house, and maybe be able to focus on her work. She admitted that delving into Anita's murder was a huge distraction. The orders for jewelry were piling up, and these last two nights she'd come home from meeting Roman and gone straight back to work for several hours. If she could get another solid day under her belt, she'd be almost caught up.

Still, even after the walking break, she couldn't bring her mind under control and finally gave up. Sure, she could put the jewelry together because the assembly was nothing more than a learned skill. Without the focused mental and emotional energy, though, the customers would end up with beautiful pieces that didn't touch them on anything other than the physical realm. Before long, people would lose interest. Her work would be written off as nothing more than a pretty novelty item.

Putting her tools down again, she sighed. Mac immediately popped up from his bed by the window and laid his head onto her lap, pressing in hard against her as if in comfort. "It's okay, big guy. Nothing's really wrong. It's this Anita thing. If only I could figure out what happened to her, maybe I could finally let it go and get on with my life."

He groaned in agreement, rolling his eyes to look up at her.

"I know," she said, stroking her fingers across his head. "I should go into town and talk to Luke and Brooke myself. I'm a big girl. I don't need Roman with me."

With the decision made, she changed into a flowy cotton skirt and fitted blouse. Finding a pair of wire cutters in one pocket of the discarded jeans and pliers in the other, she took the tools back down to her work table and tidied the area. Then, making sure the doggie door was open, and the water bowls full, she locked the front door and jogged to her car.

Mia decided to approach Brooke first. She'd googled the dance studio the night before and knew roughly where it was located. In under ten minutes, she was parked outside the sunny yellow building.

Music blasted out through the speaker system in the main studio—Taylor Swift if she wasn't mistaken—and five tiny girls laughed and leapt about in time to the beat while a young woman wandered the room calling out instructions. Glancing over at Mia, she gave her a come-ahead gesture with one hand.

"Are you Brooke Adams?" Mia studied the instructor's face. Can't be, too young, she thought.

"No, I'm Callie," the girl said. "Brooke's in her office back there."

Glancing over her shoulder, Mia spotted two doors along the side wall. One of which had the word OFFICE painted in bold blue. The blinds on the window were up, and she could see a blond woman sitting at a desk. She knocked hesitantly on the door.

"Come on in, Callie. Problem?" The woman didn't look up from the laptop on her desk.

"Excuse me, I'm looking for Brooke Adams."

"You found her." Now the face lifted and Mia saw china-blue eyes, large and stunning, in the delicately featured face. "How can I help you?"

"This is going to seem a bit odd, but I'm Mia Reeves, a friend of the Mancini family. I was hoping you'd talk to me about Anita." Mia held her breath while Brooke studied her.

"Wow, I've never met a private investigator before. You're not what I expected."

"I'm not really—"

"It's okay, I know you're probably not technically supposed to tell me who hired you, but Roman called yesterday and asked if I'd mind speaking with you. Everyone was saying you're some kind of psychic or something. A PI makes more sense. Roman told me his mom was having a hard time with it coming up to the ten year anniversary." She shook her head and blew out a breath. "It's still hard for me, too. Sometimes I imagine Anita will walk in the door one day and tell us she was on this amazing adventure. Anyway, I have no problem talking to you. Callie's taking the next class, and I'm not back on the floor until five, so I have some time now."

Stupidly, Mia wasn't prepared for this outcome, and she gulped involuntarily. Seeming not to notice her unease, Brooke smiled at her.

"Oh, I'm sorry. Where are my manners? Can I get you a coffee or maybe something cold?"

"I'm fine, thanks," Mia said, shifting uneasily while she tried to formulate a jumping off point into the conversation about Anita.

"Here, I could use a break from the desk. Let's sit over there and be comfortable."

Lithe and graceful, Brooke moved across the room and sank into a Windsor chair arranged by the window. Breathing out a sigh of relief, Mia followed and settled on the love seat.

"Maybe you could tell me about the last time you saw Anita," Mia began.

Brooke's eyes immediately clouded with emotion. "It was the Monday she disappeared. I was working here at the studio for the summer, and I had the morning off. Anita and I met for lunch at Gabe's. We were both tired after the weekend. It was right after the Fourth of July festival, and Dalton really got into celebrating. I was doing dance demos all the way through, and our younger students were in the parade. Anita had worked double shifts on Saturday and Sunday at the diner."

"Other than tired, she seemed okay?"

"You know, I've gone over it a million times in my head. She didn't say anything was wrong. Yeah, we were both seriously bagged, but she did seem a little…I don't know what…at the time I thought she was clumsy because she was tired, but now I wonder if it was maybe something else."

The scene flashed into Mia's mind, the two girls at a booth along the back wall of the diner. Brooke was wearing a pale pink leotard and had a sarong wrapped around her waist. Anita was in the same outfit she died in. They were both slumped back against the padded bench, and Brooke was talking about some boy named Bobby. She was furious because he went off with his friends and got drunk on the Saturday afternoon while she was working. Then he was passed out for the fireworks and party later that night.

Anita commiserated, saying guys were so lame sometimes, but she checked her watch several times. When the food came, she knocked her cutlery on the floor before finally spilling her drink all over the table.

"Did she mention anything? Like she was nervous or scared for some reason?"

Brooke shook her head. "No. She just seemed distracted or out of it or something."

"This wasn't in the police report, was it?"

She sighed and looked away. "No, because I honestly forgot about it until much later. And then it seemed stupid to go to the police and tell them I remembered Anita knocked her Diet Coke on the table. Do you think it's important?"

Mia sensed the tension climbing in the other woman and worried she might lose focus. "Probably not. So, she was tired and distracted, but otherwise okay. What did you two talk about?"

"The usual girl stuff. Our boyfriends. I was dating a total douche bag, but Anita was with Luke McNally. You probably already know that. Well, she was gone on him. Like, let's get married gone. She had this whole plan about finishing school and starting their careers before doing the big wedding thing. Not that he'd asked her yet." Brooke's words seemed to pour out without a breath. "But everyone could see they were perfect together. Even from here, at the wise old age of twenty-nine, I can't help looking back and thinking they might have actually made it."

"You liked Luke?"

"Sure, he's a nice guy. Even as a teenager he was decent. Kinda serious and definitely knew what he wanted to do, but also really sweet with Anita. It's still hard for me to see him and Mandy together."

"Someone mentioned Luke and Mandy started dating the same year Anita disappeared. Did that make you wonder at all?"

Her lips pressed into a hard line, and she shook her head. "At the time, I was devastated when he and Mandy hooked up. It felt like such a betrayal. Like he'd never loved Anita. I was a total bitch to him. I couldn't let it go. I'd call him up all the time and yell at him, cry, basically melt down on the phone."

Brooke got to her feet and stepped up to the window overlooking the studio where she stood for several seconds, head bowed and breath hitching. "He never blocked my number. Never told me to get lost. Just kept saying he was sorry. He missed her, too. It took me a long time to realize what he said was true. He could be with Mandy and still have a broken heart for Anita. You know what I always wondered though? Why would Mandy want him like that knowing Anita was always the one?"

She turned and stared at Mia.

"I understand Luke and what he did after, but I still don't get Mandy. Not at all."

Mia frowned. "Are you suggesting she had something to do with Anita's disappearance?"

Brooke let out a long breath and sank back down onto the chair. "No, I mean, it doesn't seem likely. She was home with her parents that night. I know the police looked into her because as soon as she and Luke got together, I kept hounding Roman about it. She couldn't have done it, but it seems weird to me."

"Is there anyone else you can think of whose behavior seemed suspicious after Anita disappeared?"

Brooke dabbed at her eyes and let out another sigh. "I'm sorry. It's stupid to cry after all this time, but I still miss her so much. Me and Anita and Ashley were friends all through high school. Ashley was probably always going to move away, but I could picture me and Anita staying here in Dalton. Maybe raising our kids together. Not that I have kids, but I might have if Anita was still around…her disappearing totally messed me up, and honestly, it only feels like I'm getting myself together now. I know I was seeing someone back then, but I'd always kind of had a crush on Tony."

"I've met him. Did you guys ever date?"

"No, but I would have in a hot minute if he'd asked me. After Anita, well…we were all lost for a while. Then he was gone to finish school and live in Nashville. I guess it wasn't meant to be."

"Yeah, sometimes life really does suck," Mia mumbled. "I'm sorry talking about this upset you. I really appreciate your time."

Brooke hiccupped once and then blew her nose. "That's okay. To be honest, it feels sorta good, like I'm glad she's not being forgotten."

"From everything I've learned, I doubt Anita will ever be forgotten. All right, I'd better go. Thanks again." Mia opened the door to the studio and stood for a minute watching the little girls do stretching exercises on the floor. "Hey, Brooke, do you have beginner classes for adults?"

"Sure." She smiled and walked over to join her. "We have a class on Wednesday nights. It's only a handful of ladies, but they really enjoy it. You should come. Dancing is great exercise and a limber body ages really well."

Mia glanced back at Brooke. "If dancing will make my body look like yours, I'm all in."

"Next block starts July tenth. I'll look for you." Her smile slipped away. "I hope you find out what happened to Anita. Good or bad it'll maybe give me some peace, you know?"

"I'll do my best."

Chapter Eleven

Shortly after nine the next morning, Roman called. "Hey, I heard you talked to Brooke yesterday."

"Is that a problem?"

"Down girl, chill out. No, it's not a problem. I'd hoped to be with you because four ears are better than two, but progress is progress. How'd it go?"

Mia shrugged, forgetting he couldn't see her. "Okay, I think. She's really sweet. I didn't know you were going to tell everyone I'm a PI."

He chuckled. "It seemed the easiest solution. And besides, thanks to TV and movies, people have a romantic notion of private investigators, so I figured it'd only help our cause. Did you…were you…did you see anything when you were with her?"

"Not really. Nothing that helps at least. But Brooke did say she thought Anita was *off* when they met for lunch."

"Off how?" His tone switched to full-on cop mode in the blink of an eye.

"She isn't totally sure about it but said Anita was sort of clumsy and distracted. At the time she thought it was to do with being tired from the July fourth weekend, but it still niggles at her."

"She never said anything to the police."

"I know. I asked about that. She said with all the upset at the time Anita disappeared she forgot about it and later, she felt stupid going to the police."

Roman was quiet for several beats. Mia could hear his breathing, short and harsh. "It doesn't really help us much, does it?" he finally asked.

"Not so far, but who knows, maybe it's a part of the jigsaw, and we can't see the whole picture yet."

"Yeah, okay. Anyway, I thought we could talk to Luke tonight. He said he'd meet us at Bean Time around six thirty. Does that work for you?"

"Sure. I'll be there."

Bean Time had a very different vibe compared to Gabe's Diner. Inside, the décor consisted of exposed brick, industrial lighting, and metal tables. The crowd it attracted was also the polar opposite of the family atmosphere in the diner. These customers seemed young and hip, and Mia felt as though she had walked into a big city downtown coffee shop. Every other person was wearing tiny glasses and a scarf—even though it was summer—and pointy shoes.

She stared around in amazement. Had all these urban looking creatures really come from this town? How come she'd never noticed them walking around the streets or in the stores? Out of the corner of her eye, she caught movement and turned to see Roman waving from a table in the back.

He stood when she approached and flashed a smile, his dark liquid eyes seeming to sparkle. When her stomach started a series of flips, she ruthlessly shut it down.

"Hi, Roman," she said, purposely making her tone brisk. "Luke's not here yet?"

He slid in opposite her and stretched his arm across the backrest of the neighboring chair. "Called and said he'd be here in ten. I guess that means we have a couple of moments to hang out first. So…how was your day?"

"Fine, thanks. Yours?"

"Oh, you know, kinda dull. Nothing like yesterday. That domestic sure was a highlight."

"You have a sick mind."

He leaned forward in his seat, eyes lasering in on hers. "No, you don't understand. It's not that I like seeing people hurt, but in this case, the outcome was good. The woman had been beaten around some these last few years, and every time it happened either wouldn't file charges or dropped them the next morning. This time she's sticking. Even got herself a lawyer. I love when you do your job and get a happy ending at the same time."

Mia nodded slowly. "I guess that must be very satisfying." She paused, and he didn't look away but remained intent on her face. It was disconcerting, and she glanced around the cafe, searching for something to talk about. When her mind remained stubbornly blank, she gestured to the front counter. "Do you want a coffee or anything? I'm going to get a latte. I could use a little boost."

"Sure, I'll take another hit of caffeine. Make mine an Americano, black."

He smiled and leaned back against the chair, and for a moment she was distracted by the way his biceps flexed against the sleeve of his T-shirt. After what she was sure was too long of a gawking session, she got to her feet and turned away.

It was a relief to stand in line for several minutes while she waited to order. In the beginning, she'd seen Roman only as a cop and the brother of a dead girl…not to mention someone to be avoided because he might dig up her unsavory past and make trouble for her in the almost-too-good-to-be-true present.

Now, though, she was starting to know him a little. What she saw was a seriously hot male specimen. He loved his family, especially his mother. That fact alone was enough to melt her heart. Roman was passionate about his work, had a definite dominant streak, which could end up being annoying, but was also a pretty big turn-on. And lastly, she was fairly sure he wasn't dating anyone, so it would seem he was unattached and available.

All in all, Roman Mancini was quite the catch.

But not for her, she amended, remembering her vow. She tended to be a loner, happy with her own company and her dogs. People, in general, were too much damned work. When it came to men, they were nothing more than an invitation to get messy. She didn't do messy. By the time she returned to the table with the coffees, she'd talked herself and her libido all the way back down to earth.

Roman's hand lingered on hers when she passed him the mug. "Thanks. I'll get it the next time."

Mia refused to be thrilled at the thought of them getting together again for coffee. Without thinking, she took a sip of her latte, burning the roof of her mouth. "Dammit," she sputtered.

"Yeah, it hurts like a bitch, doesn't it," Roman said. "I'll get you a water or something."

When he sprang to his feet, Mia reached out and touched his arm to stop him. "No, it's fine. I'm already okay."

He glanced down at the hand on his wrist and smiled. "Okay. If you're sure."

The flush raced up Mia's chest and neck and landed on her cheeks, and she snatched her hand back and put it in her lap. God, she was behaving like a teenager on her first date, and this was the farthest thing from a date.

"Hey, Mia, it's okay for us to be friends." Roman's voice was soft. "I know I was kind of a jerk to you in the beginning, but I appreciate everything you're doing to help find Anita. It means a lot, so thank you. And now that you've stopped showing up at the police station and lying right to my face, I can see you're a pretty cool chick."

She lifted an eyebrow at him. "A pretty cool chick? Wow, there's a compliment."

"Yeah, I didn't want to get too sloppy and ruin our dynamic." He shrugged and winked at her before his attention shifted over her left shoulder. "Hey, Luke, you made it. Thanks for coming."

Roman got to his feet and held out a hand. The man was almost as tall as Roman's six-foot-two but leaner and rangier. They shook hands, and Mia stood and offered hers as well.

"It's nice to meet you. I'm Mia Reeves."

Luke smiled at her briefly. In his pale green eyes, she saw both fatigue and wariness. "Hi, Mia. My wife loves your jewelry. She bought a necklace and a pair of earrings at the fair last week. Hasn't taken them off since."

"Oh, that's nice to hear. Thank you. Can we get you a coffee or anything?"

"Nah, I'm good."

Roman gestured to the seat beside him. Luke sat with a sigh while he and Mia returned to their chairs. "How are Mandy and the kids?" Roman asked.

"Good. Busy. It seems like the boys are on the go twenty-four seven. Neil started soccer this summer, and I can tell it won't be long before Patrick will be ready, too. Then there's judo, swimming, skating. You name it, and they're doing it." He paused and swallowed. "I didn't tell Mandy I was meeting you, by the way. It can get awkward sometimes. You understand?"

"Yeah, sure. I get it." Roman nodded and spread his hands on the table. "Anyway, I asked you here because Mia thought it might help to talk to you, ask some questions."

Before Mia could follow her cue and wade in, Luke turned to her. "It's weird that you're a jeweler *and* a private investigator. How do you have time for both?"

"Oh, well…the PI work is really secondary. I'm pretty much easing out of it, in fact. The hours are lousy sometimes. Besides, my jewelry business is going really well, so I think I'll stick with that. I'm sorta doing this as a favor."

Luke nodded, seeming to accept the explanation. "What do you want to know?"

"Let's see…um…when was the last time you saw Anita before she disappeared?"

He frowned and glanced at Roman. "I already told the police a million times. Isn't it in the report?" He sighed and bowed his head. "We met on Sunday night at Pizza Hut. Anita only had a short break. She was working until closing, so we grabbed a bite around five thirty."

"What about the next day? You talked to her, right? I remember that showing in the phone records."

"Yeah, I did. A couple of times. We were supposed to meet for lunch before she started her shift but I…couldn't…I got tied up at work. I was interning at my dad's office that summer and you know how it is, especially when you're the son of the boss. Can't just cut out whenever you want."

"I guess she ended up eating lunch with Brooke that day?"

"Yeah, I know. I shoulda pushed harder to get away. I don't even remember what it was that kept me back now. Stupid. So stupid."

His fist pounded down on the table, and Mia felt the anguish in her own body. His emotions were so raw it was easy to push into him. What she saw was a surprise though, and her breath hitched when the snippets of a scene flashed by. Inside a restaurant she didn't recognize, Luke and Anita were leaning close together across the table and talking intently. Arguing maybe? Anita wiped at a tear on her cheek. Luke's eyes were hard and his face infused with red.

"Was everything okay between you and Anita before she disappeared?" Mia blurted out.

Luke shrank back, but seeming to catch himself, squared his shoulders and turned to face her. "Yes, of course. We were crazy about one another."

Mia was aware of Roman's sudden interest. His foot shifted over and rested lightly against hers under the table. When she flicked her glance across to his face, the message was clear in her mind to keep pressing this button.

"Oh, I know you two were tight. But couples, even the most loving and connected ones, have disagreements from time to time. I've heard Anita wasn't herself the day she disappeared. You know, distracted and out of sorts. Maybe you guys had a fight the night before, at dinner?" she pressed.

"We were fine," Luke insisted. "Nothing was wrong."

Mia couldn't see into him anymore, but she felt his fear rising up like a tidal wave followed by the most devastating pain. Then everything in her mind went dark. With a nod at Roman, she pushed away from her connection with Luke and exhaled quietly, trying to rid herself of the panicky sensation. She hated allowing anyone's negative energy to invade her.

Unfortunately, the energy wouldn't budge, and now her own uneasy fear joined in until her heartbeat pounded in her head and spots appeared in her line of vision. She climbed unsteadily to her feet. "I need to use the ladies room," she said in a voice that sounded miles away from her.

She caught a glimpse of concern in Roman's eyes and saw him pushing to his feet, but she shook her head, turned away, and fled to the restroom.

* * *

Mia stepped out of the ladies' room to see Roman leaning against the wall swiping the screen on his phone and obviously waiting for her. His head snapped up the minute she appeared.

"Hey, you okay?"

She nodded, ignored the rising rush of embarrassment, and glanced over his shoulder toward their table. "I'm fine. Did Luke leave?"

"Yeah. He was pretty frazzled after you bolted though trying his damnedest not to show it. Then he pretended to get a text, which he didn't because I was near enough to see his screen. He made some lame excuse about getting home to help with the boys."

"Oh, I'm so sorry. I shouldn't have left like I did. I just…couldn't stay."

Roman's eyes scanned her face for a long moment. "What happened back there? You went ghost white. I swear you looked as if you were gonna drop like a stone. Did you see something again?"

Mia sighed and leaned against the wall beside him. "Not exactly. I think maybe Luke and Anita had a fight the night before she disappeared, but it was only a glimpse. I have no idea what it was about. That's not what got to me though. It was his fear and pain today. As soon as I started asking about that stuff, he was terrified and it…okay, it's hard to explain without sounding like a lunatic, but when the feeling gets into me, it's…it's horrible. I had to get rid of it. Except I couldn't while I was sitting right across from him. I needed some distance." She paused and stared down at her feet.

"Hey, I'm sorry." Roman's voice was barely more than a whisper. "I didn't realize helping me would bring you so much pain. Look, we can drop it for now. If something comes to you—like before at the park—then great, but you don't need to put yourself through this. The truth is, Anita's gone. She's not coming back. Nothing we figure out is gonna change that."

Her breath caught, and she raised her eyes to meet Roman's. In them she felt his genuine concern and sorrow. Steeling herself, she pushed out with her mind. Now his sadness and what was it?...remorse, maybe...filtered into her.

She stepped away from the wall. "No, absolutely not. We keep looking. Keep asking. I can handle it. Sometimes I'll need a moment to stabilize myself and sometimes, if it's too much, I'll have to back away entirely for a bit, but I'll be fine. Honest."

His head shook back and forth like a dog with a bone. "No, I can't ask you to do this. It's not right."

She grabbed his arm and squeezed tight, taking more of his despair into herself...taking as much of it as she could stand so he'd be sure to feel a good, solid lift of mood and energy. He gazed at her hand for a moment and then back into her eyes, the question showing clearly on his face.

What the hell? Why did she care so much all of a sudden? This was so unlike her. She couldn't seem to think her way through the feelings to even begin figuring it out.

"It's my decision," she insisted stubbornly. "I'm going to keep looking for your sister whether you want me to or not."

The silence stretched on for a few more moments, but she was content to wait while he stared down at her. Finally, he smiled, and his eyes warmed all the way through.

"You know something, Mia? You fascinate me. I've never met anyone like you."

His hand reached out, and soft fingers stroked her cheek, causing her breath to once again catch in her throat. Carefully, painstakingly slowly, he lowered his face to hers while she stared back at him, heart galloping. When their lips met, Mia stopped thinking entirely and threw herself into the kiss. He tasted of coffee. His lips were warm and soft and somehow exactly perfect against hers.

A moan rose up from her chest, and she pressed into him, chest to chest, while his arms wrapped around her shoulders and stroked down her back. Somehow her hands were in his hair, all the masses of glorious black silk, and he eased her against the wall as their lips parted and tongues stroked in.

The wanting, the needing, clawed at her with such force she felt dizzy. Heat washed over her, and she closed her eyes against the too bright lights of the hallway before wriggling her hands up in between their bodies and pushing him back.

"No," she said. "This isn't going to happen."

"From my point of view, it's already happening," Roman said, but he shifted away and released her from the wall. "There's something here. Don't you think we owe it to ourselves to figure out what it is?"

She shook her hair back and brushing by him, walked several steps before turning to face him again.

"It's nothing more than some basic sexual heat. It happens all the time. I don't know about you, but if I followed every hit of lust to its obvious conclusion I'd never get anything else done."

She didn't like the look of the smile breaking over his face.

"That was more than basic sexual heat, and you know it, but I get it might have scared you some. My powers with women are an awesome responsibility," he drawled. "No worries. I can wait until you've wrestled your fear back down to manageable levels. But know this. I'm not done with you. Not by a long shot."

"Oh, please, get over yourself," she snapped. "I'm not twelve. Come to think of it, that 'you're scared and I can wait' crap wouldn't have worked on me even back then. I'm not scared. I'm just saying no."

When he crossed his arms over his chest and kept right on smiling as if some all-knowing wise man, she growled and whirled away.

"I'll go and talk to Luke again tomorrow. Alone," she called out over her shoulder before disappearing around the corner and back into the coffee shop.

Chapter Twelve

It took a bit of pleading, but eventually Luke agreed to meet with Mia, this time in his office at the clinic. And while he was courteous and answered her questions, there was now a definite mental barrier erected between them. Although it was unlikely he'd have known Mia probed into his mind the day before, some part of him was blocking her out nonetheless.

When she realized she was getting nowhere with him, Mia decided to throw caution to the wind and go for it.

"Luke, I can't help having this feeling something was going on with Anita the day she disappeared. If you know anything, please tell me because it could really help. The Mancini family is desperate to have some closure." She grimaced and held up her hand. "I know, I hate that word, too, but in this case, finding her body would perhaps bring them some peace. I'm sure it must be the same for you?"

He scowled and leaned back in his chair. "Of course, I want that, but I don't know anything. Frankly, the way you're pressing this point—as if I'm the one who...made her disappear or know what happened and have been withholding the information all these years—is insulting. I think we're done here." He stood and walked around the desk. "I've given you more than enough of my time, and I won't talk to you about Anita again."

Mia got to her feet and trailed after Luke to the door. It was only as she pulled her purse strap over her shoulder that she remembered what she'd brought and unzipped the outside compartment. She withdrew a slim, silver box embossed with Healing Crystals on the lid.

"I brought this for your wife." She held the box out for Luke who studied it through narrowed eyes. "You said she enjoyed my jewelry, so I thought she might like this bracelet." When he continued staring at the box, she sighed and lifted the lid. "Look, it's not a bribe or anything, honest. I'm passionate about my art, and if Mandy appreciates it too, I'd love for her to have another piece. The stones are rose quartz for relaxation. Please, take it. No strings attached."

Finally, he reached out and grasped the box, turning the bracelet over with his finger. "It's nice. I think she'll like it. Thank you."

"You're most welcome. Thanks again for talking to me."

Mia shrugged internally while she walked back to her SUV. All in all, it could've been worse, she supposed. Yeah, Luke had more or less tossed her out of his office, but he hadn't been nasty, and she had the feeling he was the type of man who wouldn't necessarily hold it against her.

Turning back toward Main Street, she caught sight of Gabe's Diner and found herself pulling into a parking space out front. Gabriel got off his stool and walked over to the take-out counter to greet her.

"Good afternoon, my friend. Is the Lord smiling down on you today?"

"Um…yes, thanks. How about you?"

He grinned. "Of course. For this is the day the Lord has made. Let us rejoice and be glad in it. Now, what can I get you?"

She couldn't help returning the smile. Gabriel loved his Bible quotes, that was for sure.

After placing her order, she slid into an empty booth by the door and settled down to wait for her food. A woman and two small children were the only serious diners with a smattering of older couples enjoying coffee or tea in this lull time between lunch and night service.

The waitress circled the room topping up beverages. Mia studied the woman's turquoise skirt and golf shirt with its piped chocolate trim. Gabe's Diner was stamped in large block letters across the back. She found herself musing that while the color washed out the woman's skin and made her dishwater blond hair look even drabber than it probably was, it would have suited Anita perfectly.

Mia waved her arm, catching the older woman's eye. She came straight over, lifting the coffee pot in question.

"No, thanks. I'm waiting for take-out. Are you Mary by any chance?"

"That's what it says right here," she said, pointing to her nametag.

"Of course, it does," Mia said.

"You're Mia Reeves, girl detective and jewelry maker and mama to a pack of dogs. It's a wonder you have time for everything."

"Yes, well, the PI stuff is really, really part-time, if you know what I mean. You worked with Anita Mancini?"

"Sure did. I was the one who trained her when she started here. There were just eight of us waitressing back then. Anita did a couple nights a week, not too late though causa school, and weekends of course. The diner was smaller then. Those two party rooms were added on about five years ago." She slid in opposite Mia with a sigh.

"You were here the night she disappeared?"

"That's right. I talked to the police 'til I was blue in the face, but there was nothing I could really tell 'em. Me and Anita were standing there by the front door after she finished her shift. I still had a couple of hours to go."

"What did you talk about?"

"Oh, well, this and that. A bit about the work schedule for the upcoming week. A bit about the fair and July fourth celebration. I'd heard some gossip about one of our regular customers, and we were chewing over that."

"Did she seem her normal self? Someone else told me she was distracted at lunch before she started her shift."

Mary shook her head. "She seemed fine to me. Tired for sure, but her usual efficient self."

"Were she and Luke fighting at all during that time?"

"Anita and Luke? Lord, no. Even as teenagers those two were already like an old married couple. None of the usual drama or tears with them. Two solid kids, getting good grades and making plans for the future." Mary's voice hitched on the last few words, and she pulled her lips tight as though determined to fight off any hint of emotion.

"Nothing unusual," Mia said, half to herself.

Mary snorted. "The most unusual thing I can think of was Anita said she needed to switch a shift at the end of the week because she had a doctor's appointment she'd forgotten to put on her calendar. That girl was so organized I think she only ever switched shifts a handful of times in the five years she worked here."

"Okay, thanks. I appreciate you talking to me."

"I have to tell you, you've given a lot of us around here some real hope. You think you'll be able to find out what happened to her?" Mary asked.

Mia sighed. "I'll try."

Back in her car, Mia set the bag of food on the passenger seat and rested her head against the steering wheel. Mary's words made her feel useless. Why couldn't she figure out where Anita was?

And if she didn't find her, what she'd done with stirring everything up was doing more harm than good. The Mancinis didn't need more pain. Neither did Tony or Brooke or even Luke. She'd only been trying to do the right thing. If she hadn't been so certain they'd find Anita's body in the woods by the park, she never would have started all this in the first place.

The park. There had to be something else there. Something to point her in the right direction. Starting the Escape, she pulled away from the curb and drove across to the far side of town. The parking area held some cars, and the playground was covered with small children. Of course, the school was out for the day. The weather was perfect for playing.

Mia grabbed her food and wandering over to the edge of the forest, chose a spot in the shade of an oak tree. Lowering to the ground and tucking her legs up underneath her, she pulled out the veggie wrap and ate it slowly while watching the people come and go in the distance.

This section of the park was blessedly free of humans, and she relaxed degree by degree. Squirrels dashed about, galloping up and down trees. Birds chattered to one another, a symphony of tweets and chirps. Leaning against the trunk of the tree and thankful the girl at the take-out counter hadn't paid attention when she said she didn't need cutlery, Mia opened the lid of the quinoa salad and spooned some up to her mouth.

When the food was gone, she leaned back and closed her eyes, letting the sounds of the forest wash over her. The breeze was warm across her skin, and it ruffled her hair gently against her neck. She allowed her mind to wander, skipping from Mary's well-worn face under the bright lights of the diner to the children climbing the jungle gym to her latest jewelry orders before finally settling on Roman.

That kiss. Holy cow. He'd been right. It was a whole lot more than simple heat, but the sad fact of the matter was she couldn't let it go any further. Roman was looking for more than a hookup and getting involved with a police officer was about the stupidest thing she could possibly do.

She thought back to when she'd come out of the bathroom and found him waiting. The way he'd brushed his fingertips along her cheek and the concern in his eyes. It had touched her deeply. She couldn't remember the last time anyone had shown such caring.

And if she was being honest with herself, she cared for him too. She knew she shouldn't. It was dangerous. Especially after everything she'd done to distance herself from her past.

Pushing up, she slowly climbed to her feet. There was nothing to agonize over. Self-preservation meant she couldn't pursue a romantic relationship with Roman. *Maybe you could just have sex* a sly voice whispered in her mind, but she immediately shook her head. He wasn't like the others she'd chosen for bedmates over the last few years. She was already attached to him. Sex would surely strengthen her feelings and make it even tougher to walk away.

With determination, she marched through the woods and straight back to the place she'd had the strongest part of the vision. There had to be something here. Something that would lead her to either the killer or Anita's body.

But there wasn't. She stood among the trees listening to the rustling and creaking of the forest, the steady tap-tap of a woodpecker, and the absolute silence in her mind.

* * *

Roman couldn't settle. He wished his mood was only about Anita, but he couldn't lie to himself. Sure, Anita was part of it, but a bigger chunk of the restless, twitchy feeling was because of Mia.

He'd actively loathed her when she'd shown up at the station claiming to have seen a vision of an attack on his sister. Oh, yeah, he'd wanted to slap her face and make her take it back. Then his mother had dragged Mia into the bosom of the family and guilted him into working with her. And dammit if he hadn't been slowly sucked in.

If she was attempting to scam him, he couldn't see it. At least not anymore. In fact, he got the distinct feeling she'd rather not know anything about Anita. And more than that, helping him was costing her a great deal. The pain he'd seen in her eyes—when she'd sat across from Luke last night and later, outside the bathroom, more composed but pale as milk—had squeezed his heart like a vise.

He was good at reading people. He had to be. It was an essential part of his job. To his mind, she wasn't faking any of it.

She tugged at him, and he couldn't seem to do anything to turn off the attraction. The only two times he'd sunk into a relationship, it had sputtered out on him faster than he'd have thought possible. *So what? It didn't mean he should stop trying, right?* He paced back to the table, picked up his cell and tapped her number without giving himself time to think.

"Hello, Roman," she said in her quiet, contained voice.

"Yeah, hi. How're you doing?"

"I'm fine. I went back and talked to Luke. I guess I should have called you."

"No worries. You get anything from him?"

The sigh was small, but it carried weight. "Nothing of value. He essentially kicked me out of his office and said he's done talking about Anita."

"That's too bad. It was worth a try though, so thanks for going." He paused and crossed the few steps over to his window, pulling apart the blinds and glancing down at the darkened street below. "I'm basically out of ideas about Anita. Maybe we could get together tomorrow night to talk it over. I'll bring take-out to your place. Pizza okay?"

The phone went silent for several beats. "I don't have any ideas either, so there's not much to say," she said at last.

"Okay, that's cool. We could still have dinner. We'll take the subject of Anita off the table for the night."

"No, Roman." She sighed. "I thought I was pretty clear last night. I'm not going down that path with you."

His breath came out in a gush, and it was only then he realized he'd been holding it. "I don't understand why you're fighting this, but sure, we'll table it for now. No problem. Sooner or later, though, we're going to get together."

"God, you're frustrating," she hissed.

"Yeah, I know. Though some might call me tenacious."

"I can think of other words."

"Best keep them to yourself. Give Layla a pat for me. Good night, Mia."

"Good night, Roman."

He stared down at the phone in his hand. Well, hell. She'd brushed him off like a piece of lint. Roman searched his mind and couldn't remember the last time a woman had turned him down like that. He knew he was good-looking, not that he dwelled on it or anything, but as a rule, women tended to be attracted to him. Kevin often joked he was the guy they wanted to be friends with and Roman the one they wanted to catch.

When his phone signaled, he had a brief moment of thinking *Thank God, she called back* before seeing his mother's picture pop onto the screen. He sighed.

"Hey, Ma."

"Hello, my handsome boy."

Apparently not handsome enough. "How are you?"

"Very well, thanks. You keeping out of trouble?"

"You'd better believe it." The pause lasted just long enough where he could practically hear the wheels turning in her mind. "I don't know anything else about Anita. We may have hit another dead end," he said.

"Bite your tongue. You and Mia are going to find her. I know it. Anyway, that's not why I'm calling. Your father and I were talking, and we've decided we should have a little get-together next weekend. It would've been her thirtieth."

"Yeah, I know." His finger rubbed at the tension between his eyes.

"Let's have a barbeque at the cottage. We don't use it enough. Lina's coming home and Tony too. I thought maybe Brooke might like to be there. I'll talk to her tomorrow. I want you to invite Mia."

"I think it'd be better if you asked her. Besides, I doubt she'll want to leave her dogs for the day."

"Well, they can come, can't they? Lots of room to run around and swim in the lake."

"I guess, but I'm not asking her."

"What's the matter with you?"

"Let's just say I think she's had enough of me."

"Nonsense. Besides, maybe being with us on Anita's birthday, she'll sense something."

"Maybe. It'll be good to see Lina."

"Yes, family should be together. Did you have dinner?"

"Of course."

"I mean a proper nourishing dinner that wasn't pizza or a sub."

He crossed his fingers behind his back. "Sure, Ma."

"Good, boy. Don't stay up too late. It's a school night."

"Scout's honor. Good night."

He smiled when he put the phone back on the table. Mia might have brushed him off, but there was no way she'd shake his mother so easily.

Chapter Thirteen

All morning Mia brooded. She so didn't want to go to the cottage, but faced with the formidable Molly Mancini, couldn't see any way out of it. At least she'd managed to convince the woman she could drive up on her own and had politely refused the offer to bring the dogs.

"You guys are my ace in the hole," she said, swiveling her chair so she could rub her foot along Mac's back. "I figure I'll put in an hour or so and then use you as an excuse to escape."

Mac grunted and rolled onto his back so she could give his tummy some attention.

"It probably won't be that bad, right? And even if it is stressful, at least I know I'll be coming home to you guys. We can go for a nice walk when I get back, and then maybe I'll make popcorn and watch a movie."

Even thinking of it, she sighed. If only she could stay home and not have to deal with all the people. Especially Roman. God, she did not want to spend any time with him right now because she was very afraid she'd weaken.

More than once in the last few days, she'd picked up her cell and had been at the point of accepting his offer to have dinner. And each time she'd fought a mighty internal battle to prevent herself from calling. She knew darned well she was at the tipping point and all it would take was one small thing from him: a sexy smile, a brush of his hand on her arm, anything really, and she would likely throw herself at him.

Sighing again, she returned to the task of printing out shipping labels. The last few days had been a time of regrouping, and she was happy to be caught up on her orders. In fact, as of this very moment, she was ahead of the game and could actually coast until Monday. Maybe tomorrow she'd even take the day off from work.

By the time Mia drove out of her driveway a few hours later, she had her game face on. *Get in. Do the social niceties. Get out. It's like a special ops mission,* she thought, but without the guns and violence.

She wasn't sure what to expect from the gathering. Maybe everyone would be sad and introspective. Maybe most of the day would be spent sitting around sharing memories of Anita. The only thing she had to contribute on that point was a vision of the poor girl's death.

As it happened, she couldn't have been more wrong. When she stepped out of her car, laughter and screams filled the air. Scooping up the container of potato salad and the bottle of wine from the back seat, she made her way along the path at the side of the cottage. Peeking out to the back deck, she saw Molly and Frank sitting with two other couples. The deck extended out and down several stairs ending on a dock where Roman and Tony appeared to be patrolling, water guns in hand.

"You can run, but you can't hide," Tony called out before motioning to Roman.

Roman sidled back toward the house, hopped off the side of the deck and—dropping straight into a squat—fired a stream of water. The screams were amazing, and he threw back his head and howled with laughter. Brooke and two other girls ran out from under the deck on Mia's side and bulleted toward Tony, who stood his ground and took aim with his gun, hitting the first girl full on in the face. She howled and dropped her weapon, launched herself at him, taking him over the side of the dock and into the lake.

"Children, enough." Molly clapped her hands. "No more shrieking. Oh, Mia, there you are. Come on in. Join us. I promise everyone will behave. You brought food? You shouldn't have."

"It's only a potato salad," Mia said, handing over her offerings.

"Frank, you put these in the fridge." Molly took the bowl and bottle out of Mia's hands and passed it to her husband. "What would you like to drink? We have wine and beer and soda, of course. I think there's juice as well."

"Um…ginger ale if you have it. Or Coke."

"Coming right up," Frank said.

Tucking her hand in at Mia's elbow, Molly towed her over to the four sitting around the table. "This is Beth and Alan Wexler and Claudia and Ed Morris. They're old family friends."

Everyone nodded and smiled and said hello.

"Hey, you made it," Roman said. When she turned to him, the heat went straight down to her core.

He was shirtless, and his hair was damp so that it curled around his face and over his ears. His chest, wide and well-muscled, gleamed with water and his skin was the color of golden brown sugar. When he smiled at her, his teeth flashed impossibly white against the dark stubble. She couldn't see his eyes since they were covered with aviator glasses, but she imagined the corners crinkling in amusement.

"Yes, I made it. It's a beautiful cottage. The lake is breathtaking."

"No more water guns for now," Molly said pointedly. Roman scowled.

"Aw, come on. You always say that when Tony and I are about to win. It's a conspiracy, I tell you." He cocked his head at Mia. "You want in?"

"Ah…no…thank you."

"Figures. That's the problem when you're as good as Tony and me. Everyone's afraid to take you on."

She bristled. "I'm not afraid, but I didn't bring a bathing suit or even a change of clothes."

He tipped his sunglasses up and rested them on the top of his head. Then he winked at her. "A likely excuse."

Her belly did one slow summersault, and for a moment she couldn't tear her eyes away from him.

"Hi, Mia. I'm Lina, this degenerate's older and wiser sister. I've heard a lot about you."

Mia turned to face the girl who had pushed Tony into the lake. Her hair was slicked back, and she'd wrapped herself in a beach towel. "Oh, hello. It's nice to meet you."

Lina's hazel eyes bore into her. "Likewise. Even under these circumstances."

Brooke and the other girl walked over to join them. "This is Brooke, one of Anita's best friends all through school, and this is Morgan, daughter of Claudia and Ed.

They live in Memphis now, but they used to be our next-door neighbors. All us kids played together."

Mia nodded to the two girls, and Brooke smiled at her.

"Hi, again. I'm glad you came."

"And you know Tony of course," Molly added when he sauntered over. "Okay, children, go play."

"Who's up for a swim?" Tony asked, tipping his head at Mia.

"Not me," she said. "You guys go ahead."

"I think I'll sit it out too," Brooke said. "Come on, Mia. We can lounge on the dock and enjoy the sun."

Molly gestured to the table, laden with a variety of snacks. "Help yourself to food, and I'll see where Frank's gone with your drink. Oh, there he is. Well, come on. The girl's getting dehydrated standing here."

"My apologies," Frank bowed and handed her a bottle of Coke.

"Thank you," Mia said.

She took a sip and lowered the bottle, glancing casually around until her eyes magically locked on Roman. He stood at the edge of the dock with the others. They were lined up and apparently counting down to diving in.

"Come on, let's go dip our feet in the water." Brooke tucked her hand in at Mia's elbow. "I'm really glad you came. I know we've only talked once before, but I have a good feeling about you."

A burst of joy spread in Mia's chest.
"Um...thanks...I guess. I have a good feeling about you too."

Mia kicked off her sandals, and they sat at the end of the dock, lowering their legs over the edge and letting feet sink into the refreshingly cool water. Mia wiggled her toes and sighed. It did feel good.

"This is the life, huh? Anita would have loved this place," Brooke said. "The Mancinis only bought it five or so years ago, so she never got to see it."

"Oh, that's a shame. But I thought...didn't Tony's father have a cottage? I guess I assumed it was this place."

Brooke shook her head. "Well, he did, but it wasn't this one. They sold it years ago. It was across the lake over there. The one with the flag." Mia's eyes tracked to where Brooke pointed. "Tony talks about it sometimes. He has a lot of memories of his mom from there."

"It must be hard for him," Mia mumbled.

"Listen, I don't want to bug you, but have you found out anything about Anita?"

"No, not so far. In fact, I feel like I've hit a dead end."

"You're not going to give up, are you?"

Lina swam toward them.

"No, I'm not giving up. If I find any new information, I'll follow it. Right now, though, I've got nothing. That's how it goes sometimes."

"What are we talking about?" Lina asked, treading water and pushing her hair out of her eyes.

"Anita, of course," Brooke said.

Sinking down and tipping her head back, Lina stared at the sky. "It's crazy thinking of her turning thirty." She twisted her head to look at Mia. "So, Wonder Girl, how's it going with finding her?"

Her tone was light and teasing, but Mia caught the flash of another woman, face soft with lines, her hair a dramatic shade of red. She took a check from Frank while Molly cried and begged her to find their daughter. Mia stiffened.

"I'm doing the best I can."

"I'm sure you are. Just make sure you don't break my parents' hearts over this."

"Mia would never do that," Brooke said in a shocked voice.

Lina's shoulders lifted up and down in an exaggerated shrug. "I hope not, but we don't really know her, do we? People do all kinds of fucked up things."

"Why are you being so mean? Mia's only trying to help."

Mia swung her legs up and climbed to her feet. "It looks like me coming today was a bad idea. I think I'll go."

"No, you won't," Brooke said, clambering up to stand beside her. "Lina's always had a sharp tongue. I'm sure she didn't mean it the way it sounded."

Lina swam closer so she could grab the edge of the dock. "Mia, you don't have to go," she said in a weary voice. "I probably shouldn't have said that. I guess I'm just tired of having another piece of my soul crushed every time it seems like we're going to find Anita and then never do. Sometimes I think it'd be better if we accept we won't ever know what happened to her."

Except I know, Mia thought as a weight of sadness settled on her. It was an impossible choice deciding if it would be worse for the Mancinis to know all about Anita's violent death or to perpetually wonder what happened to their daughter and sister and cousin.

Mia zoned back in to hear Lina saying, "…please stay. I promise to play nice. I need to remember this is a day of celebration. We may not have Anita with us anymore, but we can still celebrate her life."

"Yes, you have to stay," Brooke urged.

"Okay." Mia nodded her head. "If you're sure. I don't want my being here to ruin the day."

Roman swam over and splashed at Lina. "Everyone looks so serious. What are we talking about?"

"Girl stuff," Brooke said with a strained smile. "What happened to the other two?"

"Tony and Morgan decided to swim over to the O'Reilly's cottage. She used to be friends with Megan and wanted to say 'hi' to her and her family. You guys have got to come in. The water's amazing."

His eyes lingered on Mia, and she swallowed while looking away from him and out across the lake. "Oh, I see them. Morgan's really fast. She's miles ahead of Tony."

"College swim team," Lina said with a smile. "That'll put a considerable dent in Tony's ego."

"He's not like that," Brooke protested.

"Believe me, sister, he's exactly like that. All guys are. Even this big dork right here." She tipped her head at Roman.

Nobody said anything for a beat. Roman spread his arms. "So what if I'm a confident guy? Maybe I have reason to be," he said, flicking his eyes over to Mia and smiling broadly.

Well, damn, thought Mia. *How the hell am I going to walk away from that?*

Soon after, Frank fired up the grill. Within the hour, everyone was gathered on the deck, helping themselves to steaks and grilled vegetable kabobs and loading up plates with various salads and side dishes. Roman followed Mia around the table and slid onto the seat beside her. He bumped his thigh against hers. When she looked over, he smiled sweetly. Mia swallowed and stared down at her plate.

"Mia, why don't you have a steak? There's plenty," Molly prodded.

"Oh, no thank you. I'm…well, I don't eat meat."

"But…oh, I see." Molly's brows pinched together, and she sighed. "Anita was the same. Wouldn't eat my Sunday roast. Wouldn't so much as look at a strip of bacon. She watched some movie about factory farming, and that was that."

Mia took a bite of pasta salad and chewing vigorously, smiled at Molly. "There's so much food, and it's all wonderful. Thank you again for inviting me."

This time Molly smiled back at her, and when conversation resumed around the table, Mia let out a silent breath of relief. It wouldn't take long for dinner to be over and then she could finally make her excuses and head back home.

It's not that she didn't like them, but between Lina's hostility and the constant pull of Roman, it was a struggle to stay calm…even more so during dinner with his arm somehow seeming to bump against hers…or the way he shifted his chair closer until she could literally feel the warmth of him. On top of all that, she fought the typical mental spillover from being around so many people. Factoring everything in, she was exhausted from the effort of it all.

Clearing his throat, Frank stood and lifted his wine glass.

"First of all, I want to thank all of you for coming. It's really wonderful having everyone together like this. Both old friends and new." He gestured toward Mia on the last few words. "I know it's been a long time since we lost Anita, though to Molly and me it sometimes seems like she was here only yesterday. Still, it helps knowing all of you hold her in your hearts. It makes us believe she lives on even if she's no longer physically with us. Thank you, everyone. Thank you for honoring our Anita."

Molly leaned forward and reached for her glass. "And now that the wonderful Mia's come into our life, we'll find our baby girl and bring her home."

Frank turned to Mia and nodded, leaning across the table. "Yes, to Mia."

Feeling incredibly guilty, Mia raised her water glass and clinked it against Frank's to complete the toast. She could sense the wave of hope rising up from around the table. Considering she was surrounded by Anita's family and friends, she should have been inundated with scenes of her. Why would Anita's energy have reached out and grabbed her so forcibly the first time in the park if there was no hope of finding her body?

As soon as Molly and Lina started gathering plates, Mia leapt to her feet and grabbed her own.

"Good night everyone. I really must get back home. It was a wonderful afternoon. Thanks for having me."

She heard choruses of good nights and nice to have met you. Careful not to make eye contact with Roman, Mia picked up several side dishes to bring inside the cottage.

"Thank you for a lovely dinner," Mia said to Molly. "I really need to get back to the dogs."

"Oh, but you haven't had dessert. I made a cake. Red velvet. It was Anita's favorite."

"I'm sorry, but I'd best go."

"Okay." She patted Mia's arm. "You'll let us know if you get any closer to finding her?"

"Yes, of course. Bye, Lina. It was nice to meet you."

"Same here. Mom, which dishes do you want for serving the cake?"

"The glass ones with the flowers. I'll walk you out, Mia." Molly crossed over to where Mia was inching back from the kitchen and put a hand on her shoulder. "Thank you for coming. Having you here meant a lot. It was a real comfort. I can't tell you how much I appreciate everything you're doing for my family. You're a good girl, Mia."

When she reached out for a hug, there was nothing for Mia to do but follow suit. With Molly's arms wrapped around her shoulders, she leaned into the tiny woman, doing her best to block out any mental crossover. She was already feeling enough guilt and inadequacy and couldn't bear to take on one ounce more.

"Good night, Molly. Thanks, again." Mia said when she was at last able to disentangle herself.

With a giddy sense of relief, she turned and strode across the main room and out the front door. The bubble quickly burst when she saw Roman. He stood leaning against the front bumper of her car, arms crossed over his chest and a ready smile. Gathering herself, she approached slowly, stopping several feet away from him.

"That was a fast getaway if I ever saw one," he said.

"My dogs are at home. I hate leaving them for so long."

"Sure, that's true, but I also know you couldn't wait to get out of here. You're good at hiding it, but I'm a trained observer. You have so many tells."

She shrugged unapologetically. "I'm not much of a social girl. It's nothing against your family. They're wonderful people. Everyone has been so nice and welcoming to me."

"Even Lina?"

"Well, no. Not her." Mia snorted. "She doesn't like me one bit, but I understand. She's only trying to protect your parents."

"That and she's not naturally friendly. Never has been. It's a miracle she managed to snag herself a husband."

"Such a shame they're getting divorced."

"What makes you think that?" Roman demanded.

"Oh…sorry. I thought you knew. I shouldn't have said anything."

"Nope. No sirree. She hasn't mentioned that little tidbit to anyone. Why the hell would she tell you before her own family?"

"She didn't exactly tell me." Mia paused, and her eyes slid away from his. "It was the barest flash of a vision, I swear. I didn't go poking around in her mind if that's what you're thinking. Sometimes stuff comes spilling out of people, and there's nothing I can do about it. Hence my desire to be by myself. Please don't say anything about it to your family." Her words finished in a rush.

Roman stared at her for a full ten seconds. Mia knew because she counted it out in her head. "You know, I forgot all about that today. Forgot you could…well, you're something, that's for sure. You have my word I won't say anything until Lina tells us herself. I guess that explains why Greg wasn't here. Pretty sure there was no work trip."

Mia exhaled. "Okay, thanks. Well, I'd better book. Good night, Roman." She sidled around him and made a beeline for the driver side door.

"Wait. Hold up a sec. We need to talk about this thing between us. You have to be feeling it too?"

Her shoulders sagged, and she stopped, bracing her hand on the front of the car when she turned to face him. "There's no *thing* between us."

He cocked his head. "Why do you insist on lying to me? There is most definitely a thing. I felt it in the kiss and today, I caught you sneaking glances at me when you thought I wasn't looking. I'm not a bad guy or anything. It's okay for you to like me."

"I know you're not. In fact, I think you're a very good man. Aren't there any other single women in Dalton? What about Brooke? She's sweet and so pretty. You guys would make a great couple. Mary-Ellen from the bank just broke up with her boyfriend. I think you two might mesh really well."

"Except I'm not interested in Brooke or Mary-Ellen from the bank. I'm interested in you."

"Please don't be," she said softly, turning away. "Go back to your family and your life, Roman. If anything comes to me, you'll be the first to know. Otherwise, I think it'd be best if we keep our distance. Good night."

Starting her Escape, she backed out of the driveway and onto the dirt road in front of the cottage. She didn't glance back at him.

He walked the short distance down to the middle of the road and stood there watching her drive away.

Chapter Fourteen

Mia didn't think she'd sleep. The afternoon spent with the Mancini family—and the way things had ended with Roman—left her stomach twisting like a writhing pit of snakes. Even after walking for over an hour with her dogs, followed by a lengthy and somewhat violent session of weeding the flower beds at the back of the house, she was still strumming with anxiety.

Yet, when she finally got into bed and turned over on her side, she dropped straight into sleep. The dream came in the early morning. Not of Roman, which had been her fear when she went to bed, but Anita.

Mia saw the scene as if hovering some distance above. Anita, dead and wrapped in a greenish material, being carried through a forest in the dark of night. The man, bent under the weight on his shoulder, trudged through the undergrowth, a shovel hanging from his left hand. The trees were a mixture of deciduous and evergreen, and in the distance, beyond the forest, a lake gleamed under the moonlight.

The next flash brought her flying down through the leaves, past branches and tree trunks and zooming to ground level. Anita was in the grave. The rough green material had been left on the pile of dirt at the side of the hole.

The man was nowhere to be seen, but when Mia looked down, she saw the path of footprints leading away. Turning back to Anita, she noted the body had been laid carefully, her hair fanning out slightly and her hands clasped on her chest. The vivid marks on her neck were the only sign of injury.

Feeling sick, unable to look at the poor girl any more, Mia stumbled back several paces, tripping over a tree root and falling on her butt. The idea the man could reappear at any moment filled her with panic. He would surely hurt her if he realized she'd seen Anita's grave. Scrambling to her feet, she leaned against the nearest tree and fought back a sob.

The trunk was massive. *It must be a very old tree.* Her fingers traced back and forth across the bark and over the ridges of carvings. It seemed to Mia they were letters inside hearts. She glanced over her shoulder and saw the first spark of light pushing its way through the trees. Dawn was breaking. Birds chirped away in a happy chorus. In the distance a loon made its eerie sound as though calling back the night.

Mia blinked when air rushed by her face, and she realized she was rising again. Up and up she went, above the trees, above the lake, and higher still until, far away, she saw the sun on that teetering edge ready to breach the horizon.

The dogs were whining and rustling around her bedroom. Mia groaned and reluctantly opened her eyes. It was not fully morning, though some light seeped into the room. She realized Mac was standing beside the bed staring at her with worried eyes. Tucker let out a yip of excitement when he realized she was awake and bounded onto the bed beside her.

"Everything's okay, guys. Relax. It's way too early for breakfast. Go back to sleep."

Tucker burrowed under the sheets and molded himself around her, a hot little ball of fur at her hip. Mac sighed and rested his head on the duvet. Mia let her head fall back on the pillow and closed her eyes. She was so tired. Another hour might give her at least a fighting chance of feeling like a normal human for the remainder of the day.

She lay quietly for several minutes, listening to the dogs settling back into various sleeping arrangements. Her mind was mushy, hardly able to hold a single thought. Something pushed at her, something important.

And then, like a bolt of lightning, the dream flashed into her mind.

Except it wasn't a dream. She was certain what she'd seen had actually happened. This wasn't the first time she'd experienced one of her visions this way. Rubbing at her eyes, she blinked them open again.

Holy shit. She knew where Anita was buried.

Okay, not exactly where, but she had some landmarks to help her find the place. Throwing the covers off, she slid out of bed. What should she do? Call someone maybe? No. This time she wouldn't involve Roman in it unless she had to. First, she needed to find the location and make sure it wasn't another false alarm.

With the decision made, she rushed through her morning bathroom routine, throwing on a pair of jeans and a tee and feeding the dogs before booting up her computer. She started a search for lakes in the area, quickly discarding two before hitting on one that looked similar to what she'd seen in the vision.

Crawford Lake. The same one where the Mancini cottage was located. She wasn't sure how far into the woods to estimate for the gravesite, but there was only one section that didn't have a road immediately along the shoreline. Moving her mouse over that portion of trees, she zoomed in but couldn't find anything else to aid in the search.

"Who wants to go for a ride?" she asked the dogs.

They must have sensed the excitement in her tone because the entire pack rushed over to the table, rubbing and banging against one another while they vied for her attention. She grabbed a couple of water bottles from the fridge. As an afterthought, she picked an apple from the fruit bowl. Then she and the dogs piled into her Escape and hit the road.

Mia tried not to speed, but adrenaline was making everything around her seem slow and syrupy. Part of her was terrified she wouldn't be able to find the spot, and another part of her dreaded discovering the burial place. How would Molly and Frank react?

And what about the killer, she suddenly wondered? How would he take the unearthing of his heinous crime? A chill hit her square in the chest making the hairs on the back of her neck stand up. Mac leaned around the seat and licked her cheek.

"I know, buddy, but we have to try and find her," Mia said.

She passed by the Mancini cottage, noting the family car in the driveway along with two others. But of course, it had only been yesterday she was there. Between the…thing…with Roman and the vision, time seemed distorted, and it felt like days ago she'd attended the barbeque.

Driving carefully now since the road was narrow and full of twists and turns, she made her way around the lake to the far side. A tiny parking area, empty of cars, marked the entrance to the national forest.

Hopping out and opening the back door, she called the dogs, not bothering with leashes. It was early yet, and the path at the entrance looked unused. She doubted there would be much pedestrian traffic. Layla yipped with delight and raced ahead bringing Tucker with her while Mac and Fifi kept pace with Mia.

She walked for hours. With the vision firmly in her mind, she'd thought it was going to be so easy. She could see the formation of trees around the grave and the slight downhill approach to the site. The reality, though, was that all the trees looked familiar, and there were plenty of downward slopes. None of them seemed right.

When she pushed through a thicket of leaves and realized she'd reached the lake, yet again, she exhaled and sank to the ground. Fifi, looking quite bedraggled with twigs and burrs and various other debris caught in her fluffy coat, crawled into Mia's lap and sighed.

Maybe this was a fool's errand, she thought, carefully freeing the trapped hair from around a particularly entrenched burr behind the little dog's ear. Should she call someone now or give up and go home? Sooner or later she'd surely get another flash of Anita's final resting spot, and maybe when it happened again, there'd be enough detail to actually lead her to the place.

She was tired and the dogs, while still apparently game enough, had started sending questioning looks her way as though wondering if their pack leader had lost her mind.

"I probably have lost my mind," she muttered, rubbing Fifi's back until the dog writhed in ecstasy. "Come on, let's find our way out of here and go home. I'm hungry enough to eat bark off a tree."

She had a general sense of where the road was but wasn't sure how far along the entrance to the trail lay. Deciding to shoot for the middle of the area, she pushed her tired legs up a rise. Ducking under a branch, she crested the hill.

Mac whined and pressed against her thigh. Mia stumbled and was forced to reach out and steady herself against the nearest tree trunk. Her body tingled. Tiny sparks of electricity raced up and down her spine. Details from her vision flashed into sharp focus in her mind. She knew this tree. Running her hand up, she found the carvings. Hearts enclosing initials.

Spinning, she surveyed the ground beyond. It was barely more than a clearing, but she knew now. This was the place she'd seen. It was mostly free of trees and covered with a blanket of brilliantly green ferns. Treading gently, she walked several feet to the left and knelt down, her dogs gathering around her. She was a hundred percent certain…knew it deep in her bones. Anita was buried right beneath her.

Bowing her head, tears poured from her eyes, dripping off her chin and falling to the earth below.

* * *

Roman walked back to the police station after being out on a call with Kevin. He dug a quarter out of his pocket.

"Heads, I take the paperwork. Tails, you do it," he said.

Kevin crossed his arms over his chest. "Nope, I did it last time. You're up, buddy boy."

"You did it last time because you lost the flip."

"Okay fine, but I'm going with heads," Kevin said.

Roman tossed the coin and watched it fall to Kevin's desk before raising his fist. "Heads it is, you shouldn't have switched. Loser, loser," he chanted in Kevin's face

"You can be such a jackass sometimes, but at least you've finally found something to smile about."

"We're cops. We don't smile."

"Yeah, sure, but while you weren't smiling, you were grumpy as hell."

Roman rubbed his hand across his head. "I didn't have the best night."

"Anything you want to talk about?"

He gave Kevin a withering look. "We're cops, and we're guys. We don't talk."

Checking his watch Roman realized he was off duty as of right now. He went to his office to collect keys and wallet. When the phone rang, he snatched it up. "Mancini," he said automatically.

"It's Mia. I need you to come meet me."

Though his heart clutched, his voice stayed calm. "What happened? Are you hurt?"

He heard her drag in a breath. "It's Anita. I've found her grave. I'm in the Crawford Lake National Forest. I can bring you to the exact spot."

* * *

He found her sitting in her car with the seat tipped back and the two smallest dogs sprawled across her. The Doberman and golden lab mix popped up from the back seat when he approached, one full of distrust and the other wagging an enthusiastic greeting. He pulled open Mia's door while she pushed the little dogs to the passenger seat.

"What's the story?" he asked. "I'm assuming it was another vision or something?"

"Yes, in a dream this time. I'll show you," she said, sliding out. "Come on, guys, let's go."

He followed her down the path at the edge of the parking lot. The dogs trooped along with her, occasionally darting away and then back. For the most part, they all walked quietly, almost somberly. The trek made Roman's stomach clench.

Soon Mia steered him deeper into the forest, weaving and dodging branches, all the while keeping her silence. Bits of leaves were stuck in her hair. The bottoms of her jeans and shoes were covered with a layer of dirt. The dogs, too, were also looking very grubby.

By the time they had been walking for several minutes, he was at the point of asking some of the questions swirling around in his mind, but he noticed her shoulders stiffen and saw the Doberman press in against her leg and tip his head up at her.

"We're almost there," she said, glancing back at him briefly.

She stopped beside a huge oak tree, her hand resting on the trunk and turning, pointed at the ground ten feet away.

"Are you positive?" Roman asked. "How did you even find this place?"

Saying nothing, she took his hand and placed it on the tree until he felt the carved letters. He gasped and stared at it in wonder.

"We used to come here when we were in high school," he said. "It's called Sweetheart's Clearing. If you were a guy and you'd been going out with a girl for a bit, you brought her here and carved your initials on the tree. When she got all gooey over it, you had a decent chance of getting lucky."

Stepping around her, he circled the tree. "There." He pointed to a large heart with RM plus PN in the center. "I brought Penny Norris out here as soon as I got my driver's license. We dated in eleventh grade, and I wanted her more than my next breath. Man, I'd forgotten all about this place."

He walked around the enormous tree, stopping when he came back to where Mia stood.

"I saw this tree in my vision," she said. "I've been searching the forest since early this morning. Maybe I should have called you first, but I wanted to be sure."

"If you'd called me, I could have saved you most of that walking." He turned and looked across to the patch of ferns. "You really think someone buried Anita here?"

"Yes, I do," she said simply. "She's right here. I'm sure of it."

She walked over and knelt down by the far edge of the area. He stared across at her and noted the dogs were arranged around as though in support. Her head was bowed, and Mac licked her hand. She looked exhausted, but more than that, she appeared sad and defeated.

"I believe you," he said.

* * *

They didn't start digging until two days later. Roman decided to independently contact a GPR company before bringing the Dalton police into the mix. After the last time at Carlton Park and all the expense, he wanted to have unassailable proof there was something worth investigating before talking to his boss.

He called Mia when he got the report from the company.

"The ground-penetrating radar found evidence of skeletal remains," he told her. "My lieutenant is taking over the investigation. They're going to send a team out at first light."

"That's good," she said. "Except why were you taken off the case?"

"I'm not off entirely…just not in charge. We want this to be strictly by the book. If this really is Anita, it could be said I don't have enough objectivity, but you can bet I'll be there every step of the way. I'll call you when we know more." He paused and sighed. "I'd like to say thanks, but I guess it's a weird thing to thank someone for."

"That's okay, I know what you mean. I'm really sorry about Anita," she said softly.

Because each layer of soil had to be excavated with care and screened for forensic evidence, it took until the next afternoon before they reached the bones. They unearthed a ring he immediately recognized as the one his parents had given to Anita for her sixteenth birthday along with ragged pieces of fabric that matched the color of the clothing she'd been wearing the night she'd disappeared. There was also a second ring that Roman had never seen before. A square-cut emerald on a gold band. No sign of the silver heart bracelet anywhere. When the dirt was gently brushed away from the intact skeleton, Roman knew he was staring down at his sister.

Despite how calmly he'd explained it to Mia and his family, he'd been furious when Lieutenant Schmidt had taken over. Now, he understood entirely. He kept his face blank, his voice steady, but inside waves of emotion battered him mercilessly.

He'd always imagined being the one to find her. That had been the driving force for entering the police academy in the first place. But now when faced with this reality, all he wanted to do was walk out of the forest, get in his car, and drive away without looking back. His mom and dad were going to be gutted because no matter what anyone said, Anita wasn't really dead to them. Now she would be.

"Mancini, take the bagged evidence to the station for processing. I'm sending Latterly to bring your family in. We need documented statements from them on everything we've found so far. Forensics will be running DNA, but you know it'll take days to get it back. We should be able to do dental matching by tomorrow, so we could have a positive ID by then."

"Okay," Roman said.

Schmidt called after him. "We'll be bringing Miss Reeves in tonight for questioning. You and Latterly can observe. I don't want you contacting her before then, understood?"

Roman nodded once before turning and striding away.

Near the end of the day, when they were finished with the questions and paperwork, Kevin brought Roman's parents to the office. Molly's eyes were red-rimmed, and Frank had an ashen, haggard look to him.

"You have to find who did this to our baby," his mother said. Her voice was strong, and she looked him straight in the eye. "I want this person caught and punished and hopefully put to death. All my life, I've gone to church, tried to be a good person. If wanting this damns my soul, so be it, but we must have justice for Anita. For our baby girl."

His father put a hand on her arm, and she reached up and patted it once before stepping forward and squaring her shoulders. "You will do this, Roman, for our family and for everyone who loved Anita. Come, Frank. Let's go home."

"I'm sorry, man," Kevin said when they were gone. "Why don't you take off? Go be with them."

"No, I'm gonna see it through. They've got Mia down in interview B. I might as well go observe."

Mia appeared small and defenseless sitting across from Lieutenant Schmidt and Cooper, another detective on the small police force. The two of them worked her hard, but she held strong, occasionally flicking her eyes to the one-way glass as though she knew Roman was standing there.

"She's tough," Kevin commented.

"Yeah. She is."

"Have you hit that yet?"

Roman clenched and unclenched his jaw and continued staring through the glass.

"Come on, man. I'm your partner, and this is a murder investigation—of your sister—you know I have to ask."

"No, I haven't hit that yet," Roman said bitterly. "Any other questions about my sex life?"

Kevin nodded once. "Nope, no questions and that's good to hear. It'll only make things stickier if you're involved with Mia, and she turns out to be a suspect."

"She's not."

"How'd she find the burial site?"

Roman rubbed his hand across his eyes and sighed. "Okay, look. It's not like I totally believe in all this woo-woo crap, but I've seen Mia do some pretty unbelievable things. She somehow knows stuff she shouldn't."

"So you think it came to her in a vision?"

"Maybe...shit, I don't know. The whole thing is fucked to hell and back."

With a sigh, Roman turned back to the glass and sent up a quiet prayer of thanks that Kevin kept the silence.

When at last the interrogation concluded, Schmidt and Cooper exited the room. A uniformed officer led Mia out to the processing area since she'd agreed to give a DNA sample. They came by where Roman and Kevin stood in the hallway.

She stopped in front of Roman and reaching out, placed her hand on his arm. "Are you okay?"

He smiled briefly before stepping back. Her hand fell away. "Thank you for coming in tonight. If you think of anything else pertinent to the case, please don't hesitate to call the department."

"Yes, of course. I understand. I'm sorry about your sister."

Chapter Fifteen

The investigation into the murder of Anita Mancini was front and center in the town. Mia knew word had leaked about her finding the burial site because Brooke had called to pump her for information. She told her what she felt she could and left it at that. Not up to dealing with all the whispers and chattering in town, Mia kept to her own property.

After working steadily through the day, finishing orders, and starting the process of setting up her greenhouse now that some of the equipment had started arriving, she settled in her sitting room, attempting to lose herself with Liam Neeson in *Taken*. She liked imagining what she would do in such a situation. It would be the perfect opportunity to use her abilities to not only free herself but make sure the bad guys faced justice.

The driveway sensor pinged from the kitchen, and she bolted up from the couch…the dogs with her step for step. Looking out, she saw headlights approaching slowly. Who would come to her place at this time of night? It was almost ten o'clock for Pete's sake.

She paused the DVD and keeping to the wall, peeked through the curtains and out to the parking area. Her muscles released when she recognized Roman's car. She hadn't spoken to him since she'd seen him outside the interview room at the police station.

It wasn't hard to figure out why he'd been so stiff and formal with her. She was the one who'd found the remains of a murder victim, so she'd naturally be a person of interest. At least at first. Not only that, it wasn't great for one of the investigating officers to have a personal relationship with her and especially when that officer was the brother of the victim.

"Shush, no barking," she ordered the milling dogs. "You guys, stay in."

She pushed through the front door and shut it firmly behind her before the dogs could weasel out. Mac, deeply aggrieved, howled in protest. "Hey, none of that," she said through the closed door. With a grumble of a growl, he went silent.

Outside, a car door slammed. She crossed the sunroom, and Roman met her at the base of the stairs. The security lights had activated, and he was fully lit.

"I shouldn't have come," he said. "I didn't realize how late it was until I turned onto your driveway and well, I was already here by then."

"Are you okay?" she asked.

His hand came up to his face, rubbing back and forth across his eyes. He let it fall away then shrugged and with a sigh said wearily, "I honestly don't know."

He looked shattered, she realized. There was a day's growth of stubble, and his hair was sticking out at odd angles from where he must have been running his hands through it. His eyes were heavily shadowed, but what tugged at her heart the most was the bone-weary posture.

"Is this an official visit?" she asked at last.

His head snapped up. "No. It's just me coming to see you."

Blowing out a breath, she turned and opened the screen door at her back. "Come in then." She didn't wait for him but continued across the sunroom and pushed through the front door where the dogs waited in breathless anticipation. They threw themselves at her.

When Roman brushed by, Layla broke away and went to him. He lowered to the floor and patted the golden lab, his hand running nose to tail in long, smooth strokes. She positively preened at him.

"You're a good dog, aren't you?" he said. She pushed into him, licking his face, and he smiled briefly. Then holding her head still, he pressed his forehead to hers. "Such a good girl. Best dog in the world."

She wiggled, her tongue darting out to his neck, and he turned his head and looked at Mia. "They identified the remains. Anita's hyoid bone was broken. She was strangled exactly like you said. There are a million tests to be done. We don't have an exact timeline yet, but anyone can tell she's been in the ground for a long time."

Mia nodded slowly, her eyes fixed on his face. "I'm sorry, Roman. It's awful. Your poor family."

"Yeah. It sucks." Gently, he pushed Layla away and struggled to his feet. "I wanted to explain about the other night in the police station. It's because of…well, department policies and—"

"I know," she said and reaching out, brushed her fingertips down his arm. "Don't worry about it. I'm a big girl. I understand how the world works. Your life has got to be a nightmare right now. You shouldn't have come all the way out here to tell me that."

"I wanted to see you." Moving toward her until they were only inches apart, he blinked down at her. "I could really use a distraction right now."

There was no way she could block out his mental energy anymore. It was pouring off him like Niagara Falls. Unable to blunt the anger and grief and sense of utter helplessness, he was crying out for something to hang onto…someone to bring him back to himself. He wanted it to be her. She wanted him too. So badly. Yet, she could also hear the chanting voice in the back of her mind to get him out of here.

Closing her eyes, she pushed his energy away and got as still as she could inside. With mind clear, she knew there was no real decision to be made. She'd already chosen her path when she'd let him in the house tonight.

Opening her eyes again, she stepped closer to him. She framed his face with her hands and stood on tiptoes until her mouth met his. He didn't react at first, simply remained still as a statue while she breathed against his mouth. Lowering her arms, she wrapped them around his broad shoulders.

"It's okay," she whispered. "I'm here."

His chest heaved, and he pushed his body up against hers while his hands grasped her hips and lifted her. She wrapped her legs around his waist, and he turned, mating his mouth to hers in a hard, desperate kiss. Somehow, they were at the couch, and he lowered back onto it, keeping her tight in his arms.

Mia pushed fully into his mind. So much sorrow. But as she ran her hands through his hair, as she stroked down the back of his neck, she felt the change. He was letting himself sink into the moment and with that came some relief from the despair.

She could do more, give more. He'd come to her for comfort, and in her whole life, no one ever had.

Wriggling free and pushing back slightly, she started unbuttoning her shirt. He watched while she pulled the fabric apart and slid it down her arms until she sat on his lap in a simple white cotton bra. Reaching down, she took his hands and placed them on her breasts.

"Go on," she said. "Take what you need."

His eyes came to hers, dark and full of grief. "Thank you," he whispered.

She thought he would dive in. Indeed, all she could hear in his mind was the unrelenting chant for physical release, but he kissed her softly, almost reverently, while fingertips traced the edge of her bra and slowly, so slowly, drew the straps down over her shoulders. She changed angles, deepening the kiss, and struggled to reach behind her back before finally managing to unclasp the bra.

Still, he held it in place. Cupping his hands, the fabric caught between his palms and her breasts. He kneaded with mounting arousal until she shifted and pulled the bra free. Even then he took his time, gazing down at her naked torso before slowly reaching out with his right hand to play his fingers across her nipples.

She moaned and arched her back. It had been so long since anyone had touched her. So long since she'd let herself go. When he leaned down and brought his mouth to her breast, the bolt of heat arrowed straight to her groin. His teeth closed around the nipple, and his tongue darted out, fluttering across the peak. She couldn't contain the sensation and flexing her hips, ground against his leg in rhythmic strokes.

"Oh, yes," she groaned.

His lips latched onto her neck, nipping and sucking, while his hands took possession of her breasts again. She couldn't think, could barely breathe. The sensations he brought to her were overpowering, stronger than a gale force wind, and she was being swept along.

Rather than resisting, she tried to race ahead, determined to catch the front of the storm. All thoughts of giving comfort were wiped clean out of her mind to be replaced by the driving drumbeat to mate, to join her body with his as though her very survival depended on it.

She found herself unable to maintain her usual detachment. Everything meshed together in her mind.

She registered each touch of his fingers, every flutter of warm breath across her skin. His feelings and thoughts bled into her and mixed with her own needs.

When she tried to block out the emotions, she simply couldn't do it. It was as though every line of defense she'd painstakingly built up over a lifetime had been stripped away, and she was laid open, vulnerable, and unable to protect herself.

Yet, even though a part of her whispered to claw back the control, she didn't want to. Her body responded in a way it never had before, the nerve-endings honed to a paper-thin response with the corresponding waves of pleasure spreading and multiplying lightning fast.

Couldn't she let herself have this? Was it so wrong to want to connect with someone even for a few moments? She was human, after all, and this was a basic human need. Later she could worry about taking back the control.

She spread her knees and pressed down until she felt the hard ridge beneath her. Oh, yes, this was what she wanted. Working herself against him, she braced her hands on his shoulders, and he drew her in to his chest, arms clamping around her back. When she felt the waves crashing closer and closer together, she forced herself to slow the pace.

He lifted his head. "What's wrong? You don't have to stop."

"I want you naked," she said, unsnapping the button of his jeans.

He rested his forehead against hers. "Fair's fair. I want you naked too."

With that, he lifted her and swung her around until she stood beside the couch. Before she could so much as blink down at him, her yoga pants and panties were on the floor. She stepped out of them while he kicked off his shoes and then standing beside her, stripped away his jeans and boxers.

His shirt remained, so she reached out and grabbed the hem, pushing it up his chest. Obediently, he raised his arms, and she lifted it over his head, letting him deal with untangling himself.

Roman's bicep flexed when he bent his arm to toss the shirt away, and she brushed her fingers over the cut of muscle. His chest was a masterpiece of the male form, broad and muscular, with a sprinkling of dark hair across the pecs. She loved the way everything angled down to his flat stomach with the ripple of well-defined ab muscles.

Taking her hand and pulling her to him until they were center to center, he stroked up and down her back.

"I wasn't expecting…I didn't think to bring anything…protection, I mean."

"It's okay," she said. "I have condoms. Let's take it to the bedroom."

"Thank God," he breathed against her neck. "I was prepared to be totally cool about it, but if I can't have you right now, I'm not sure I'll ever recover from the disappointment."

When he laid her out on the bed, when he finally pushed into her, she couldn't ever imagine why she'd considered denying herself. Her body stretched around him, almost painfully at first, but soon turning to breathtaking pleasure. The heat of him both deep inside and along her thighs and chest where he covered her, gave her a sense of completeness. A sense of belonging.

Waves of liquid ecstasy washed over her, building, building, until she went up and over the peak, shattering on the other side. With heart hammering and heat turning her body to molten ash, there was nothing else in the world but Roman. His body thrust hard and deep, his hands linked with hers above her head, and his eyes laser-focused on her face.

Reaching out with her mind, she realized his release was right there waiting for him, but he held back, slowing, changing angles, and forcing it away time and again. His control was a thing of beauty.

Understanding he was doing it for her, she let herself sink back into the sensations, let herself savor the slap of flesh upon flesh, and the way he pressed down and rocked sensuously forward and back, enjoyed the delicious friction.

Her next orgasm built like a gently rolling sea, wave upon wave layering softly until the focus of her entire body was a single, throbbing nerve. When everything in her screamed for relief, she worked her hands free. Reaching up, she framed his face.

"I'm with you," she gasped. "It's time to let go now. Please, let yourself go."

Stilling briefly, he brought his forehead to hers while his eyes fluttered closed for several seconds. Then he reared up, and his hands came under her hips, lifting her. He drove into her again and again, his teeth fixed on his lower lip while his breath hissed out with every thrust. She lost herself, shuddering, crying out, her fingers scraping along his arms while her climax spun on and on until there was nothing left of her.

Briefly, she registered Roman push into her one last time. Holding himself deep, he groaned out a release before collapsing onto her chest. He pinned her to the mattress, his chest heaving and the stubble on his cheek rasping against her shoulder.

Mia could have stayed that way forever. She felt safe and sated and insanely alive. Gently pulling his hair, weaving her fingers through the dense, dark strands, she allowed herself to drift. When Roman cleared his throat and shifted to roll to his side, she had to stop herself from pulling him back.

His eyes were sleepy and so satisfied. "How you doing?"

"I'm pretty frickin fantastic."

"Yeah, I think I might have seen God."

"Me too. Plus, all the Apostles and maybe an archangel or two."

He ran a finger up and down the side of her neck before leaning in and kissing her cheek. "Thank you."

She laughed. "You're quite welcome. Though I think it was a two-person operation, so I can't take all the credit."

"You know what I mean. Even if it was pity sex, I'm happy to take it."

She punched his shoulder. "I don't do pity sex. And besides, this was a one-time only thing. I'm sure your lieutenant wouldn't be too happy knowing you're in my bed. Don't worry. I'm really good at keeping secrets."

He stilled, and his eyes turned to slits while he studied her. "The only reason you slept with me is that you think it's a one-off?"

Swinging her legs over the bed, she shifted into sitting position. She glanced over her shoulder and gave him a smug smile. "That's right, Mr. Law and Order. Now, can I get you anything to eat before you head out? I'm sure you don't want to hang around too long in case anyone happens to see your car here."

He collapsed back onto the bed with a grunt. "You think you've got this all figured out, don't you? Well, Miss Smarty Pants, they're going to clear you before too long and then it won't matter so much. As for my car, you live outside of town, and your driveway is as long as the Amazon River so nobody's seeing anything. And no, thanks, I'm not hungry. I could go for a beer though."

"A beer I can do," she said, pushing to her feet.

"You know," he said a few moments later, setting his beer on the kitchen counter and swiveling his stool to face Mia, "I don't think they've found a damned thing to help us get Anita's killer. Maybe we'll get lucky and he lopped off a bunch of his hair to bury with her or something. But even still, unless he's already in the system, we won't be able to find him."

Mia sighed and dropping her head in her hands, squeezed her temples. "I'm still not getting anything on him, just a blank guy. He could be anyone."

"Except you said Anita knew him," Roman pointed out.

"Okay, he could be any guy she ever met."

"See, that narrows it down a whole bunch. All we need is a starting point. There has to be something to send us in the right direction."

Mia pushed to her feet and wandered over to the window. She stood looking into the darkness until Mac nudged her hand with his head.

"I do have an idea," she said, stooping to rub Mac's ears. "It's maybe not the best idea, but it might help me see something."

Picking up his beer bottle, he pointed it at her. "I'm up for anything you think will get us this guy."

Straightening up again, Mia blew out a breath. "I think I need to touch Anita."

Roman's arm stalled with the bottle partway to his mouth. Setting it back down, he stared at her before slowly nodding his head several times. "You mean her bones? Yeah, that makes sense. It's kinda creepy, but it makes total sense. I think I can make that happen. Can you come to the station?"

"Okay. When?"

His fingers tapped against his mouth.

"Um...they're pretty much done processing her remains. Later tomorrow. How about I text you when we're in the clear. And Mia, I think this is something we should keep to ourselves. If anyone asks what you're doing at the station, tell them you're wondering how the investigation is going or something like that. Okay?"

"Sure, no problem. How is your family doing?"

"So-so. Ma's acting tough, but I can see it's ripping her apart inside. Dad's barely saying anything. I swear he aged ten years overnight. Lina's out for blood as you might expect, and Tony, well, he's keeping up a good front, but I can tell he's wrecked. I should really go and check on them." He glanced at his watch. "Too late now. I'll swing by in the morning on my way to work."

"Well, let me know if there's anything else I can do."

He reached across and placed his hand on her arm. "You've already done it. Thank you. I'm glad we've found Anita. It helps. More than you can know but…"

"You won't be at peace until you catch her killer," Mia finished the sentence for him. "Once again, I can't promise anything, but I'm really hoping I'll get something from her tomorrow. If Anita left such a strong echo in the park, it would stand to reason having direct contact with her should net us something good."

"One can hope," he said, squeezing her arm. "All right, I'm off."

He clambered to his feet, and she followed suit. She gazed at him for several seconds. "Thanks for stopping by," she said at last.

His smile was brilliant against his weary, grief-stricken face. "You're completely welcome. Seriously, though, thanks for being here."

He eased closer to her and without warning laid his lips against hers. The kiss was hot and possessive, and her heart hammered in response.

"My sister's murder may have brought us together, but there's more than that between us. I wouldn't feel what I do if it was only flat-out proximity and circumstances," he said, drawing back.

She frowned, her eyebrows creasing together. "Stop. Don't say things like that."

When she tried to step back, he grabbed her shoulder and kissed her again…this time soft and dreamy. "Good night, Mia."

"Good night. I'll wait to hear from you about the…about coming to the station."

The dogs roused from their various places of slumber and followed the humans out to the front door. "Make sure to lock this behind me," Roman said.

She watched the tail lights of his car disappear down the driveway. *Did that really just happen,* she wondered? It may have been a mistake, but from her point of view, it was so worth it. Fifi whined and performed a pirouette at her feet. Mac nudged up against her leg.

"Okay, okay, stop nagging," she said. "Let's go to bed."

Chapter Sixteen

The text from Roman didn't come until late the next day.

Can you come now? Text me when you get here. I'll go down and bring you up.

The police station was relatively quiet when Mia walked in. A man sat at the reception desk, but other than Roman waiting by the elevator, there wasn't anyone else in the area.

"I've got this, Mike," Roman called out to the man before he could say anything to Mia.

Roman still looked tired, but he was clean shaven and had his badge clipped to the waistband of his jeans. Gone was the grief-stricken man. In his place stood a sharp-eyed cop.

He pressed the button on the wall, and the elevator doors sprang open. Mia followed him in and waited while he selected the third floor. The doors closed again with a ding and Roman turned to her, reaching across to squeeze her hand briefly.

"Thanks for coming."

"Anything new today?"

"Not so far. Lots of reports on soil composition and foliage and stuff like that. Nothing that's helping us get this guy. Thank God, I have you in my pocket, or I'd be seriously pissed off right about now."

She stepped back and crossed her arms over her chest, her hand clutching the strap of her purse where it lay against her shoulder. "You know I can't promise anything," she began. "It's not predictable—"

"Hey, I know. Don't worry. If you see something today, great. If not, I know you will at some point."

She shook her head. "No, I can't—"

Once again he cut her off. "Mia, I have infinite faith in you. One way or another you're gonna help us get this bastard."

The doors slid open, and they stepped out into an office space. Half-walled cubicles filled the floor, though it was mostly empty of people. She could hear two men talking about an upcoming baseball game. As she and Roman walked along, a woman spoke into a phone reassuring someone that everything was being done to find the person who'd vandalized their car. Roman strode ahead to the far wall and turning left continued to the second door. He stopped and gestured Mia inside.

It was small, barely enough room for a desk and two visitor chairs. There were no personal mementos on display. She'd expected sports trophies or photos or something, but the décor was completely generic.

"You need some plants in here," she said as she continued surveying the small room.

"Do I?" His smile was warm.

"Plants are proven to reduce anxiety and increase the oxygen in the air. It's not healthy to spend your day inside breathing recycled air."

"And what about when I forget to water them, and they die a slow and painful death?"

"We could get you the hardy kind that barely needs any water. A couple of aloes and maybe a snake plant or two."

He closed the door and leaned back against it. "And when the guys make fun of me, will you come here and set them straight?"

"Absolutely. I'll tell them that you're sexy and sensitive and extremely attentive to my needs in bed." She smiled a wicked smile. "Or are those the kind of things I'm supposed to keep to myself?"

"Definitely things to keep to yourself."

He walked over to her. "Hi, Mia."

She stepped back. "No, Roman."

"Are you serious? We had sex less than twenty-four hours ago."

"Yes, but that was a one-time thing. Come on, we can be grown-ups about this. Let's not make it all weird, okay? Why don't we get started?"

He gazed at her for several seconds then gave a jerking kind of shrug. "Sure. No problem. Go ahead and sit in my chair," he said and waited until she'd walked around the desk and slid onto the seat. "Open the top right drawer."

She followed his direction and immediately saw the clear plastic bag with the red band across the top and Evidence stamped in black letters. Inside were two long bones. Mia guessed they were from the lower arm. She placed the bag on the blotter of the desk and looked over to Roman who leaned against the wall by the window.

"Hang on a sec. There should be another bag in there. Do the ring first. None of us recognize it. Luke swears up and down he never bought or gave her a ring."

Mia found the smaller evidence bag and pulled it out. "It's okay to touch?"

"Yeah, everything's been processed, so go ahead and take it out."

The ring was gorgeous. The emerald stone sparkled, and the ornate carving on the band caught the eye. She cupped it gently in her palm and saw all kinds of things. A middle-aged Latino man with a dirty red bandana tied around his neck who wore a yellow hat with a lamp fixed above the brim. An open-air market with table after table of gemstones. A man in a tiny office scowling over a form titled Import Duties and Taxes. A Caucasian woman's reflection in a glass display case. Nothing with Anita or a grave or anything else that could help find the killer.

She shook her head and placed it back inside the plastic before turning to the larger bag.

"I thought they'd be white," she said.

"Bones that have been in the soil for a long time like these ones are typically discolored."

Sliding the tab across the top of the bag, Mia reached in and pressed her fingertip onto the longer of the two bones. The edge was rougher than she'd expected. It reminded her of a pumice stone. She wrapped her fingers around it and closed her eyes.

"Hello, Anita," she thought. "It's nice to meet you. I'm sorry you're dead. And since you are, it's really important you tell me who hurt you."

Nothing happened.

Mia focused on her breath. Slowly in. Slowly out. What if Anita didn't show her anything? No, worrying wouldn't help. She kept her mind as blank as possible and pushed away the anxiety. She brought to mind some of the flashes she'd already seen of Anita with Luke, with Brooke, with her family. She pictured her soft brown eyes and sweeping curls. Still, the bones remained silent.

Eventually, she became aware of Roman shifting nearby and heard him clear his throat.

"I'm so sorry," she said finally, opening her eyes and turning to see his hopeful expression. "There's nothing at all. I really thought if I—"

His expression smoothed out. "It's fine. We had to try, right?"

Looking down again, she ran her finger around the bulbous end of the bone before withdrawing her hand and sliding the tab across to seal the bag. "Should I put them back in the drawer?"

"Yeah, sure."

"I'm really sorry," she said again.

She carefully nestled the bag in the drawer and began sliding it closed. Out of nowhere came a wave of intense nausea, and she clutched at her stomach.

"What's wrong? Are you okay?" Roman knelt beside the chair.

For a moment, Mia actually thought she might vomit, and she closed her eyes, breathing fiercely. In the next instant, she was in the scene.

Anita leaned against the wall of a bathroom stall. She was lightheaded and nauseous. She rubbed a hand over her sweaty forehead then turned her wrist and glanced at her watch. Five after twelve. She waited, counting to sixty then let out a long breath before turning to the toilet.

Balanced on the seat was a rectangle of white plastic. She picked it up and stared down at it. Two pink lines. Pregnant. She shoved the test stick into her purse and pulled free a handful of toilet paper, swiping furiously at her eyes.

"Mia. Mia. Talk to me. What's going on?"

Roman's voice penetrated her consciousness, and the scene flashed away.

"Anita was pregnant," she whispered.

"What? Are you sure?" Roman leaned toward her, his eyes searching her face.

"Yes, I'm sure."

He shot to his feet and paced away, his hand rifling through his hair. "My sister was pregnant," he mumbled.

Mia pushed off the chair and walking around the desk, reached out and grabbed Roman's shoulder.

"Wait. I don't know when she was pregnant. Maybe it happened long before she was killed. She could have had an abortion."

Roman whirled to face her. "What do you mean?"

"Look, I saw her in a bathroom stall reading a pregnancy test. She was feeling sick and crying. What I don't know is when it happened."

"All right, you have a point. I want you to sit right here and think about the scene and tell me everything you remember," he demanded, pushing her down into the nearest visitor chair. "You said she was in a bathroom. Was it at my parent's house?"

Mia shook her head. "No, it was a stall in a public restroom. The side was metal, and there was dark grey tile on the floor."

"What was she wearing?"

Mia closed her eyes. "Tan capris, red sandals, and a red short-sleeved blouse."

He nodded. "Okay, so it was summer then. What else? Did she have nail polish on? Jewelry? Could you hear anyone else in the bathroom?"

"Um…I think she was alone. She wore a silver watch with a square face on her left wrist and a silver and gold ring on her middle finger. I'm not sure about her other hand. 'I Kissed a Girl' was playing on the sound system. That's all I remember."

"Okay, this is good. My parents gave her the ring for her sixteenth birthday, and I think she got the watch a Christmas or two later. I'll have to ask my mom. That Katy Perry song, when did it come out?"

"A long time ago. I don't remember exactly."

Roman whirled around and went to his chair. He pulled the keyboard shelf toward him and started clicking and typing. He pointed at Mia. "'I Kissed a Girl' was released in two thousand and eight. April twenty-eighth to be precise. The very year Anita went missing."

He turned back to the screen and typed some more, nodding his head as he read. A huge smile broke over his face.

"What is it?" she asked.

The weather in the early part of two thousand eight was not typical. The first day to hit eighty was May fifth. Anita hated the cold. There's no way she'd be wearing a little blouse and sandals unless it was at least that warm. It's likely your vision is from somewhere between May fifth and July sixth of the year she disappeared."

"Do you think Luke knew?"

"That's a really good question. I think we might just have to ask him, don't you?" He leaned back in his chair and rubbed a hand over his face. "I'll have to figure out how to introduce this into the investigation."

"Or we could go and talk to him ourselves," Mia suggested.

He blew out a breath. "Yeah, but it'd be a whole lot better to do it by the book. If he had anything to do with what happened to my sister, I want it all official."

"Can't it be a follow-up interview now that you've found her remains?"

He nodded his head. "Maybe. I'll run it by the lieutenant, I guess."

"I wonder if Brooke and Ashley knew. And what about Lina? Don't sisters talk about that kind of stuff?"

"I don't know. Lina was so much older, and she'd been away at school and working for a while by then. I'd be real interested in finding out if Brooke knew."

"I'll bet Anita went to the doctor. You should get her medical records."

"That's a tough area. She was an adult when she died, and they have that whole patient confidentiality thing going on. If I can get someone else to admit to knowing, then a judge will probably be willing to sign off on a subpoena for anything from her file related to a pregnancy. Otherwise, I don't see us getting too far on that front."

"Well, somebody had to know," Mia insisted.

"Yeah." Roman nodded his head. "Now all we have to do is find out who."

* * *

Mia mulled over the revelation all the way home. The fact Anita was pregnant didn't necessarily have anything to do with her murder, but it seemed entirely too coincidental to be dismissed. Added to that, if it wasn't somehow important, why would she have seen that exact moment in time shortly after touching her bones. It had to mean something.

Determinedly, she did not think about Roman. Last night had been wonderful, but they could never be together long term. He was a cop, for heaven's sake, and she…well…if he ever found out about her past, he wouldn't want to be with her anyway. It was best to look on it as a mutually happy indulgence and leave it at that.

She turned onto her driveway and had gone barely ten feet when an animal streaked across in front of her SUV. She slammed on the brakes, heart thudding. What the heck was that? She gasped when something bounced against her window.

Holy hell, it was Mac. Flinging the door open, she called him, and he leapt at her, his feet digging into her thighs while he lapped her face.

"What on earth are you doing out here?" she cried, grabbing his collar. "Do not tell me you jumped the fence. Come on, buddy, let's get you in the back seat."

Mac hopped in obligingly then proceeded to whine and fidget when she slid behind the wheel. She put the car in drive, and Mac lifted his nose into the air and howled. Once again she stomped on the brakes, and the dog shifted forward, his front paws sliding off the seat. He bounced back again and continued whining.

"Look, I get it," she said sympathetically. "It was scary running around on your own like that, but I'm home now, and everything's okay."

When Mia turned back once again and prepared to continue to the house, she saw the tiny snowflake dog sitting in the grass up ahead beside a tree. She bolted out of the car.

"Fifi, come. Come here, girl. Come on. That's my good girl."

She crouched down and worked to keep her voice calm and reassuring. It wasn't easy since they were steps away from the road. Although hardly a traffic hub, it would be her luck to have Fifi run out and get hit.

Thankfully, the little dog galloped toward her, hair rippling back in the breeze and eyes bright with excitement. Fifi leapt straight into Mia's lap, and she hugged the dog tight to her chest.

"Oh, my poor baby. Come on, let's get you and Mac home."

She drove cautiously down the driveway, terrified that either Layla or Tucker might suddenly throw themselves in the path of the tires. Neither appeared. Once at the house, she took the dogs inside. The absolute quiet told her what she feared was true. The other two dogs were nowhere to be seen.

It didn't make any kind of sense. The gate by the house was closed and locked, just like always. How the heck had they escaped?

No time to solve that now. She had to find the missing dogs. Since twilight was falling, she grabbed her heavy-duty flashlight by the back door and putting Mac and Fifi on leashes, walked the property while calling for Layla and Tucker. It was a windy night, and it was hard to hear much beyond the rustling of tree branches and field grass, but she screamed their names and continued walking around and around her acreage.

The moon started to rise, and gradually the wind died down, but still nothing. Her flashlight beam crisscrossed back and forth over the fields. She turned again, dragging a now reluctant Mac toward the brook at the back of the property. He whined and twisted against the leash and all at once let out a series of triumphant barks.

She heard an answering yip and held her breath, ears straining, flashlight scanning left and right. Something brushed by her knee, and she spun around to see Layla jumping on Mac. Their reunion was noisy, even more so when Tucker leapt through a nearby bush and threw himself into the fray.

Mia crumpled to the ground. Her pack ran over her, licking, whining, bumping, while her breath sobbed out, and tears of relief poured down her cheeks.

* * *

The beam of Roman's spotlight lingered on the jagged cuts. He and Mia stood near the end of the dog run behind her house and silently stared at the section of fencing that had been opened up. The post at the corner stood unmolested, but someone had taken wire cutters and ripped away a whole panel where it attached to the edge. The cuts were uneven, and some of the wire was bent back so violently it resembled broken fingers.

Giving it a wide berth, he walked around to the far side and shone his light along the ground. He growled in his throat.

"The dirt's too dry to find any tracks. If we get real lucky, maybe the perp dropped something. Otherwise, this is a dead end."

Mia nodded. "And everything about the note is so generic, I'll bet there's nothing there either."

"Let's go back in and look at it again before I take it to the station."

When they walked toward the house, he placed his arm around her shoulders and pulled her against him. "It was a crappy thing to do. I'm so sorry."

"Yeah, well nobody got hurt."

"This time. As soon as they're done processing the area tomorrow, I'll help you fix the dog run. Do you have anyone who can come and stay with you tonight?"

She shook her head. "Not really. Besides, I'll be fine. The dogs will keep me safe."

"It may seem like a prank, but you need to take this seriously."

"Trust me, I am," she said grimly. "And nothing that puts my dogs in danger is a prank."

Back in her kitchen, she pointed at the piece of paper on her counter. Pulling a Kleenex from the box on the fridge, he carefully used it to pick up the note.

Stop helping the police or worse things will happen

Mia had found it tucked into the window frame on the side door off her kitchen. The envelope was plain white with no writing. The note was typed or generated by a computer on a sheet of eight and a half by eleven with the single line spaced roughly in the center.

That was it. No other marks could be seen with the naked eye other than a smudge of dirt along one side of the envelope consistent with the edge of the window. Roman doubted they'd find anything to help locate the person who did this.

He glanced over at Mia who stood with her arms crossed over her chest and hip cocked against the counter. Her face was set in resolute lines. Despite her show of bravado, she seemed very small to him. So defenseless.

"Why don't I stay here for a few days? At least until we have a chance to track whoever did this."

She immediately shook her head. "I told you, I'm fine. I have the dogs. Roman, you don't need to worry about me. I've been taking care of myself for a long time now."

"Okay, fine. But I want you to text me morning and night. You carry the cell with you everywhere you go, got it?

"Yes, sir. Boss man." Using the first two fingers of her right hand, she gave him a mock salute.

His face creased with concern. "I want to make sure you stay safe. You mean a lot to me."

Her smile was wistful. "Thanks, Roman. You're a really good guy."

Chapter Seventeen

By the time Roman had logged the items into evidence and written up his notes to the case file, it was too late to go back to his parents' house, so he drove the three blocks over to his apartment and climbed the stairs to his front door.

He was bagged. All told, it had been a hell of a week. What he needed was some serious down time, and he hoped to God he'd finally get a decent night's sleep. Ever since Anita's body had been found, he'd been too strung up to stay asleep for more than an hour or so at a time. The fact there was proof someone had murdered his sister left a ball of rage roiling in his gut and made him twitchy and over adrenalized.

With Mia's problem added to the mix, like a cherry on top of a fucking sundae, he certainly didn't feel any calmer. There came a point when the body would take what it needed, and he sensed tonight was the night. He brushed his teeth, splashed water on his face and stripped down to boxers before collapsing face-first onto the bed. Within moments he slipped away to sleep.

Getting a solid six hours helped, but even still, his first thought upon waking was coffee. He pushed to his elbows, lifted his head, sniffed the air. Nothing. Dammit, he'd forgotten to set up the coffee machine the night before. For a moment, it all felt like too much, and he wondered what would happen if he put the pillow over his head and refused to get up.

A vision of Mia floated across his mind, eyebrows furrowed and hand rubbing up and down between her breasts the way she did when agitated. Then came his mom's red-rimmed eyes and father's ashen face, and finally Anita's skull with the empty eye sockets and discolored teeth. He thought of how much she'd hate knowing all the whitening strips in the world hadn't stood a chance against a decade of soil.

He rolled off the bed and stood up, stretching his arms overhead and leaning back until his shoulders cracked. It was time to take on the day and hopefully get closer to catching himself a murderer.

By the time he'd showered, caffeinated, and driven the few blocks to the station, he was firing on all cylinders. His phone pinged while he walked across the lot to the front door and looking down, he saw it was from Mia.

All okay here. No sign the intruder returned. How are you?

Instead of texting back, he waited until he was at his desk with another cup of coffee in hand. He punched her number. She picked up on the second ring.

"Good morning," he said. "How'd you sleep?"

"Um…okay, I guess."

"That good, huh? You should've taken me up on the offer to stay. You never said if you got any…I mean, if you…you know, saw anything when you touched the note the perp left on your window."

He heard her exhale. "That's because I didn't get anything from it. Nada. It's infuriating. I see all these random visions from people and objects, but when it's something seriously important to me and my safety, I get a big fat goose egg. Maybe if I try again when I'm not so emotional, it might work…" She trailed off and sighed.

"Hey, don't get so down about it. You know what occurred to me? It's likely the person who cut your dog fence is Anita's killer."

"Knowing that a murderer was on my property and left me a threatening note does not make me feel better," she snapped out.

"Okay, yeah, that part isn't great, but on the flip side, it means he's still around here, and he's damned nervous. Nervous criminals make mistakes."

"I guess that's a good thing," she said.

"Look, the tech guys will be at your place soon. They'll probably be there for several hours processing the scene, especially now we're looking at it in the context of Anita's murder. I'm going to put in for some black and whites to patrol your place, and I'll be there tonight. FYI, I'll sleep on the couch if that's what you want, but I'm staying."

"It's…okay, we'll see how the day goes, I guess, and decide later. Did you get a chance to find out if anyone in your family knew about Anita being pregnant?"

"Nobody did, and it was another arrow in their hearts, let me tell you. We're gonna bring Luke in this morning and see what he has to say."

"Good luck." She paused for a beat. "I honestly don't know what to wish for. Luke seemed like a really nice guy, and he has the two little boys and everything. It's hard to believe he could have killed her."

"Well, if he did, he's going down." Roman took a second to unclench his fists, and when he spoke again, his voice had softened. "I'll be in touch later. Let you know what time I'm coming out to your place. Remember, cell phone with you at all times."

"Aye aye, Captain. See you later."

Kevin poked his head in the door. "They brought in Luke McNally. Schmidt said if you want in, we can do the interview. Otherwise, it'll be him and Cooper."

Roman placed the receiver on its cradle and pushed up from the chair. "I want in so bad it hurts."

They went downstairs at a jog, but before Kevin could pull the door open, Roman stepped forward to block the way. "Listen, man, I don't know if I'm gonna go there right now, but I want you to be ready for some questions about Anita being pregnant."

Kevin raised his eyebrows. "And you've been keeping this to yourself, why?"

"Because I only found out last night. I have to think McNally knew. I don't know how it plays in yet but…"

"Yeah, but…" Kevin said. "Where'd you get the info?"

Roman stepped to the side and grabbed the handle to the door. "Mia," he said before stepping into the main lobby.

"Oh, man," Kevin said under his breath before hurrying after him. "Hey, Roman, are you out of your mind?"

Roman didn't reply until they were outside the observation room to interview A. "I'll feel him out first and see how it goes. I've gotta believe Anita being pregnant is important. If it had nothing to do with her death, how come McNally never said anything about it?"

"Schmidt isn't going to like this," Kevin warned.

"Yeah, well, Mia found her, didn't she? I can't think of any way we would have stumbled across Anita's remains without her pointing us straight to the spot, can you?"

"No, but come on, you know what the brass thinks about psychics and the like."

"I know. Me too, mostly. Except this time, it's different. This time we have someone who actually does see stuff. Real stuff. And it's for my sister, man. I've gotta push on this. I understand if you want to stay out of it."

Kevin hissed out a breath. "No, we're partners. I've got your back. Do me a favor? Make sure it gets us somewhere. I don't want to take a bunch of crap from the guys."

Roman nodded before pushing into the room. With a sigh, Kevin followed in his wake.

"He's lawyered up," Lieutenant Schmidt said when Roman and Kevin stepped up to the glass beside him and looked in at Luke McNally. "Jessop from Nashville. He's a big wig. Done some high profile murder one cases. I'd say our local doctor is feeling the heat. You boys ready?"

"Yes, sir," Roman said.

"Okay, good. I'll be watching. No need to go in hard since it's a routine follow-up. I'm giving you a chance to keep your finger in the investigation, so check your personal feeling at the door, Mancini."

"What personal feelings?" Roman asked.

"He's got ice in his veins," Kevin added, clapping a hand on Roman's shoulder.

When they entered the interview room, the lawyer got to his feet. "Detectives, I'm Walter Jessop. Mr. McNally has retained my services."

He was a tall and extremely thin man. His navy suit fit him like a glove. *Must be made-to-measure,* Roman thought. Glancing down, he noted the lawyer wore the much-favored black wing-tips shined to perfection. The briefcase on the table probably cost more than Roman's car.

Kevin pointed to Roman. "This is Detective Mancini, and I'm Detective Latterly. Hi, Luke. Sorry to bring you in here again. We'll be recording this."

Roman walked across the room. After pulling out his key fob, he opened the cabinet in the corner. He selected one of the digital recorders and brought it back to the table before turning it on and setting it squarely between both parties. Kevin recited the case number, date, and names of those in attendance before sitting back and turning to Roman.

"Excuse me, Detectives, but I'd like to start by asking why my client is here today? Unless you have any new evidence and are planning to charge him, this is completely unnecessary. I'm fully aware that you, Detective Mancini, questioned Mr. McNally at a café last week and then had your assistant go to his office the very next day. I think I could make a strong case for harassment."

The lawyer leaned back in his chair and spread his arms in a gesture of a man attempting to be reasonable under extraordinarily trying circumstances. Roman would just bet Jessop was a killer in the courtroom. The juries probably loved him too. Luke had chosen well, but it was bound to be costing him an arm and a leg and possibly his firstborn.

"We have a few follow-up questions," Kevin said in an easy voice. "I'm sure your client is as eager as we are to find the person who killed his girlfriend."

Roman shifted to face Luke more fully and at the same time dismiss Jessop. "Luke, tell us again about the dinner you had with Anita on Sunday, July fifth. How did she seem?"

Luke's eyes shifted to Jessop and then back again to Roman. "Um...she was tired. We all were. As you know, it was a busy weekend."

"What did the two of you talk about?" Kevin interjected smoothly.

"Oh, the parade and the fireworks. Stuff like that. We were both looking forward to some downtime at the end of the week."

"Why was she crying?" Roman asked.

"She...wait, what?" Luke stuttered. "Who said she was crying?"

Roman paused for a beat, locking eyes with Luke. "Let's say I had an interesting conversation with Brooke the other day. Turns out something was up with Anita, isn't that right?"

"Brooke couldn't have known...I mean, Anita didn't—"

Jessop raised his hand. "A moment, please. I'd like to confer with my client."

Kevin reached out and hit the stop button on the recorder, and both he and Roman got up and walked back out to the observation room.

"What's going on, Mancini?" Schmidt all but pounced on Roman when he stepped into the room.

"You better have something, or Jessop will tear us to shreds."

Roman blew out a breath and turning, stared into the room. Jessop and Luke were huddled together with the lawyer apparently doing most of the talking. Luke occasionally nodded.

"He knew," Roman said to Kevin before answering his lieutenant. "I've recently discovered Anita was pregnant in the weeks leading up to her death."

Schmidt's icy blue eyes pinned Roman. "Why didn't you come to me with this?" he demanded.

"Because the information only came to light last night and the source can't go on record. I had to find out if McNally knew. This seemed like the best way of doing it."

"Am I to take it that Brooke Adams did not provide you with this fact?"

Roman shook his head. "No, I just used her in there with McNally."

Schmidt sighed. "Mia Reeves then? I should have known. You'd better make this work because I'm not gonna save you from whatever that high dollar shark hits you with if you're wrong."

"Understood," Roman said.

"You too, Latterly."

"Yes, Lieutenant. I understand."

Back in the interview room, Kevin reengaged the recorder and nodded at Roman.

"Why was Anita crying?" Roman asked.

"Because…there was…we were having a discussion about our future, and she got emotional, that's all." Luke's eyes stayed on his hands which rested on the table.

"Were you breaking up with her?" Kevin asked.

Luke's head shot up, and he faced Kevin. "No, absolutely not."

"So, she was happy about whatever you two were talking about?" Kevin pressed.

"Not exactly happy. We were trying to decide some things."

"Why would you attempt to make important future decisions at a Pizza Hut during Anita's short dinner break on a night when you were both admittedly exhausted?" Roman asked.

"It wasn't planned. It just sort of happened," Luke said.

"My client has answered your questions about the conversation he had with the victim on the night of July fifth. Was there anything else?"

Roman blew out a breath and thought *fuck it*. "Come on, Luke. We know she was pregnant. It must have been a bummer. You were barely into your second year in pre-med, and now you'd have a baby to support. I'm sure that wasn't in your carefully organized life plan."

Luke said nothing. With head bowed he kept his eyes fixed on the table.

"Maybe you were pushing her to have an abortion?" Kevin suggested. "Is that why she was crying?"

Jessop slid the cap on his gold pen and placed it along with the yellow pad of paper in his briefcase. He closed the lid down with a snap. "We're done here, gentlemen. My client has nothing further to add. Unless you're charging him with something, we're going to get up and walk out."

"I always liked you, Luke," Roman said. "And I know without a shadow of a doubt Anita loved you. It's too bad when the chips were down, and she needed you the most, you weren't the standup guy we all thought you were."

Roman pushed back from the table while Jessop pinned him with a stare. "That was completely unnecessary," the lawyer said. "I won't have you pestering my client. He's a pillar of this community. If I discover any evidence you are sullying his name, we'll see you in court. You can count on it."

"Yeah, I can see how awful it would be to have his name sullied. It's not like we're talking about the murder of an innocent young woman or anything," Roman said in a low voice.

Kevin put a hand on his arm, and Roman merely nodded and moved away from the table.

"Yes, she was pregnant. Yes, the baby was mine. But I never pushed for an abortion and as God is my witness I didn't kill her," Luke said, his eyes blazing into Roman's.

* * *

"Luke knew, didn't he?" Mia asked within seconds of Roman stepping inside her house that night. "Do you think he killed her?"

"You know something? I could really use a beer." He handed her the two pizza boxes and crouching down, patted the dogs, most especially Layla.

"I'm sorry. Of course, come in. I have Rolling Rock and Desperado. Why don't you sit down and relax."

"I'll take a Rolling Rock."

He followed her back to the kitchen and refusing an offer of a glass, took the beer bottle from her and drank deep. Leaning his hip against the counter, he shifted his head back and forth to stretch his neck and sighed.

"Do you want me to reheat this," Mia asked, lifting the lid off the larger of the two pizzas.

"Nope, as is will do me fine. You know, I've never ordered a pizza with no meat and no cheese. Gus looked at me as if I had a head injury. You're really disciplined about your diet, aren't you?"

Mia turned away and opening a cupboard, pulled down two blue plates. "I guess," she mumbled. "It's not what you think though."

"What is it then?"

She didn't say anything for a minute. Instead, she heaped four slices of pizza, loaded with pepperoni and sausage and dripping with cheese, onto one of the plates and handed it to him. "Napkins are on the table."

He watched her open the smaller pizza box and put two slices on the second plate. She stepped around him and made her way over to the table in the kitchen nook. Reaching for the macramé napkin holder, she placed one on the setting across from her and one on her lap. Mac wandered over and sat by her chair. Roman stood for another moment while she picked up a slice of pizza and took a delicate bite. He walked over and slid in across from her.

"You're not going to tell me?" he asked.

She continued chewing and swallowed before meeting his eyes. "It's going to sound crazy."

"Try me."

"I sometimes get things from the food. Flashes, I mean. What I see from meat and dairy is...let's say there's no way I can eat it after seeing what I see. Fruits and vegetables can give me things too, especially if the person picking or harvesting or whatever was in a state of emotional distress. But at least I'm not eating something whose misery and death are firmly rooting in my consciousness. And more than that, the animal's suffering was in essence caused by me."

Roman stared at her then abruptly sat back against the chair and crossed his arms over his chest. "Are you trying to make me feel bad, so I convert to veganism because it won't work? I love my meat."

"No, I'm not. I firmly believe each person has to make up their own mind," she said. "Though I think it'd be darn interesting if everyone saw what I saw."

He looked down at his pizza and back to her again. "Then I guess I'm glad I can't see it." Picking up a slice from his plate, he took a huge bite and chewed. She smiled placidly at him.

"Okay, I'm dying here. You have to tell me what happened with Luke," she said once he'd finished the slice and taken another pull from the bottle.

"After some pushing and prodding, he admitted he knew Anita was pregnant. She'd only taken the test at work on the day they met for dinner at Pizza Hut. They were both shocked and upset and hadn't decided anything by the time she had to go back to work. Luke admitted he kinda lost his mind for a bit. They were supposed to have lunch the next day and talk some more, but he canceled at the last minute. Said he needed time to think."

"And when Luke canceled, Anita reached out to Brooke. That's why she was so distracted during their lunch. Except it doesn't seem she told her about the pregnancy."

Roman shrugged. "I'd lay money she didn't, but we'll follow up with Brooke tomorrow."

"Back to Luke. Do you think he killed Anita?"

"I dunno. It doesn't read that way. He comes off as telling the truth or at least now he is. Plus, he's alibied tight unless his parents lied for him. Parents will do that, sure, but in this case, I can't see Doc McNally living with the fact his son killed a girl."

She knocked her fist on the table. "I wish I could get a better read on Luke. The only things that came to me were pain and loss and regret. None of it felt violent."

"And if it's not Luke, we're back to having nothing."

"Can you think of anyone else she might have told?" Mia shook her head. "I guess it doesn't really matter though because the only person who would care enough about the pregnancy was Luke."

"Beyond Brooke and Ashley, I can't think of a single person. I might have considered Tony, but he said he didn't know. In fact, he was more shocked than anyone when I told the family the other night." He shook his head and putting his elbows on the table, slumped down. "Man, I really thought this pregnancy news was the break I'd been hoping for, but all it is is another dead end."

Reaching across, she closed her hand over his. "I'm so sorry, Roman. I still believe it means something because otherwise why would I have seen it?"

"I don't know. You said random things come to you. It could be just that, completely random."

"I wonder why she did the pregnancy test at work? Do you think that other waitress, Mary, knew about it? Not that it matters but still an interesting question."

Straightening up, he turned his hand under hers and linked their fingers together. "Yeah, it can't hurt to check that out too. Okay, no more Anita talk tonight. I need to decompress."

She pulled her hand free and stood to gather the plates. "Sure, absolutely. Let's take the dogs for a walk. It's going to be a beautiful sunset. I can just tell."

Their view from the porch was spectacular with rays slanting low and producing pink and orange streaks across the sky. Light filtered through the trees at the back of the property and turned the brook into a painter's palette infusing the water with hues of red and gold. In the background, a chorus of crickets sang their approval.

All the dogs romped. Ecstatic to be out in the sweet evening air, they chased one another through the grassy field and with noses down, followed scents among the trees. Back out in the open, a hawk circled, hunting. Tucker, taking his presence as a personal affront, leapt into the air, barking ferociously. His actions had zero effect on the bird of prey, but he seemed well pleased with himself and jostled against Layla, smiling his doggy smile.

Mia breathed deeply, tipped her head back and gazed up at the sky. "Nothing can beat a night like this," she said.

"I've always been a town guy. I like having neighbors, knowing them enough to say 'hey, how's it going?' I like walking half a block to grab a coffee or a sandwich at lunch, but this beats all. The land and the colors and the sense of it happening just for my pleasure. It's pretty freaking great, isn't it?"

"Yeah. I love it. I knew as soon as I could manage, I'd get a place in the country. The city life is so not for me."

"Which cities have you lived in?"

"Here and there. Nowhere special." She shrugged nonchalantly before lifting her arm to point over his shoulder. "Oh, look, the moon's rising. Not a full one, but a solid three-quarters."

"It's not a hard question, Mia."

"We should probably start heading back." She let out a whistle. "Mac, Layla, let's go. Time to go home. Come on, guys."

Mac came bounding up with Fifi half a length behind. A few seconds later, Layla and Tucker raced over to join them. Mia had only managed to walk a few steps before Roman grabbed her arm.

"Why won't you tell me where you've lived? Surely it's not a state secret?" he pressed.

She looked down at his hand on her arm then across the field to where the sun was dropping below the horizon. "The past isn't important. Where I've lived isn't important. I prefer to stay in the present."

He took her shoulders and turned her to face him. "What the hell happened to you that makes you so afraid?"

"Nothing happened to me. I make my own way in this life. My own choices. I know you have this idea I'm some kind of victim, but I'm not." Reaching up she gently pushed back a lock of hair from his forehead. "You need to accept the fact that you and I are never going to happen. I'm sorry for it because you're a great guy, but I want you to back off."

She walked away, striding up a small rise with her dogs flocking around her and the dramatic sky framing her silhouette.

The longing hit him like a punch to the solar plexus. Why the hell did he want her so much? It defied logic. She was good looking—that was true enough—but not especially his type since he'd gravitated to willowy brunettes in the past. At times she was prickly and evasive and seemed to have no trouble turning him down. She'd told him no at least a handful of times, and yet it seemed to make no difference to him.

Come on, he growled inside his head, *you're making a fool of yourself. It's time to move on.*

Chapter Eighteen

The next morning, with Roman back in town at the police station, Mia admitted it had been a tough night. Having him sleeping in the spare room—knowing he was just steps away and glad to welcome her under the sheets—had been the worst kind of temptation. Especially now that she knew first-hand how much pleasure they could bring to one another.

If only he could be casual instead of getting all intense about everything. Most guys would give their left arm to have a no-strings-attached sexual fling with a willing woman, but not Roman. *Figures I went and picked him out of the herd.*

She sighed. It would be cruel to sleep with him again knowing how he felt. She couldn't do it. Could she? No. It was wrong. She was a better person now. Damn. Living the straight life was harder than she'd thought.

Using iron-willed control to rein in her distracted mind, Mia concentrated on crafting her jewelry. Still, when her cell phone signaled in the afternoon, she pounced on it.

"Hello, Brooke. How are you?" Mia said.

"I'm fine. Are you busy?"

"I don't have to be."

"That's good. I wondered if you wanted to meet for coffee?"

"Um…sure, okay. What time?"

"Now would be great if that works for you. I'm at Gabe's dinner."

"Now would be fine. I'll put myself together and see you in twenty minutes."

Once at the diner, a hostess Mia hadn't seen before showed her to Brooke's table. Brooke smiled up at her.

"Thanks for coming. It's been a pretty rough day, and I could use a friendly ear."

Mia easily sensed the sadness. It radiated out from Brooke in steady waves. She slid in across from her, reached out and closed her hand over the one clenched on the table. "Did something happen?" she asked.

"No, not really. Well, sort of. I came from…" Brooke paused and pulled her hand from under Mia's when the waitress approached.

"What can I get you?" the woman asked Mia.

"Mint tea, please."

"Sure, hon. You want a top up?" She motioned to Brooke's cup of coffee.

Brooke shook her head. "No, thanks. I'm still working on it."

When they were alone again, Mia raised her eyebrows at Brooke and motioned for her to continue.

Brooke exhaled and clasped her arms across her chest, hugging herself. "I was called down to the police station. They wanted to talk to me again. That's where I heard about Anita being pregnant. Since you've been helping Roman investigate, I guess you knew." She raised her eyes to meet Mia's.

Mia tilted her head. "Yeah, I heard. You really didn't know before?"

"No." Brooke's face dissolved, and tears began dripping down her cheeks. "I can't understand why she didn't tell me. I was her closest friend. She must have been so scared. Why didn't she say something when we had lunch that day? Her being distracted makes so much sense now."

"I don't know, Brooke. I'm sure she was planning to tell you. I guess it was so new. It sounds like she and Luke barely had time to talk it through themselves."

The waitress reappeared. When her eyes flicked to Brooke, she said nothing, simply sliding the mug in front of Mia before silently departing.

Now Brooke was the one reaching out. She clutched Mia's hand. "That must have been why she was killed. Otherwise, the police wouldn't be asking about it. Do you think it was Luke?"

Mia shrugged. "I honestly don't know. I'm sure the police are following every line they can."

Brooke swiped at her eyes with her free hand, her lips trembling. "I know it was a long time ago, but ever since they found her in the conservation park last week, it feels like it's happening all over again. I miss her so much."

"It must be awful," Mia said in a soothing voice. "I've never had a close girlfriend, so I can only imagine how hard this is for you. I'm sorry for your loss."

"If she hadn't been killed, the baby would be nine years old by now. I can't stop thinking about it. I wonder if it was a boy or girl."

"From the sounds of things, it was far too early to tell."

"She always wanted children. We talked about it a bunch of times. Once she was done with college and she and Luke were married, she told me she was hoping for three, but wouldn't rule out four. I know being pregnant before college wasn't her plan. Still, I have to believe she would have been happy about it."

The grief was overpowering now. Mia let her eyes slide away from Brooke for a moment. She saw Mrs. Bird from the post office sitting with her husband and sharing a pot of tea. Gabriel came out from the kitchen, a dish towel slung over his shoulder and a ready smile on his face.

"Every child is a blessing," Mia said, finding it difficult to look away from Gabriel. Finally, she turned back to the sobbing blond woman. "You're right, I'm sure Anita would have been happy."

Brooke nodded several times and released Mia's hand, then grabbing a napkin. She blew her nose and wiped her eyes. "Everyone keeps telling me I should get past it. I think my mom and my other friends think I'm purposely wallowing in the grief. I'm not. I swear it. I just can't seem to let Anita go."

"I obviously didn't know Anita, but I've heard so much about her. She sounds like the kind of person who embraced life and was always looking to the future. I have to guess she wouldn't like seeing you this way. Don't you think she'd want you out there living your life to the fullest? If you had died, would you want her to still be so sad?"

Brooke blew out a breath. "I know. People have told me that before. For some reason, hearing it from you, right now, feels different. Like it's actually true.

Thanks for talking to me. You're really nice. I'm sorry for being such a mess." She blew her nose again then swiped her arm through the air. "Okay. I'm all right now. No more crying."

After that, they talked about easy things. Brooke took all the pressure away from Mia having to make conversation because she was happy to chat about anything and everything. She explained her plans for the fall dance gala and once again urged Mia to join her adult beginner class. Brooke also asked about the process of making jewelry and wanted to know the history of each of Mia's dogs.

Mia found it relaxing whiling away an hour with the other woman. She was warm and funny and didn't seem predisposed to asking a lot of personal questions about her past. Maybe, if things worked out, she and Brooke would become good friends. Maybe they'd meet for lunches and dinners and talk just like this. The idea of it filled Mia with a warm glow. It would be fun to have a girlfriend.

"Is it true you and Roman are having a thing?"

Brooke's question jolted her from her daydream. "I...um...no. We're not," she managed at last.

"That's too bad because I think you'd be great together. Well, okay, I don't actually know you very well, but I have this feeling you guys would really hit it off. Oh, of course..." She slapped her forehead dramatically. "You probably already have a boyfriend. I'd have heard if it was someone from around here, so you must be doing the long distance thing. That's got to be hard. Will he move here?"

Mia's head started to spin. Had it only been a moment ago she'd thought conversation with Brooke was easy?

"No long distance thing and no boyfriend. I'm single and happy to stay that way."

"I'm sorry." Brooke giggled. "Okay, not entirely sorry but still, I know I can be pushy. Let me just say you should think about Roman. He's one of the good guys. I think maybe the thing with Anita turned him darker than he would have been otherwise, but he's still rock solid."

"You're sure doing a great selling job on him. How come you two never dated?"

"I don't know exactly. It's not like I don't look at him and think *oh yum*. Somehow though, we never went in that direction. Who knows, if things had been different maybe we would have, but I don't think it would've lasted. I'm a firm believer in the power of the gut. Mine never said a peep when he was around."

"But it turned into Chatty Kathy whenever Tony showed up?"

Brooke paused and stared down at her cup of cold coffee. "You listen too much."

"Oh, it's okay for you to put me through the ringer over Roman, but when it comes to Tony you're practically mute?"

"Yeah, well, for me I guess he was the one who got away. And now it feels like it's too late. With some things you just can't go back, you know?"

"I'm sorry. I didn't mean to bring up a difficult subject."

"No worries. It's old news." Brooke checked her watch and pushed the mostly full mug away from her. "That's my cue to go. I've got a class in fifteen. Thanks for coming, Mia. Talking to you helped more than you can know. And about Roman, maybe you should give him another look."

Mia shook her head and waved Brooke off. She sat a moment longer, finishing her tea before she checked her watch. Almost four o'clock. Although she'd tried to dissuade him, Roman had insisted on staying at her house again to make sure she had no unwanted visitors. She'd originally planned to cook, but since she was already at the diner, the idea of picking up something to bring home suddenly seemed a whole lot more appealing.

At the take-out counter, she put in an order for two large salads, one topped with sesame chicken and the other garbanzo beans and lentils. She knew Roman would turn his nose up at salad, but if she also made herbed garlic bread and offered him some apple crumble for dessert, she figured he wouldn't grouch too much.

Gabriel pushed up from his stool behind the main counter and walked over to join her while she waited for her order. "How's it going, young lady?"

"Well enough. Are you having a good day?"

"Always. Every day the Lord gives me breath is a good day. Will I see you at service on Sunday?"

"Um…I'm not sure…"

"Think about it. Everyone's always so busy working on their minds and their bodies when the really important work takes place in the soul."

"I'm sure you're right." She glanced around, desperate to come up with another topic of conversation.

"I'm sorry, dear. I can see I'm making you uncomfortable," Gabriel said. "I don't normally push so much, but with Anita being found, it's on my mind. None of us ever know when we'll be called from this earth, so it's important to be prepared to meet our Lord."

"Yes, of course. Oh, look, my food is ready. I guess I'll see you later."

"Take care. And no more lectures, I promise. I guess I'm feeling melancholy today."

She softened. He did look sad. "That's okay. Thanks for caring enough to…well, thanks. I'll see you later."

It wasn't until she'd stepped over to the cash register and dug into her purse for her wallet that the vision came to her. All she could do was stand there and watch it play out.

"Twenty-one dollars and seventeen cents. Mia. Are you okay? What's wrong?"

The woman came out from behind the counter and touched Mia's shoulder. "I'm…it's…I'm okay. Sorry, how much did you say?"

With shaking hands, Mia counted out the money, reached for the containers of food, and held them to her chest. She paused by the door and slowly turned back, searching the diner for Gabriel. He'd returned to his usual spot behind the main counter.

Nodding to a man on a stool, he pointed to the baked goods housed below the glass. The customer said something. Gabriel reached down, producing a muffin the size of a small bowling ball. He placed it in front of the man. When Gabriel stepped back, his head came up, and his eyes met Mia's. Smiling, he lifted his hand in a brief wave before turning back to the man on the stool.

The skin at the back of her neck crawled like a skitter of spider legs. She pushed through the door and hurried to her SUV. In less than two minutes, she was parked in front of the Dalton Police station.

* * *

"Tell me again what Gabriel said to her," Roman said.

"I still can't believe it. Surely it wasn't him?"

Mia's hand rubbed back and forth across her jeans. Roman reached across the console and closed his hand over hers, stilling it. He waited until she brought her eyes up to meet his. "Don't worry about any of that now. What's important are the details of what he said to Anita."

She nodded briskly. "You're right. Okay. What he said was, 'No one of illegitimate birth shall enter the assembly of the Lord; none of his descendants, even to the tenth generation, shall enter the assembly of the Lord.' That's weird, right. It sounds like he's quoting from the Bible or something."

"And you're sure Anita told him she didn't want to get married yet?"

"Absolutely. And she was crying. That's when he patted her arm and told her to take an extra-long dinner break."

Roman sat back against the seat and continued writing in his notebook. "Okay. That's good," he said when he clicked his pen and flipped the cover over on the small spiral pad. "Now all I have to do is figure out how to officially get him in here for questioning. I guess I'll talk to Schmidt. Are you okay?"

"To be honest, I feel kinda sick. I didn't want it to be Luke, and that goes double for Gabriel. He's always been so nice to me. It's starting to feel like anyone around here could be Anita's killer."

"Welcome to my world."

"I'm sorry. This isn't about me. These are your people. You've known them your whole life. It has to be a million times worse for you."

"Let's just agree we both feel crappy about it. Why don't you go on home? I think I'm gonna let this sit for a while. It's almost end of shift anyway, and it'll give me more time to figure out how to get Schmidt on board. I have a couple of things to finish up, and then I'll join you. Do you want me to bring food?"

"That's okay. I already picked dinner up at the diner. Don't get your hopes up," she said quickly when his face lit up. "We're having healthy salads tonight. You need to start taking better care of yourself."

"Maybe I should have a pre-dinner snack before I head out. I think I have a coupon for KFC somewhere in my car."

"Don't you dare. There'll be plenty of food, and you'll like it, I promise."

"Sure. Sure. Drive safe…and Mia, thanks for coming straight over with this."

"No problem."

She was more than ready to go home. Back to her four-legged boys and girls and the quiet where she didn't have to wonder if she was rubbing elbows with a murderer. It was doubtful she'd be able to concentrate on work, but sitting in the sunroom with a glass of wine sounded just about perfect.

The dogs seemed especially energetic when she pulled the SUV up to the house. They ran at the fence and Mac actually hit it so hard the wire sprang and bounced him back. It was strange. She'd only been gone a few hours.

Naturally, they raced in through the doggie door ahead of her and practically bowled her over when she stepped inside. Layla did something she knew was against the rules. She jumped up so her front feet landed on Mia's chest, knocking the food containers out of her hands and slamming her back into the closed door.

"Bad girl," she hissed. "What's wrong with you? You haven't done that since I first adopted you."

Layla cowered at her feet. Tucker whined and licked the golden lab's face. Rubbing her butt, which had taken the brunt of the impact with the door, Mia stooped over and picked up the food. Oh well, there'd be no need to toss the salad, she thought.

Subdued now, the dogs followed steps behind her as she made her way to the kitchen. Mac let out a little whine and sat at her feet. Fifi crouched in between Mac's front legs, gazing up at Mia. The other two dogs paced back and forth across the kitchen.

She stared at them for several seconds. "What the heck is up with you guys? Do you want to go for a walk, is that it? I was thinking porch and wine, but maybe a walk would be better. Okay, troops. Let's do it."

They perked up slightly when Mia said the word *walk* but remained quiet when she unlocked the kitchen door and stepped out. Not only was Mac pressed up against one leg, but Layla, uncharacteristically, stayed glued to her other thigh. The two small dogs slotted in beside their bigger companions, and Mia felt like she was marching in formation. When Mac whined for a second time, she finally looked up.

Her heart lurched in her chest, and her hand involuntarily flew to her mouth. "Get back," she screamed before she'd fully registered what was in front of her. "Come on. Everyone in the house. Now."

Grabbing Layla's collar, she turned and ran to the side door. The dogs followed as one unit, and Mia had everyone back in the kitchen, safe and sound, within seconds. Whirling around, she slammed the deadbolt into place. Her breath came in short gasps while she grabbed up her cell phone and punched her contact list and Roman's number.

"Hey," he answered. "I'm almost ready. Should be able to head out in fifteen. Did you change your mind about eating healthy?"

"You need to come *now*." Her voice sounded wrong in her ears.

"Where are you? Are you safe?"

"I'm…yes, I'm safe. The dogs and I are locked in the house. Someone was here. The greenhouse is smashed to bits."

"Don't go out there. Don't answer the door no matter who it is. I'll be there in ten minutes."

He made it in eight.

Chapter Nineteen

Even in the short amount of time Mia waited for Roman to arrive, she managed to find her equilibrium. She was okay. The dogs were fine. Anything else could be fixed or replaced. From the front window, she watched Roman and Kevin exit the Impala with guns drawn. A black and white police car roared in after them. When it slammed to a stop, two officers jumped out.

Roman motioned them to the house, and Mia saw him nod at Kevin before cautiously walking toward the back yard. She returned to the kitchen and peered through the window over the sink where she was able to track their progress around the greenhouse. All was quiet. Whoever had smashed the glass panels was apparently long gone.

Eventually, Roman and Kevin approached the side door where she stood waiting.

"It looks like a total demo. I'm really sorry," Roman said.

"What about the equipment inside?"

Kevin shook his head. "Maybe some of it can be repaired, but wires were cut and most of the trays dented or cracked."

"Dammit. That's my new hydroponic setup. I literally just got it last week."

"I know." Roman took her hand in his. "It's seriously crappy. Why don't we sit down? You can take us through the timeline of the afternoon."

"It couldn't have been Gabriel," she said once she'd reached the end. "I talked to him right before I went to see you. There wasn't enough time to get out here and trash the greenhouse before I got home."

"Yeah, I agree. But what about when you first got to the diner? Did you see him then?"

Mia closed her eyes. "The new girl was at the hostess station. She's the one who seated me. Brooke was already there. Um…Jim was working the counter then. I guess I didn't notice Gabriel until later when he came out of the kitchen."

"So there might have been time, especially if he was watching your place and saw you leave?" His eyes flicked over to Kevin. "We'll have to follow up on that. I'd also like to know where Luke McNally was this afternoon."

"This is so stupid," Mia said. "I may have found Anita's body, but I still don't know who killed her."

"From the killer's point of view, nobody has had any interest or clues for ten years, and then you came along and blew the whole thing wide open again. My guess is he wants you out of here. The sooner, the better," Kevin said.

"Makes me wonder if he's getting desperate enough to kill again," Roman said.

"But there wasn't a note this time. We don't even know for sure it was the same person," Mia protested.

"Odds are good it was," Kevin said.

She rubbed a hand over her face. "I know. None of this seems real."

"I think it'd be best if you moved into town. It's so remote out here. You're making the killer's job ten times easier," Roman said.

She stared at him. "I have four dogs, and I work from home. I doubt the local bed and breakfast would be willing to take me on."

"I meant to my place."

"Well, since I've never seen your place, I can't actually say for sure, but it sounds like an apartment. A one bedroom apartment," she said, emphasizing the last few words before pointing to the dogs pacing at the kitchen door. "How exactly do you think that'll work?"

"Okay, you're right. My parent's house then. It's big enough, and I'm sure they'd be more than happy to let you stay until this guy is caught."

"Roman, thanks. I mean it. But I'm not moving into your parents' house with a pack of dogs and an online jewelry business. So far it's only happened when I'm not home. From now on, I'll stay put. I can get practically anything I need with an internet connection and FedEx."

"We'll put a uniform on the house," Kevin said.

"Yeah, for a day or two, but you and I both know we don't have the manpower long-term," Roman said.

"I have the dogs and a cell phone, and I'll be careful," Mia insisted. She didn't know why the thought of leaving her home made her feel so panicky, but it did.

"And I'll be here at night," Roman added. "Non-negotiable. During the day, you'll text me every hour."

"Every hour? Come on. Don't you think you're taking it a little too far? How about two times during the day?"

"Four times," he countered. "Every second hour."

"Three times," she said firmly. "Ten, noon, and three o'clock."

"And we'll add a couple of drive-bys," Kevin said. "That should do it. Mia doesn't strike me as the sort of person to take unnecessary risks."

"No, she doesn't, but I can't say the same for this psycho."

When everyone except Roman had gone, Mia went out and walked cautiously around the remains of the greenhouse. Every single panel except those on the roof had been damaged. Most were smashed into countless pieces. The grass was littered with debris. It would be a job and a half to clean it up, and she'd have to keep the dogs well clear of the area until then.

She moved slowly, picking her way among the larger jagged pieces of glass. *How long will it take to do this,* she wondered? *And what did he use? A baseball bat? A tire iron?*

Flash. The briefest instant of a vision. A sledgehammer. *That's what he used.* Old, the metal carrying a sheen of rust and the handle wooden. She saw the black leather glove and a dark blue sleeve. Then it was gone. Although she strained, standing still and keeping her eyes closed while frantically reaching out with her mind, she couldn't bring the vision back.

"Nothing else?" Roman asked when she finally gave up and went inside to tell him. "What about shoes or pants? Anything in the background like a car maybe?"

"No. It was barely a second, and the vision was tight. I saw it as though looking down. The arm was swinging forward. One arm, one hand, and the sledgehammer. Nothing else. The edges of my sight were smudged out and grey."

"Could you hear anything? Were the dogs barking?"

She thought for a moment. "It was more like a snapshot. Just a single moment frozen in time. Wait, there was…" She paused and rubbed her temple with her right hand. "There was…he was happy. No gleeful. That's the right word. He was filled with glee."

When the shiver traveled down her spine, she hugged her arms around her chest.

"It's okay. Try not to worry. We're going to get this guy."

"I know. I'm not worried," she lied.

* * *

The next week was enough to fray every last one of her nerves. During the day, she kept all the doors locked and only went out on the back porch whenever the dogs were in the run. She was terrified the killer would try something again. Something more sinister than cutting a hole in the fence.

Other than the porch outings, she didn't leave the house.

Her only reprieve was a nightly walk with Roman and the dogs. It was arranged that one of the uniformed officers followed him to Mia's house at the end of shift and sat on the place while they took the dogs around the property to stretch their legs. Roman carried his gun and said little on the outings, his eyes constantly scanning the fields and tree lines.

His laser-like focus on the surroundings made her feel completely exposed, and she was barely able to exhale while her mind filled with visions of a masked man spraying her with bullets. It would be pitifully easy for the killer to hide out somewhere and take both Roman and her down in seconds.

"Maybe we shouldn't do this until after he's caught," Mia said.

"We're fine. Don't worry. Dave and I always drive the side road behind your property on our way over. There're no suspicious vehicles parked anywhere in the area. Just relax and enjoy the night air, okay?"

"Okay," she said though she didn't feel much better.

After the first few days, Mia put her foot down and insisted she couldn't live on take-out. "It's not healthy. It's expensive, and besides, I like cooking," she told him, counting off the reasons on her fingers.

Mia came to truly treasure that time of the day. Once they were back safely from the evening walk, they settled inside the log house, and she finished preparing the food and plating up dinner. She and Roman ate in the kitchen nook. The dogs, totally used to having an extra human around, lay in pools of the late evening sun filtering through the front room windows.

This new routine was homey and relaxing. Rather than feeling hemmed in, she found it nice having someone to talk to every night. Roman told her funny stories about the guys at the police station or about some of the small events that happened in his day. He talked about his family and the sports teams he followed, particularly the Atlanta Braves. She'd never really watched baseball, but now sometimes joined him on the couch to catch a few innings.

And, of course, the discussion often wound around to Anita's murder.

There were still no new leads on whoever had come to Mia's property and destroyed the greenhouse. Luke McNally had a rock-solid alibi. He'd been seeing patients at the time and hadn't left the office building the entire afternoon. As for Gabriel, he was basically in the clear. Roman couldn't officially bring him in for questioning since the only link they had to the case was Mia's vision of him lecturing Anita about children born out of wedlock.

Still, Roman had quietly asked around town about the day the greenhouse was vandalized and was told that Gabriel had been at home. This, apparently, was his typical weekly schedule since he closed the restaurant every night without fail. Even with more probing of the employees at the diner, he hadn't been able to confirm the man's whereabouts for the rest of that afternoon since he was supposedly running errands.

It frustrated the heck out of him that Gabriel might be a possible suspect, but, as of yet, he had no way of questioning him.

The forensic evidence at Anita's burial site had netted them nothing. Using the internet, Roman found the emerald ring was part of a signature line carried by Zale's, one of the largest chains of jewelry stores in the country. None of the suspects had purchased anything at any Zale's store the two years before Anita was killed with either credit or debit. Since there was no way of tracing a cash sale, it didn't actually clear any of them either. For all intents and purposes, the ring was a dead end.

Given the murder had happened ten years ago…no one in town remembered anything about vehicles parked at the entrance to the forest…nor had anyone stumbled across the freshly cultivated ground shortly after Anita had been buried. Really it had been a risky place to hide her remains since it was a known hangout spot for teenagers.

Roman couldn't decide if the choice of burial site made it more or less likely that the killer had been a teenager. Did adults even know about Sweetheart's Clearing or had the guy simply stumbled upon the location by chance?

"How's your family doing?" Mia asked once they were both seated at the table one night.

"Sort of okay. I can tell it's wearing on them, but after all this time they're basically used to dealing with this kind of stuff. Lina's gone back to Atlanta. She still hasn't said anything about getting a divorce. I guess she figures there's enough going on right now without adding to the bad news in the family. Tony's in…I think it's Miami this week."

"That's good, about Tony I mean. Is he away long?"

"Not sure. I think he's keeping it loose at work until we figure out when to have the memorial." Roman forked up a mouthful of mashed potatoes and sighed. "These are really good."

"Thanks. I hadn't thought about the memorial. When will Anita's remains be released?"

He swallowed and put down his fork. "Any day now would be my guess. They've tested and retested everything. I don't think there's anything more her bones can tell us. Ma's thinking maybe July sixth."

"The day she went missing and was likely killed?" Mia murmured. "Very fitting."

"Yeah, it makes a nice circle I guess. Whenever it is, I want you to come."

Before she could stop herself, she'd reached across and placed her hand on his arm. "Of course. It would be an honor."

He nodded. "Good. Having you there…it'll make it easier."

"And maybe I'll sense something," Mia said, squeezing his arm.

He leaned back in his chair and moved her hand until he could thread his fingers through hers. She looked down at their joined hands for a moment, her brow drawing together, but said nothing.

"It will be good to lay her to rest. I'd rather we catch the killer first. Still, even this way, it'll feel like we've done something for her," Roman said.

"I know. I'm sure your mom and dad will be relieved."

"That's for sure. They hated the thought of her buried in unconsecrated ground. These things are important to them."

"Not to you?"

"The Catholic stuff?" He shrugged. "I like some of the ceremonies and rituals, but I'm not especially down with everything they preach. Did you know I was an altar boy?"

"What? Really? What was that like?"

"To be honest, it was cool. I got a kick out of being behind the scenes, going places other people weren't allowed to go like the altar or into the sacristy. I still like it, I guess. As a detective, I can be right in the thick of things behind the police tape, and everyone else has to stand back. What about you? Any religious affiliations?"

"No. Some of the homes…I mean, my parents were Anglican but didn't go to church."

He stared at her, blinking rapidly. "What homes?" he finally asked.

She released his hand and leaning forward, gathered their plates and cutlery. "We moved a couple of times, that's all. I made brownies for dessert."

"Why won't you talk about it?"

"About what?"

"About anything from before. How many times did you move? What was it like being an only child? How come you have a degree in art history, but there aren't any paintings in your house or books on art? Most people have personal photos and relics of the past scattered around. Where are yours?"

She paused before stepping into the kitchen. "Three. Lonely. I realized I wasn't passionate about art and most of my effects were lost in a fire. Do you want me to heat your brownie?"

Picking up their glasses, he followed her. "I guess that's a start. Though it only makes me want to ask more questions."

She put the plates down and gripped the edge of the counter before squaring her shoulders. "Roman, why do you keep pushing on this? My past is my business. I don't share it with anyone."

"Whatever you're afraid of, whatever you're running from, I can help. Is it an abusive boyfriend or husband? You don't have to tell me right now, but I need to know if someone might come looking for you."

She shook her head and made a growling noise in her throat before turning to face him. "You've got to get this stupid idea out of your head. I'm no damsel in distress, and I don't need saving," she snapped. "I simply choose not to talk about my past. Get over it already."

He raised a hand as though to ward her off. "Okay. All right. Message received."

They stood staring at one another while the seconds ticked by, and then she nodded. "Hallelujah. Finally. Okay, do you want ice cream with your brownie?"

The tension remained for the rest of the evening. Mia decided to make it an early night. *This is exactly why I don't want anyone in my life,* she thought, as she brushed her teeth. *All the emotion and negotiating and upset. It's so much better being alone. Just me and my dogs.*

She tried not to remember the hurt in Roman's eyes or the jerky half-shrug he'd given the way he often did when he was battling with his emotions. Even thinking about it made her mad. She'd told him and told him she didn't want a relationship. He kept pushing for intimacy anyway. She simply wasn't built that way. Why couldn't he be content to leave things on the surface, just coast along and enjoy each other's company while they were in this strange situation and forced to live together?

She was tucked up in bed with her laptop when Roman knocked on the bedroom door.

"Yes," she said impatiently.

"Can I come in? I need to say something."

She heaved out a sigh. "I guess."

He opened the door and stepped into the room. Layla immediately leapt off her bed and rushed up to him as though his presence was the greatest thing ever. He smiled down briefly and patted her head. Mia saw he'd showered. His damp hair was slicked back from his face. If she wasn't so mad, she might have enjoyed perusing all six foot two of prime male specimen. Instead, she said "Yes?" and raised her eyebrows at him.

"Here's the thing," he began. "You're absolutely right that your past is your business. I'm sorry I keep pushing on it. I won't ask again. Promise. Maybe one day you'll trust enough to tell me more about yourself, but if all you're willing to share is the here and now, I'll take it."

"You'll take it?" she said slowly.

"Yeah. I've hardly made my feelings a secret, so you have to know I like you. Let me try keeping it casual, like you said. I'll be happy enough to hang out with you or whatever with no promise of anything more. We'll go day by day."

She pushed herself farther up the headboard and studied him with narrow eyes. "I don't think you can do it." She pursed her lips. "No, you're way too intense. You'll never be able to keep it casual."

He tipped his head before his lips slowly curved into a smile. "Are you seriously daring me? Listen, Missy, I can keep it casual, no problem. In fact, I bet you'll be the one who starts to slip. You're gonna get super into me because I'm a really great guy. The more time you spend with me, the harder it'll be to stay detached."

She laughed and pushed her hair back from where it had fallen forward over her face. "Okay, you're on. Except how do we set up the parameters to figure out who wins? And what are the stakes?"

He walked farther into the room until he stood at the foot of the bed. "I've got a hundred that says I can take you. As for the parameters, well, I'd say on my side no asking about your past, obviously. No talk of us having any kind of future. Also, while I'm staying here, I won't expect to have dinner with you or even assume we'll hang out every night. I'll be all easy come, easy go."

She nodded and smiled up at him. "I wonder if we should be writing this down? Nah, you won't last long enough for us to forget. I'll meet your hundred and say that on my side, no spontaneous, affectionate gestures. Definitely no declarations of loving, needing, or missing you. I will under no circumstances pry into your past relationships. If you don't call or come around, I won't mind and certainly won't call to ask where you are. Anything else?"

"Sex. On or off the table?"

Her smile was dazzling. "On. No question. The only thing I ask is no other sexual partners. When it's over, we say it's over, and then we're free to sleep with anyone and everyone. Agreed?"

"Agreed. Anything else?"

"Nothing's coming to mind. Should we shake on it?"

She closed her laptop lid and put it on the bedside table then folded the sheet away from her body. Her grin was full of fun and sex. "I can think of a better way to seal the bargain, but you'll have to get in here with me, and you'll need to be naked. Unless you don't want to?"

He stood stock still for several beats then grabbing the hem of his T-shirt stripped it up and over his head. "I guess I could fit you in since I don't have anything else going on."

She rolled out of bed and following his lead, lifted her shirt off. "Race you."

Naked, they tumbled onto the bed together, arms and legs tangling. Roman rolled until she was pinned underneath him. He framed her face with his hands and lowered his mouth bringing hot, hungry lips to meet hers. She sighed against him, and her hands stroked down his back and lingered on his ass, kneading, before she wriggled and twisted. He obligingly rolled over again.

When she reached down between them, her hand closed over him and his breath caught in his throat.

"I wasn't expecting this tonight, but as you can see I'm already getting up to speed," he said into her ear before nibbling down her neck.

"You sure are," she said, squeezing and stroking while he moaned against the side of her throat.

"I'm nothing if not a fast starter." His teeth closed over the tender skin at the base of her neck, and she gasped.

When his hands got busy, though, she slapped them away. "No. Your only job is to lie back and enjoy the ride."

So saying, she straddled his waist and slid down until she was seated in his lap. Slowly, sinuously, Mia rubbed herself against him. His hands grasped her hips. She shook her head and held his wrists, pushing them down by his sides, anchoring them in place with her knees. Rolling her hips again, she arched back and cupped her breasts. Lifting, fondling, her hands worked steadily while her eyes remained locked on his.

When she judged him on the point of desperation, she shifted back onto her heels and slowly lowered down onto him…inch by glorious inch. His eyes closed for a moment. This time when he reached for her, she gave him free rein to touch. He caressed and kneaded while she rose and fell, flexed and rocked, gently, so gently, keeping time with her breath.

But soon the need built layer upon layer until she was no longer in control. Her body tightened and plunged following its own path. The clawing desperation forced her faster, harder, deeper. Roman saw the release coming as her eyes went soft and unfocused. With a groan, she slammed down again and arched back lifting her arms around her head while her breath sobbed out in a kind of triumph.

Staring up at her in awe, he thought she looked like a goddess. Mia was lean through the waist, full breasted with the moonlight bathing her skin, glowing porcelain white against her fiery hair. Deep inside, in the heat, she clamped around him and slowly circled her hips a few times more while her body shuddered. He didn't think he'd ever seen anything more beautiful in his life.

She eventually collapsed down on him, heart hammering against his chest, and he gathered her close and rolled until he was on top again. Grasping her legs and pushing them up around his waist, he finally, joyfully, allowed himself to go. Thrust after thrust after thrust, he pounded until the heat and the pleasure shot through him. He was so close now. His body cried out for release and, oh Lordy, it was all he could do not to follow.

Yet at the same time, he wished this moment would somehow spin out forever and ever, and he could be with her like this into eternity. When he did come, when all the tension disappeared, he lay limply on top of her gasping and partially blind from the bliss, a small secret part of him already missed her. Physically, she was right there next to him, but in every other way, Mia was nowhere even close.

Chapter Twenty

The idea nagged at Roman while he and the other officers sat through roll call. It followed him out on the road when he and Kevin were sent to investigate a B and E in neighboring Walkerton. He wasn't even sure what had sparked it off in the first place, but now that the awareness was lodged in his brain, he felt stupid for overlooking the obvious. If this had been anyone else's murder investigation, he'd have thought of it immediately.

When he finally got back to the station, he shut himself in his office and logged onto the NCIC database. He started a search of homicide investigations both solved and unsolved adding details of Anita's case into the parameters. Assuming it would take some time, he wandered out for coffee. By the time he'd returned to his desk, Roman was surprised to see there were already two results showing on the screen.

The first was from July of last year in Cleveland, or more correctly Brecksville, a suburb of the city. Marla Shaw finished work at a jewelry kiosk in the

Sparkswork Mall on the night of July sixth. Security cameras showed her exiting the mall through the door by the movie theatre at nine twenty p.m. There was no visual on the parking lot. Her car remained where she'd parked it earlier that afternoon. No one saw or heard from her again.

She was found a week later by a man walking his dog. She'd been buried in a shallow grave in the wooded area of Furnace Run Park. The dog had dragged his owner into the forest, and the man saw the recent evidence of digging and what looked like a human size grave and called the police.

The tox screen showed traces of chloroform in her system. She'd been raped and strangled. She wore an emerald ring on the ring finger of her left hand. No semen or other DNA evidence was found, and no unusual fibers or other trace materials existed on her body. The case remained unsolved.

The second victim was Jenny Maple of Wilmington, North Carolina. She disappeared seven years ago on July sixth, also after leaving work. This time the victim worked at a Dunkin Donuts. The manager claimed to have seen her walk across the parking lot to the bus stop. He couldn't remember if anyone else was waiting there. He was the last person to see her alive.

Her partially decomposed body wasn't discovered until almost four months later at a park on the other side of town during a Rotary Club scavenger hunt. Like Marla, there was chloroform in her system, and she was wearing an emerald ring. The authorities had zero leads on the case.

With heart hammering, Roman clicked back onto the search he'd left running in the background. Three more hits. All abducted on July sixth. All strangled. All either wearing an emerald ring or one was found in the gravesite.

"Kevin, get in here," Roman shouted.

The detective stepped into the office, stopping to lean casually against the door frame. "What's up?"

"We've got ourselves a serial," Roman said, his eyes never leaving the screen.

"You mean the B and E? Nah, I checked. Nothing else reported in the area."

"No, a serial killer. The same as my sister. Shit. Another one just hit. That brings the count up to seven. So far, all of them occurred after Anita."

"Seriously? No way. Other than some domestics gone bad and Leonard Karl, who was killed by his brother-in-law for cheating on his sister, we haven't had any homicides in the area during the past ten years."

"Not here. Try Wilmington, Cleveland, Gainesville, Tucson, to name a few. They're spread all over the US of A. All on July the sixth."

"Well, fuck me. I never thought to look. Jesus Christ, we have to bring it to the lieutenant."

"Yeah. We will. First, let's put this thing together. I'll let the search finish and see what we end up with. In the meantime, I'm going to dig deeper into the next two victims. Why don't you take Marie Gleeson and Rhonda Ziegler? I'll email you the links to the files."

In the end, there were nine in total, including Anita. All strangled, many dosed with chloroform, and every burial site contained an emerald ring. A couple of the bodies had carpet fiber, but other than tracing it to a car type, it was a dead end until they found the killer. No traces of foreign DNA on the victims. Each one, again except Anita, had been unconscious at the time of their rapes and deaths.

Lieutenant Schmidt sat back in his chair, hands clasped over his stomach and his index fingers steepled. He said nothing while Roman and Kevin brought him up to speed.

"Okay, I want you two to split the list and call every single detective in charge," he said when they'd finished. "See if you can get anything from them that'll help us. Keep a lid on it for now until we've had a chance to look into it more thoroughly. I don't want the townsfolk breaking out in mass hysteria." He paused and rubbed a hand over his chin. "You realize if this guy stays on pace he's probably planning to kill someone else this year. That gives us ten days."

"Yes, sir," Roman said.

"And I want you to pass off some of your remaining caseloads to Cooper and White. This is your priority for the time being. Remember, if you learn something new, I'll know it two seconds later."

"We're on it," Kevin said.

"You know we're going to have to call in the big boys, but let's finish this round of investigation first and put it all together," Schmidt added.

"I figured as much," Roman said. "They'd better not cut us out."

"They will, Son. That's how it works. The only way we stay in the loop is if the killer strikes here again. That seems unlikely since so far he's never repeated a kill spot."

"Come on, partner." Kevin slapped his hand on Roman's shoulder. "Maybe we can crack the case before the FBI hones in on it."

They went back to Kevin's office and divvied up the victims. "Kinda weird this guy only kills once a year. Most serials don't show that much control and certainly don't wait so long between victims. I wonder if he did anything else in between?"

Roman rolled his printed list of victims into a cylinder and tapped it against his leg. "You're thinking sexual assaults, right? Maybe he snatched them the same way using chloroform, but I'll bet there was no ring on those gals. Probably has to kill them to make them worthy of a ring. I'll log back onto NCIC and run another search. Good thinking."

"See, I'm not just a pretty face. You know, it also occurs to me that with these murders scattered all over hell and back, it may not be a native Daltonion. When we thought your sister was a one-off, I'd assumed it was someone from around here, but maybe not. Coulda been a guy in town for the fireworks."

"Yeah. I'd been wondering about that too. Well, I guess we'll see where the trail leads us."

* * *

It was almost dark when Roman pulled up in front of the house. He'd called earlier to say he would be late. In that brief moment on the phone, Mia sensed his excitement. Now she watched impatiently while he climbed out of his car and walked across to the porch steps. She met him inside the front door with Mac flanking her left side and the other canines fanning out behind.

"You've got a new lead," she said even before the lock had clicked into place on the door.

He turned to her, and she saw the weariness in his eyes. "Shoulda known you'd be up-to-date. Yes, we got a break, but still no suspect."

"Oh."

"I'll tell you all about it. First I need a shower and a beer, and then I'll probably eat everything in your fridge."

"I have a stir-fry prepped. You go on up and wash away the day. Dinner will be ready when you come down."

When they finally sat at the table with plates of steaming food in front of them, she reached across and touched his arm. "I'm dying here. You have to tell me."

He took a deep swig of his beer, rubbed a hand over his face, and laid it all out for her.

"But…I mean…wow. All those women. You think Anita was the first?"

"Maybe. She was either the first or he slightly altered his method after her because all the other bodies were left in shallow graves. Easier to find that way. If he killed before her and buried them deep, we may not have found his earlier victims yet. May never find them."

"I guess this opens up the possibility of it being someone from out of town. If that's the case, either he's back here now and is likely the person vandalizing my property or it's completely unrelated and we've been barking up the wrong tree."

"Except for the note about helping the police," Roman said.

"Yeah, there's that," she agreed. "Who from town does a lot of traveling?"

Roman finished chewing, swallowed, and leaned back in his chair. "Um…I can think of a couple of guys off the top of my head. Chad Murray is on the road a ton. Dusty Preston works for Whirlpool and goes to sales conferences several times a year. It could be someone who grew up here and moved away but still comes back to visit family. Hell, it could be anyone really. All they need to do is go on vacation every July."

"It doesn't actually help," she said after they'd contemplated all the possibilities.

"Not right now. It'll help when we have someone in our sights because we can run the dates against his whereabouts. Until then, nothing's popping out at me."

She smacked her forehead with the heel of her hand. "I can't believe I didn't get it until now. The emerald ring. It's Anita's birthstone so they must be for her. Unless all the other women were also born in May? I think the killings might have started with your sister."

Roman shook his head. "I remember at least one of the victims had a birthday in October because the date was the day before mine." He gazed at her for a beat. "You're really good at this. Sure you don't want to become a cop?"

Mia snorted. "A million times sure." Her face settled back into serious lines. "It's not fair. This guy's running around killing woman, and it seems like there's no way to catch him." She paused and stared down at her food. "Maybe I could help somehow?"

"I'm glad you asked. I figure it can't hurt to show you the pictures of the women. Could be something will spark for you. Are you sure you're up for it?"

"Yes. Absolutely. Let's do it."

She started to push back from the table.

"Hang on a sec. I'm more than eager to get this bastard, but let's take a moment and enjoy our dinner. An hour here or there won't make much difference. How was your day?"

She scooted her chair closer to the table again and picked up her fork. "It was fine if you discount the fact I'm on house arrest. I love my place, but I have to tell you I'm starting to go a little stir crazy."

"I know. I'm sorry. It's hard on you. I wish to God I could make it all go away. Hopefully soon, baby."

She cocked her head and lifted an eyebrow. "Baby?"

"Thought I'd try it out. I think I like it. Why? You have something better in mind?"

"That would be a no. Isn't baby kind of overused?"

"Oh, I get it. You want something super unique. Asking for that seems like you might be slipping into the murky waters of serious relationship territory. I don't think people in no-strings-attached sexual deals care what kind of pet names are used."

"You know, I hadn't thought of it that way. In that case, baby will do fine."

He drummed his fingers on the table. "How about kumquat?"

At this, she burst out laughing. "Talk about unique. I think I'll take a pass on kumquat unless you want me to call you my big-daddy-yum-yum."

"If that's what you want, I'm good with it. Especially the big daddy part." He puffed out his chest in an exaggerated movement.

She only shook her head. "Why is it guys are always hung up on size?"

He shrugged. "You're a girl, of course, you wouldn't understand."

"And I guess I never will."

After they were done eating, Mia pushed back from the table, but Roman beat her to gathering plates and cutlery.

"Fair's fair. You cooked, so I clean."

"You won't get an argument from me. Thanks. I've got more work to do. Are you up for sex later?"

The question caught him off guard, and he paused halfway to the kitchen. After a beat he turned to face her, his lips curving up into a smirk. "I'm always up for sex, kumquat. Let me know when and where."

"I'll whistle when I'm ready," she said.

"Should I come running?"

"I'd say that'll depend on how eager you are."

"Pretty eager. Do you want me to roll over and shake a paw too?"

"No, I think coming when you're called will do for now."

"Are you going to tell me I'm a good boy and give me a cookie?"

"I'll tell you you're a good boy, but you'll only get a cookie if the sex is really, really hot."

He continued into the kitchen and put the plates on the counter by the dishwasher. "That sounds fair," he said over his shoulder. "And the sex will be really, really hot. Have those cookies ready."

Chapter Twenty-one

Two days later, Roman flipped open his laptop and brought up the files Special Agent Millar had sent minutes before he'd left the station. It wasn't that bad working with the big boys from the FBI. Since the murders took place in multiple states, they were heading up the investigation, but Dalton Police were still in charge of Anita's homicide.

The Bureau had larger budgets, and better resources. So far they weren't being stingy about sharing the data. Still, nothing solid was popping for anyone. Millar told Roman it was unlikely they'd catch the guy unless he killed again.

That morning a press release had been sent out to all the major media outlets warning the public of the danger and asking anyone with information on any of the murders to call a newly established hotline. This would undoubtedly start an avalanche of calls from every crazy in the country. Some poor smucks riding the desk would be left to wade through the nonsense. Roman didn't expect anything useful to come of it.

In the meantime, all they could do was consolidate the various suspects from each of the victims, re-interview everyone, check whereabouts for the times of the murders, and hope to God something hit. If this guy had been killing for a decade or more without the police getting a sniff of him, he must be very, very good at covering tracks. The only difference now was that they were waiting for him. All state police had been notified to jump on any missing persons reports taken in the upcoming week. Maybe this time they'd catch a break.

More than anything, Roman wanted it to be over…the memorial, the catching of the killer, and especially the moving on with his life now that he had Mia in his sights. He didn't care how long it took, he was going to wear her down and get her locked into a relationship.

When he finished working, he wandered out of the spare bedroom upstairs and went in search of her. Predictably, he found her in the room off the kitchen at her work table. The woman was tireless when it came to her business.

"That's really pretty. What is it?" he asked pointing to a yellow stone.

She looked up at him with bleary eyes. "Citrine. It's for enlightenment and clarity. The client is a writer and is hoping it will help her figure out a story she's struggling with. I promised I'd have the necklace ready to be shipped tomorrow. Hey, do you want me to make one for you? It might help with the case."

He ran a fingertip across the large oblong crystal. "I don't think it'll work with my coloring, otherwise I'd totally say yes."

She chuckled and took a tool from the table, twisting a silver wire around the stone. "Funny guy."

His hand rested on her shoulder. "You work too hard."

"Said the pot to the kettle." She paused and looked up at him again. "You know, that sounds like something people in serious relationships say to one another. I hope you're not about to step over the line."

He snatched his hand back. "Just a simple observation. It's what I do. Observe."

Returning her focus back to the necklace, she made a loop in the wire and wove it around the first loop, creating a serpentine pattern. "Okay. I had to check."

He stood another moment, watching her work, then cleared his throat. "Anita's memorial is set for Friday. I talked my parents out of having it on the sixth. If you still want to go, I'll arrange for a uniform to sit on the house while you're out."

She turned in her chair, giving him her full attention now. "Yes, of course, I want to go. Are you...is your family holding up okay?"

He nodded once, and his eyes briefly rested on her face before sliding away. "They are. Thanks for asking. I think everyone is eager to get it done. They'll appreciate you coming. I'm going to be tied up right before the service helping my folks. Kevin offered to drive you there. " Pausing, he bent down and rubbed Layla's head. "Okay. I'm going upstairs. Good night, Mia."

Her heart squeezed in sympathy. "Good night, Roman."

* * *

On Friday morning, Mia went to extra trouble to curl her hair and carefully apply makeup. She slipped into a navy dress with half sleeves and a fitted skirt. Since the memorial was taking place at the small park beside city hall, she decided high heels were impractical and slid on a pair of ballet flats.

At quarter to ten, she stood waiting in the front sun porch. The dogs were settled inside with the door to the dog run locked, and Officer Jensen sat stationed outside the house. She watched Kevin Latterly drive up and park in the front lot. He'd barely had a chance to get out of his car before she arrived along the flagstone path to meet him.

"Thanks for coming," she said. "Though I still think I could have driven myself."

He spread his arms. "It never hurts to be cautious."

Walking around the front of the car with her, he opened the passenger door and gestured her in.

"I saw the press release on the news the other night. Has it helped at all?" she asked once they were underway.

"Not that I know of. It was more a case of warning the public. These hotlines hardly ever produce any real leads, but we've got to do it. It's nice of you to go to Anita's memorial. I know it means a lot to the Mancini family."

"It seems like the least I can do. How is…" She paused and blew out a breath. "Roman's not saying much these past two days, does he seem okay to you?"

Kevin's eyes flicked over to her then back to the road. "We're all tired. There's a ton of data to wade through. He's holding solid."

Brows knitted together, she slowly nodded. "That's good. Will Lisa be there today? We haven't met, but I've heard so many nice things about her."

"Lisa's great and yeah, she'll be there. She grew up in Dalton and knows the Mancini family."

Mia caught a flash of Kevin and Lisa kissing across a kitchen table, napkins and cutlery falling to the floor and Lisa giggling. "I'm glad you have someone special in your life," she said before turning her head and staring out the window.

The memorial was well attended. Mia surveyed the crowd and calculated there must be close to five hundred people gathered on the grassy area over which an American flag flapped and snapped in the stiff breeze. She parted from Kevin and made her way to the far side where a few empty chairs remained. The town clock struck the hour, and a hush fell over the crowd when Frank Mancini stepped up to the podium in front of City Hall.

"Good morning everyone. Thank you for coming," he said, the microphone giving his voice plenty of reach even with the wind. "Ten years ago our baby girl disappeared, and we've grieved for her deeply ever since. As everyone knows, the police have finally found her. It's not the ending we were hoping for, and my heart will never be the same, but I'm glad she's no longer alone out in the woods. Once the police return her to us, we'll have a private family burial. In the meantime, we wanted to do something for everyone who knew her and those who've grieved with, and comforted us during these long, difficult years."

He stepped back and turning to the side, motioned to someone in the wings. Straining to see over the heads in front of her, Mia watched while Lina walked over. She hugged her father then slipped out a small stack of note cards and stood by the podium.

Lina talked about what a bubbly, happy child Anita had been. One with an open heart and a ready smile. Always popular, she'd sailed through school and was looking forward to a career in interior design and one day marrying her sweetheart. Turning her head to and fro like many of those seated near her, Mia found Luke McNally with his wife Mandy seated across the way. He didn't seem to acknowledge Lina's comment. Though it was subtle, Mia saw Mandy shift away from her husband. When Lina finished speaking, she walked down the steps to join her family in the front row.

Mia took a moment to study the pamphlet she'd been handed when she'd first arrived at the memorial. On the front was a picture of Anita, which must have been taken sometime in the year before she died. On it she was well out of the early teenage stage and looked fully into womanhood. It was a candid shot, and the pretty girl was caught in mid-spin, arms flung wide, and a smile of delight on her face.

Inside were more pictures spanning various stages of the girl's life. The sweetest one, to Mia's mind, was a snap of Anita from her early teenage years flanked by Roman and Tony. Each of the boys had their arm around her, and she had tipped her head onto Tony's shoulder.

No longer able to prevent herself, Mia glanced through the crowd for Roman. She found him way up on the front row sitting beside his mother and Tony. She could only really see the side of his face, but she stared at him for a long moment. He shifted and shot a look over his shoulder and straight at her as if he'd known exactly where she was sitting and was aware of the scrutiny. They locked eyes for what seemed like an eternity before he turned back and put his arm around his mother's shoulder.

Two more speakers took to the stage. One was Mrs. Wexler, an old family friend, and neighbor. Mia remembered her from the barbeque at the Mancini cottage. The last to address the crowd was a high school teacher. Bowing her head and closing her eyes, Mia let the words fall over her while she opened her mind. She didn't normally sit unprotected in a large gathering but hoped if the killer was here…maybe just maybe, she'd get something from him.

After several minutes she opened her eyes and once again blocked out all the mental chatter. A vicious throbbing had taken root in her head, and she feared any more channeling would give her a full-blown migraine. She used to get them all the time when she was little and hadn't yet learned how to protect herself. It was no use anyway. The sadness of everyone around her was overwhelming, and nothing else seemed to be coming through.

The Mancini family rose and walked to the stage with Frank once again speaking into the microphone.

"It's been wonderful to hear the many kind words and warm memories of our daughter, sister, and cousin. Thank you all. And now it is time to say goodbye." He turned to Molly, and she stepped up and clasped his hand. Roman flanked his other side with Lina and Tony adding on at each end. "Anita Maria Mancini," Frank said. "You will always be in our hearts. We know you are in a happy place and hope you watch over us. We have utmost faith we'll see you again. Until then we say goodbye to you, our darling girl."

A melancholy note came through the sound system, followed by the familiar voice of Eric Clapton as he launched into "Tears in Heaven." Lina and Tony broke away from the group and bending over, each picked up a decorative box from the front of the stage. They held them to their chests before lifting the lids. Twin clouds of monarch butterflies rose up. Brilliant bursts of color filled the air as countless wings beat in a quest for flight. They flew up and up while the music swelled.

When the tears gushed, Mia reached into her purse, clutched a handful of Kleenex, and dabbed at her eyes. The woman beside her sobbed. For a moment, it was too much, too intense, and Mia bowed her head and tried to center herself. How on earth had she ended up here, at a memorial for a girl she hadn't even known in life but with whom she felt an inextricable bond?

The energy of the crowd buffeted her from all sides, so she focused on her breathing, keeping it slow and steady. When at last her mind cleared, she lifted her head. The Mancinis remained on the stage, linked hand to hand and gazing into the sky, watching the butterflies gradually dispersed.

Final strains of music filled the air then faded away. Behind Roman, a cardinal swooped low, barely clearing his head before landing on the microphone stand. The bird cocked its head to the side, stretched its wings, and once again took flight. The vivid flash of red darted over the crowd, circling back to City Hall, and disappeared from view.

It seemed like ages to make her way to the front. Really, she would have been happy to leave but wasn't sure where to find Kevin. Plus, good manners dictated she pay her respects to the family. The line slowly snaked forward. Everyone wanted to talk to the Mancinis, and they continued to show a united front, standing together below the stage.

"It was a lovely service," she said to Molly Mancini. "Incredibly touching."

"I'm so glad you came. I know you never met my baby girl, but I think she would have wanted you here."

"I'm glad I came too," she said.

Frank shook her hand and Tony, his normally sunny face set in severe lines, caught her up in a strong hug.

"Wasn't it beautiful?" he asked when he finally released her. "The butterflies were my idea. I think Anita would have loved them."

"I'm sure she would have," Mia soothed. Turning to Lina, she nodded. "Your eulogy was wonderful. You speak very well."

"Thank you. I heard you've had some trouble at your place."

Mia nodded. "A little. Hopefully, it will soon be sorted out. Roman has been such a support." With her emotions so close to the surface, she forced herself not to glance over at him. "All of the police have been incredible. Speaking of which, I really should get back. I'm so sorry for your loss."

Lina nodded and in a surprising move, placed her hand on Mia's arm. "I know I wasn't very friendly when I met you at the cottage. It's not…I didn't…well, I'm sorry. Thank you for coming today."

"Of course. And don't worry about it. I understand."

Before Mia had a chance to step back, someone patted her shoulder. She turned into Brooke who caught her straight up in a hug.

"I can barely stop crying," Brooke said against her. "I wanted to speak about Anita, but I knew I'd never hold it together." She released Mia and swiped a hand over her eyes. "You should've told me you were coming. We could have sat together. Oh, I want you to meet Ashley."

Brooke turned and motioned a woman forward. "Ash, this is Mia, the woman I was telling you about. Mia, this is Ashley. Anita, Ashley and I were best friends all through high school."

Ashley was one of those perfect petite types with delicate hands and a tiny waist. She had long coffee-colored hair and soft, doe brown eyes. When she smiled at Mia, a dimple winked in her left cheek. "It's very nice to meet you. Brooke said you helped the police find Mia."

"Well, yes. I guess I did. I'm sorry about your friend. Brooke tells me you live in Nashville."

"That's right. I got a job straight out of college, and I've been there ever since. It's perfect because it's not far to come back to Dalton and visit my parents."

Roman walked over and all but picked up Ashley. "I didn't realize you were here," he said as he held her to his chest in a hug. "It's good to see you, even under the circumstances." Putting her down he stepped back and flashed a smile. "If you're sticking around, we should all get together and catch up. It's been awhile. I have a couple of things to do at the station, but I could probably get away early."

Mia could have sworn someone had punched her in the stomach at the same time a giant fist closed down hard over her heart. Her face felt stiff, and it was an effort of will to force her expression into pleasant lines. Taking what she hoped was a subtle step to the side, she started inching away. Brooke's hand snaked out and grabbed her elbow.

"Mia should come too," Brooke said.

"Thank you but no. I need to get back to work. Besides, I'm sure you guys want to catch up on old times and talk about Anita. I'll find Kevin and have him take me home."

Roman fished his phone out from inside his sport coat and held up a hand. "Hang on. I'm getting a text from him right now. He's looking for you."

"Tell him I'll meet him at his car."

When she turned to leave, once again her arm was restrained. "Wait. I can take you back if you want," Roman said.

She made a shooing motion with her hand. "No, that's not necessary. You go and be with your family and friends."

His eyes zeroed in on hers. "Or you could join us like Brooke suggested."

For a nanosecond, she wanted to stay with him, but with the feeling came a spurt of panic, and she ruthlessly pushed it away. "I really can't. The service was beautiful."

His hand fell away from her arm. "Thank you for coming. I appreciate it. I'll see you later?"

"You know, I think I'll be fine for one night. Why don't you stay in town?"

Ashley sidled up to him. "Would you mind swinging by my parents' to pick me up? I didn't rent a car, and I don't want to leave them without."

With Ashley momentarily distracting Roman, Mia took the opportunity to turn and walk away.

"Hey, hang on," he said.

"I've got to go. Kevin is waiting," she called over her shoulder without looking back.

Chapter Twenty-two

Back at home, Mia couldn't work. Couldn't eat. Couldn't concentrate on anything but the image of Roman hugging Ashley and the way he'd smiled down at her. The dogs picked up on her restlessness and paced around the house after her. She needed to move, burn off some of this anxiety. Finally, she motioned the dogs out the front door.

She had her cell phone. The house was locked up tight. If psycho killer came back and ruined more of the property, it could always be fixed. From now on, she refused to be a prisoner in her own home. Maybe she should move after all. Change her identity. This time though it wouldn't be her past she was escaping, but the attention of a serial killer.

It felt good imagining a new *her* in a new life. *Except you wouldn't have Roman,* a sneaky voice whispered in her mind.

Dragging her feet through the long grass, she whistled to the dogs. "Come on boys and girls, we'd better head back. My allotted brooding time is officially over."

Not surprisingly, Roman texted to say he would be late and Mia would have to forgo her walk this one time. She didn't bother telling him she'd already had a solo outing that afternoon. Instead, she texted back, again suggesting he not come and surely she and the dogs would be fine for one night. He didn't respond.

When he did arrive a little after ten o'clock, she said, "You've had quite a day. Are you all right?"

He kicked off his shoes and nudged them onto the boot tray by the front door. "I'm fine. Glad it's all over. The memorial was hard, but I have to say it was good spending time with family and friends."

"Ashley seemed…nice," she couldn't help saying.

Hit with a sudden flash of insight, he paused before picking up his knapsack. Clearing his mind, he focused on Ashley…picturing her long, mocha hair and dark eyes. He remembered how she'd taken his hand while they walked back to his car after dinner and for an added bonus, he imagined kissing her. *There you go, Mia,* he thought, *that'll give you something to chew on.* It'd be really interesting to see how Miss No-Strings-Attached would deal with a little competition.

"She is nice. Plus, she's always been a looker. She's even hotter now than she was in high school. I have to admit I have a weakness for brunettes," he said.

Mia didn't say anything for several seconds. Instead, she stepped back and wandered across the hall, finally leaning against the doorway to the kitchen. Roman hid his smile while he stowed his keys in the side pocket of the knapsack.

"I sensed Tony was in a better place. More accepting. Do you think he would ever be interested in Brooke?" she said, breaking her silence.

Now Roman straightened and gazing at her, cocked his head to the side. "I don't know. Why do you ask?"

"Just a feeling I have. I think Brooke would be open to it."

"Is that so? Can't say I've ever seen Tony show much interest in her beyond being friendly. He mostly dates city girls, if you know what I mean. So far he hasn't kept any of them for long. I think he's still in the process of finding himself. Maybe now, with Anita's memorial behind us, he'll be able to move on.

"Roman..."

"Yeah?"

"The memorial was beautiful and incredibly moving and more than ever, I wish I'd known your sister."

He sighed. "I wish you had too. See you in the morning."

For the first time since he'd started staying at her house, Mia wished she hadn't insisted they sleep in separate rooms.

* * *

Mia found the night tortuous. Her mind would not move away from the image of Roman and Ashley walking hand in hand to his car, of them kissing. She'd seen it clear as day when she'd pushed into his head. It was distressingly easy to imagine them as a couple with their similarly dark coloring and outstanding looks.

She shouldn't have gone poking around in his head. It wasn't right. Hadn't she promised herself she'd be better than that? *Sometimes old habits die hard though.* She sighed as she walked down the stairs. It seemed she had a lot more work to do in the area of personal integrity. Maybe what she was feeling now was a sort of punishment to keep her on the straight and narrow. An instant karma deal.

She hated that the idea of Ashley and Roman bothered her. He was just a casual fling, wasn't he? She'd made that plain as plain could be. If he had the hots for some sexy brunette from high school, it was no skin off her nose. She could easily say goodbye and never look back.

Except she didn't want to say goodbye. She liked having him around. Liked talking to him. The sex was outstanding, and now that he was with the program, she didn't have to deal with intrusive personal questions. As far as she was concerned, it was the best of everything.

He won't be satisfied with this for long, a voice in her mind whispered. He's a serious guy looking for a serious relationship. Maybe, then, this is exactly the wakeup call she needed because she hadn't realized she was getting attached.

No, *attached* wasn't the right word. Used to. That was better. She was *used to* him now, that was all. Like a…what? Her mind searched and finally came up with house cleaning. Okay, sure, he was like a cleaner. He was in her house, and he did things for her. Though she could hardly count sex as an odd job, plus, it was not as if she paid him.

"You're analyzing this thing to death. Get a grip," she said aloud, then realized the dogs were looking at her expectantly. "Okay, you're right. It's breakfast time. Let's get you guys some food."

Once she'd dealt with filling dog bowls and letting the canines out for their morning meander around the dog run, she sat on the back deck with a cup of coffee and gave herself a stern talking to.

This was not like her. She didn't ever get seriously involved with men. Certainly didn't spend time brooding about them. She thought about the bet she'd made with Roman and couldn't help wondering if he had some kind of sixth sense himself. Either way, it was turning out to be prophetic because she, Mia Reeves, was having trouble maintaining an emotional distance.

She felt stupid even thinking about this. She was a champ at maintaining emotional distance and always had been. It was simply a matter of letting her usual instincts take over. And the best time to start was right away.

When Roman came down to the kitchen an hour later looking sexy with his morning stubble and sleep-rumpled hair, she told herself she didn't find him attractive anymore. Getting up from the breakfast nook, she poured him a cup of coffee and handed it over with the briefest of smiles before pointing at her laptop on the table.

"I've been doing some research on cameras. There's a company not far from here, so if you don't mind watching the house, I thought I'd go in and get the ball rolling. You're not working, right?"

"What?" He took a sip of coffee and rubbed his eyes.

"You stay. I'll go. Got it?"

Glancing down at the laptop, he slid onto the chair and studied the screen. "You're getting security cameras? Don't you want me to look at them and maybe talk to the guys?"

"Pretty sure I've got this. It's not exactly complicated."

"Jeez Louise, these things are expensive."

"Yeah. It's going to hurt, that's for sure. It'll be worth it though. Even when this psycho killer is caught, I don't think I'll ever feel okay about leaving the dogs alone. The cameras will at least give me some peace of mind. I'm hoping to get them installed this weekend and then you won't have to babysit anymore. I'm sure you're more than ready to go back to your own life."

He frowned at the laptop screen. "This seems kinda sudden. Don't you want to shop around, compare prices?"

She studied his profile, pushing away the ripple of longing rising up from her belly. "No, I want to get it done. I need my space, and you surely must need yours."

Shifting his eyes up to meet hers, he blinked several times. "So this is really about getting me out of your house? Interesting."

Mia shut the lid on the laptop and gathered the computer under her arm before stepping away. "There's nothing interesting about it. The cameras make sense. And with them, I won't need someone here at night."

"Really? What if, despite the amazing cameras, the guy breaks into your house while you're sleeping? How are you going to protect yourself?"

"I have four dogs and a baseball bat under my bed. I have a cell phone. The security alarm will wake me before he gets in the house."

"Seconds before," Romans said, getting to his feet and crossing his arms over his chest. "You'll barely be out of bed, and he'll already be in the house, coming up the stairs. Sure, you've got the dogs, but I'd put money on them rushing out to confront the guy. All he'd have to do is shoot them. It wouldn't be hard if he hid in the spare room and picked them off. Or he could stay by the front door and blast at them when they came down the stairs. You might call nine-one-one, but he'll have you out of the house and in his car before they even have a chance to dispatch the first vehicle. Then you're gone. Until we find your grave in some out of the way wooded area. Do you really want to be number ten?"

"If you're trying to scare me, you'll find I'm not that skittish." Her focus leveled on his.

"I never said you were. What you are is stupid."

She laughed. "Nice try. I'm not going to let you bait me into a fight. This is my life. I get to decide how I'm going to live it. Us having sex doesn't give you license to have a say in the matter."

"Fair enough. How about this? You go get your cameras. Sign up with a security company if you want. I don't give a rat's ass what you do. But get this through your thick skull—as long as Anita's killer is out there, I'm going to be here every night whether you want me to or not. I'll sleep in my car if need be, but I'm not letting anything happen to you."

She whirled away clutching the laptop to her chest. "I'm not Anita. You don't need to protect me."

Grabbing her elbow, he spun her back to face him. "I do need to protect you. It's my job, and on top of that, I care about you. A whole lot. If this guy snatched you…if he hurt you…" He shook his head. His hand lifted to her face, and the backs of his fingers stroked her cheek as gentle as a whisper. "It's not going to happen, that's all. What's this really about?"

"What do you mean?" She jerked her head back, and his hand fell away.

"I mean, why did you get up this morning with a bug up your ass about getting me out of here? It seems kind of sudden." When she said nothing, merely meeting his gaze with icy eyes his face broke into a smile. "Oh, I get it. You're upset about Ashley, and it put you in a mood."

With some effort, she smoothed out her expression and wandered back to the table to put down the laptop. "Ashley?" she said, keeping her voice light. "Why would she have anything to do with this? I don't care who you kiss."

"Really? Because it seems like you do. And for the record, Ashley and I didn't kiss last night or any night in recent memory. Maybe way back in high school, there might have been some lip action at a dance, but that's about it. Funny, for someone who's supposed to be all about keeping it casual, you seem to have your nose out of joint over the mistaken idea that I kissed someone besides you."

"Why are you lying? Not that I care, but I know you kissed her. As far as I'm concerned, you can kiss her a thousand times, and it won't bother me."

"Good to know, but I didn't kiss her."

"I saw it. You totally kissed her in some parking lot. It was right there in…I mean…you did, that's all."

He walked up to her and tapped his finger against her nose. "Were you looking around in my head? You're a bad, bad girl."

"It's not like that…I didn't…okay, I did look. I'm sorry, but I had to know. I don't understand why you're lying about this."

Rubbing his hands together, he laughed. "God, this is good. You may have this amazing gift, but I now know how to get around it. I knew you were bent out of shape about Ashley and figured you might go snooping, so I imagined the whole thing and it totally worked."

"You imagined kissing Ashley?" she sputtered. "But…"

"That's right. I got you good. Now onto the best part of all this. You were a hundred percent bothered about the idea of Ashley and me. The only reason you'd be upset is because you're developing feelings for me. The trouble is you don't want to admit it to yourself, so you're trying to push me out with the cameras. It's okay, Mia. I promise I'm a good guy. I may hurt you because anyone in a serious relationship hurts the other person from time to time, but I won't do it on purpose. We're great together. Surely even you can see that?"

Head down, she backed away. "I can't. It'd never work anyway."

The sting hit him deep in the gut. "So you won't even try? Wow, talk about being a coward."

Now her head snapped up, and she met his eyes. "It's not fear for me. I won't get hurt. You will. I'm not built for serious relationships."

His chuckle was harsh in his ears. "Wow. How altruistic of you. Thanks for looking out for me, but sort of like what you were saying earlier, this is my life, and I get to decide how I'm gonna live it. I'm not afraid of being hurt...so bring it on."

"You don't even know me. You know weeks, a couple of months. You know what I show you and most of that's a lie anyway."

"You don't know me either. That's the whole point of this. We spend time together. Learn about one another. It's what relationships are all about, Mia."

"That's not even my name," she blurted out before slapping a hand over her mouth. A red flush raced up her neck and spread across her face.

"I know," he said quietly. Mutinous eyes met him, and he shrugged. "I've known for a while now."

"You know I'm committing identity fraud and haven't done anything about it?" she said slowly, not even aware she was inching away from him.

"Yeah, since we found nothing in the woods at Carlton Park. I ran a deep background on Mia Reeves and eventually discovered she was dead. Your identity is good. Real good. It must have cost a lot."

"It did," she mumbled, sinking to a chair at the table. Her heart hammered in her head, every beat sounding like a warning. "What are you going to do?"

He cocked his head. "I'm not going to do anything. Eventually, I'm hoping you'll tell me what you're running from, but I won't threaten it out of you. And when you do, we'll deal with it."

Looking down, she realized the dogs had gathered around her. Her family. Her heart. As always…right there for her. She couldn't risk it no matter how much she might like Roman. She'd have to leave. Move on. Change her name again. God, the thought of all that entailed made her feel exhausted.

Forcing a smile, she lifted her face to meet his again. "You're so patient with me. Thank you for not pushing. Maybe we could work. I need to think about it."

"Come here."

He walked to her and offered his hand. With barely any hesitation, she accepted, and he pulled her to her feet. His fingers cupped her jaw, and dark liquid eyes searched hers. Whatever he saw in her satisfied him, for he smiled and leaned down, kissing her with soft lips. No demands. No urgency. Just simple sweet contact.

Her heart pinched painfully, and she rubbed a hand between her breasts.

"Hey, you okay?" his voice was laced with concern. "You're trembling."

She shook her head. "I'm fine. A little rattled, I guess. I want to take this slow, okay?"

"Of course it's okay. As long as we're together, the rest is just details. I feel good about us. We're going to figure this out."

She wished it were true. Wished she could imagine a future with Roman. "I'm sure you're right. I need time to settle. Get used to the idea. I still want to get the cameras."

"They're a good idea. Especially out here. I can hold down the fort while you're gone."

Instead of driving over to the security firm, though, Mia headed into Dalton, her mind calculating. If Roman had known about her false identity for all this time, he wasn't going to move on anything in the next few days. She had some time yet.

Her first stop was to the container store. She needed boxes. She wouldn't take everything with her, but certainly all her jewelry stuff. Hit with a sudden realization, she grasped at a section of shelving to steady herself. She couldn't keep doing her jewelry business even under a new name. It would be way too easy for Roman to track her down.

Okay. Fine. She could still sell the inventory somewhere on the road. She already knew she'd likely be walking away from her house, so this would at least give her a quick infusion of cash along the way.

Once she'd loaded up on storage bins, she stopped at the bank and withdrew eight grand. It was a risky move since the teller immediately tsked when Mia admitted she hadn't called ahead to arrange the funds.

"Sorry," she said. "It's a last minute thing, and I thought I'd take the chance you had enough on hand."

In the end, she had to speak to the branch manager and go through a lengthy process to get the cash. She knew that while they wouldn't immediately go out on the streets of the town spreading the word that Mia Reeves was pulling funds, she was darned sure it would come to light once she'd disappeared.

She also planned to hit up the instant teller machines if she was in town over the next day or so. She needed as much untraceable cash as she could get her hands on. Still, it wouldn't point them in any particular direction since she, herself, hadn't yet decided where she was going.

At the grocery store, she stocked up on road supplies—dog food, and other odds and ends—so she wouldn't have to buy them once she was on the run. It was important she didn't change her normal habits with Roman. While she was out, she bought fixings for a nice dinner. She knew he'd be watching her closely in these next few days. She'd have to behave as normally as possible.

Slipping everything into the back of her Escape, she thanked goodness for the tinted windows. It was unlikely Roman would notice the supplies crammed on the floor. Next, she opened her travel toolbox and chose a screwdriver and a mini can of WD-40.

The parking lot was about a third full, maybe fifteen cars or so. She'd chosen a spot in the far corner and had parked especially close to the Nissan Sentra beside her. Pulling out her cell phone, she pretended to take a call. She leaned against her SUV before pacing back and forth behind the vehicle and scanning the area as she moved. No stock boys collecting shopping carts. No other patrons coming out of the store. This was as good a time as any.

Mia dropped to her knees, quickly sprayed the screws and slipped the screwdriver out of her back pocket, efficiently removing the license plate. She took another at the bowling alley and finally a third in the communal parking lot behind the Pizza Hut, the tanning salon, a hairdresser, and a Michaels craft store.

It would likely be blamed on teenagers messing around. For Mia, it was additional cover during the first few days. Especially if she ended up taking any toll roads. She might even steal a couple more if she managed to get back into town again.

Satisfied with these preliminary steps, she drove back to her house. For the first time since she'd bought the place, she didn't allow her gaze to linger on the log house or the gardens or the way the fields spread out beyond the driveway.

It was no longer hers.

Chapter Twenty-three

Mia got through the dinner and the rest of the night without panicking. Every time she felt something for Roman, a yearning, a tug of affection, she told herself she had to treat him like a mark. He couldn't mean anything to her. Although she wasn't actually stealing from him, she was scamming him all the same and needed to stay true to her part just like she'd done in the past with other men.

She couldn't do the sex though. When he suggested as much, she claimed exhaustion, which wasn't completely untrue, and took herself and the dogs into her bedroom for an early night.

Sleep was fitful at best. During the waking times, she thought and planned and tried not to become emotional. Still, she rose with a heavy heart early in the morning to start the day.

Roman beat her to the kitchen. She'd heard him moving around in the night so knew he didn't get much more sleep than she had.

"Good morning," she said brightly.

He stood dumping tablespoons of coffee into the coffee maker. "Not yet," he grumbled.

She puttered about, feeding the dogs, watching over them in the dog run, watering her indoor plants. *What will happen to them after I'm gone,* she wondered, then quickly closed her eyes and pushed the thought away. When she turned to walk back to the kitchen, she caught Roman studying her.

"Something wrong?" she asked.

"Not with me. I'd say you're still feeling unsettled after yesterday. Don't worry so much. It's not going to be as hard as you think."

If only that were true. "I know. It's going to take some getting used to, that's all."

His face broke into a wide smile. "Hey, I just thought of something. Looks like I won the bet. You owe me a hundred big ones."

Pretending to ponder the idea, she tipped her head. "How so?"

"You, the supposed ice queen of romance, weren't able to keep things casual. Who got jealous of Ashley? Yeah, that's right. It was you. I told you I'm totally irresistible."

"You'll have to wait until I have a chance to hit the bank unless you'll take a check?"

"I can wait. Hey, do you want to do something today? If it's quiet at the station, I could get one of the uniforms to watch the place, and we could maybe go into town for lunch then come back here and watch a movie."

She looked into his happy, hopeful eyes and her heart broke. "That sounds nice, but I have a lot—"

When his cell signaled, he groaned and fished it out of his pocket. "Hold that thought." He brought the phone to his ear. "Mancini. Yeah. Okay. Where again? I vaguely know it. Meet you at the station. I'm leaving now. Could be…it's our first real break…yeah, exactly."

"Well?" she asked.

He was already shoving his phone away and gathering up the laptop. "I'm not sure. Someone from Brighton found Anita's wallet and heart bracelet. Or at least I think it'll be her bracelet. I gotta go."

"Okay. Wow. This is huge, right? How far is Brighton?"

"It's the other side of Walkerton. About forty-five, give or take."

He jogged upstairs and returned moments later, his weapon harness in place, and his badge clipped to the waistband of his jeans. "We'll have to rain check lunch and a movie."

"I wish I could go with you. Please let me know what happens."

"I will. I need to figure out the lay of the land with the FBI. Plus, we have to see if it's genuinely her stuff. I'll be in touch."

This is good, Mia thought once he'd left. If the police finally had a solid lead to Anita's killer, Roman would be plenty occupied over the next few days. It would give her more time to plan and prepare. If they caught the guy, there'd be the added benefit of having her guard duty stand down, which would make it even easier to steal away before anyone realized she was leaving.

Should she just go now?

No, more time would be better. This way she'd be able to organize and pack more of her belongings. That would make starting over a little bit easier. Anyway, a part of her couldn't help wanting to see this through. Roman might need her help fine-tuning details of the killer or his location. Since she was planning to walk out on him with no explanation, no goodbye, the least she could do was ensure he got justice for his sister.

She left the dogs inside, retrieved the plastic bins from her SUV and brought them into the house, locking the door behind her. She couldn't pack everything without tipping him off, but clothes and general toiletries seemed like a safe bet. It took very little time to fill a few of the containers and return them to the Escape. She stacked and stowed the empty ones in the back of her closet.

After checking her watch, Mia figured Roman and Kevin should be almost to Walkerton by now. She wished she knew what was going on. *Please let this bring a resolution to the case.* Anxiety strummed through her. She paced around the front room, unsure what to do with herself. Picking up on the stress, the dogs stayed with her.

"Okay. Pacing around and wasting a morning will only make me feel worse. There's nothing I can do to either help or pack. Therefore, I should work," she said to the dogs.

Although she'd be shutting down the Healing Crystal storefront once she left town, she could still sell products to stores and fairs while she was on the road. The more finished pieces she had, the better the return on investment.

Mia cued up her New Age music mix and set it to play in the background. With a freshly brewed pot of chamomile tea on her work table and a lavender diffuser scenting the air, she went through her inventory and decided earrings were the right choice for today. They were more intricate than necklaces and would, therefore, keep her mind suitably focused. Blue lace agate earrings to be exact. The stone emitted a calming and soothing vibration which was exactly what the doctor ordered.

She'd be calmed and soothed and not look at her watch until she finished the earrings.

That lasted all of twenty-two minutes. *Roman should be well into investigating the site by now. Please let it be the big break everyone's praying for.* This guy needed to be caught before he killed again.

She let out a yelp when her driveway monitor pinged in the kitchen. No way it was Roman. Too early for his return. Rushing to the window, she recognized Tony bolting across the lawn toward her front steps. She met him in the sun porch.

"Oh, Mia. Thank God. Roman's been shot. I don't know all the details. We have to go."

"What? No. That can't be right. Someone from the station tagged him. They found some items that may have been Anita's in…" she rubbed the palm of her hand hard against her temple. "Not Walkerton. Shit. I can't remember the name of the town."

"Brighton. I know. He called us on route less than an hour ago. I guess the guy was there. Hiding. Roman and Kevin were hit. Kevin's okay, but Roman's being prepped for surgery. I knew you'd want to come. I need you with me. I'm losing my mind."

She shook her head trying to make sense of what he was saying. It couldn't be real. "Yes, of course. I'm coming."

Tony grabbed her elbow and hustled her through the screen door. "My aunt and uncle are already on the road. Lina was at the airport heading home, but I think she's going to get an Uber or something. At least they got the guy. Alive too, which is good. I want the bastard to spend the rest of his life rotting in a cage."

"Wait. I didn't even lock the door. I need my purse," Mia said when they reached the car.

"They got him, Mia. Nobody's after you anymore. We have to be there for Roman."

She nodded quickly. "You're right. Okay."

Tony put the car in reverse and spun around, spurting up gravel.

When they got to the road, Mia turned to him. "Where was he hit? He would have had his vest on, right?"

"I assume so. He is usually pretty careful about wearing it," Tony said. "I don't have all the details. I think maybe his neck and face. Aunt Molly promised to call when she gets there."

They drove on in silence with Tony pushing the speed hard and zipping through turns. Mia's heart clutched, and for an awful moment, she thought she might actually be sick. Loosening her seatbelt, she put her head down between her knees. The car slowed, and she realized he was pulling over.

"Hey, what's happening? Are you all right?" Tony asked.

"It's okay. Keep driving. I don't think I'm gonna throw up, but I'll maybe stay down here until it passes."

He put the car in park, and she heard the click of his seatbelt. A gentle hand rubbed her back. "Oh, Mia, you make this so easy for me," he whispered.

The warning screeched through Mia's mind. By the time her head snapped up, it was already too late. Tony pressed something hard to the side of her neck, and her body erupted in shocking, explosive pain with every muscle contracting in full-blown spasm. The air was forced from her lungs, and a part of her mind registered the gasping screams she heard were coming from her.

When at last it stopped, she was left completely incapacitated. So weak she couldn't even bat Tony away when he kissed her cheek. He took a Kleenex from the box on the dash and carefully wiped the drool from her mouth. Sometime later she realized he'd popped the trunk.

"Why are you doing this?" she asked stupidly, her words slurred and barely comprehensible.

"Because I must," he said, a lilt in his tone. He opened the car door and got out.

Run. Move. Go. Do something.

The words screamed inside her, but in reality, she could barely turn her head. At least the fog in her brain was lifting some. Shifting her eyes, she remembered they were on a country road. Tony had taken some back route that was apparently faster, and now she knew why. They were surrounded by woods. No traffic. The closest house was barely visible at the end of a long, narrow driveway, and probably no one was home anyway.

Tony pulled the passenger door open, and she managed to push herself back against the seat. She locked eyes with him. "Please don't," she begged.

Reaching down, he freed her from the seatbelt then pulled her out of the car. She struggled as best she could, but he was a fit man who probably had sixty or seventy pounds on her, and she was as weak as a kitten. He produced zip ties from his back pocket.

"Okay, let's turn you around and put these on."

She fell to her knees when he spun her. It didn't seem to slow him down, and before she knew it, her hands were secured behind her back. The plastic dug into her wrist when he pulled her to her feet.

"They're too tight," she gasped.

"Oh, no. That's terrible. I bet they really hurt," he said in a happy voice. "You know, it might be best if you don't talk for a while."

His hands came up on either side of her face, and he wrenched her mouth open and pushed in something soft. She tried to spit it out, but it was impossible. From a backpack on the ground, he produced a roll of duct tape and ripped off a section. When she shook her head, he held her still and pulled the tape across her mouth.

"There you go. Quiet as a mouse. Let's put you in the trunk."

Some strength was returning to her muscles, and with a chaser of surging adrenaline, she managed to kick at him and stomp on his foot.

"You stupid bitch," he snapped, pushing her against the car. "You're just making it worse for yourself."

When he turned away and reached into the trunk, she ran. She'd barely gone ten steps before stumbling and going down on one knee. With her hands bound behind her and her body still off-kilter, she couldn't get up again. In the next second, he grabbed her shoulder and waved a Taser in her face.

"You want this again? I don't mind giving you another good zap if that's what it takes. Yeah, I didn't think so. Now you're going to get up." He yanked her hair and pulled her to her feet. "And you're going to walk back to the car and climb in the trunk."

She'd thought her heart was already at maximum velocity, but it found a whole other gear and filled her head with the frantic sound of its beating. Her mind remained locked in a loop of panic where the only thing it seemed capable of suggesting was to run. If she got in the trunk, it was game over. Mia knew it, but short of a meteor crashing down on Tony, she couldn't see any way out.

Chapter Twenty-four

Roman called Mia for the fourth time in the past half hour. When she failed to answer yet again, his blood went to ice. He'd been watching her closely since yesterday morning when he'd dropped his guard and revealed he knew Mia Reeves was an alias. Although she put on a good show, he knew damned well she was rattled. Surely she wouldn't run, at least not so soon?

Then another thought hit him, making his heart lurch in his chest. What if this psycho serial killer had her? Getting he and Kevin all the way out to Walkerton was a great ruse and made it pitifully easy to swoop in and snatch her. And dammit all to hell, today was July sixth.

Without a second's hesitation, he rang through to the station and had a black and white sent out to her place to ascertain her whereabouts. He told them to go in hot. There wasn't anything else he could do from his current location.

He turned his attention back to Kevin. They were in the bowels of a dingy bus station where the techs were dusting a row of lockers for fingerprints.

"It's gonna take friggin forever to run all these prints," Kevin grumbled.

"Yeah. And chances are our guy isn't in the system anyway. We should head back. Our crime scene crew knows what they're doing, and we've bagged everything we can find. Why did the son of a bitch call this in? It had to have been the killer. Seems like he's playing with us, and now I can't get hold of Mia."

Kevin whirled around. "What?"

"I sent a uniform out to her place, but my gut is seriously having a fit."

"Hey, calm down. We're heading back there now anyway, and I'll bet they find Mia having a nap or something. She's too smart to go outside, and she'd never let anyone in. Plus, she has like a zillion dogs."

"I hope you're right. Okay, let's hit the road."

"I'll drive. You work the phone."

He flashed back to the day he'd driven home from camping with his friends and found the town in turmoil, his parents stricken, and his sister missing. Pain banged behind his eyes. His stomach churned. This couldn't be happening again.

When the call came, he closed his eyes and ordered himself to calm down.

"Her car's there?" he asked when Martins explained no one was answering the door and the dogs were inside going crazy.

"That's affirmative," she said. "I checked the front door, and it isn't locked. I've looked in all the downstairs windows. There's no sign of her. What do you want me to do?"

What he wanted to do was order Martins inside, but he wasn't entirely sure Mac wouldn't rip a chunk out of her. He looked at the GPS. They were still a full twenty minutes away. Shit. If Mia really was missing, every second counted.

"Go around to the back deck. There's a gate at the side of the house. If you can, smash open the doggie door. No, the kitchen door. That'd be better. Break in through that. Open it a touch but leave something jammed up against it. One of the deck chairs maybe. Something the dogs can push through. That will give you enough time to get back out through the gate again before they do. Once they're in the run, hoof it to the front door and get inside before they realize what you're doing. You should be able to get back to the kitchen and close them out."

"And if I don't?" she asked.

"The Doberman's the one you have to win over. The others will follow his lead. His name is Mac. Use it. Tell him to sit and point at the floor. Hold your ground. Be firm. Don't look away. I wouldn't ask you to do this if I didn't believe it was life or death. Call me when you've gone through the house."

"Okay, sir."

"What the hell, man," Kevin said when Roman clicked off. "I've seen those dogs. That Doberman could take Martins down in the blink of an eye."

Roman leaned his head back against the seat and closed his eyes. "I know. What choice did I have? If Anita's killer has Mia, we don't have any time to waste. We're already too late."

The moments dripped by like syrup, and they waited in silence for the phone to signal. When it did, Roman stabbed the screen. "Martins?"

"I'm in, and the dogs are locked outside. Mia Reeves is not in residence. There's a pot of tea, slightly warm, on a table in the room off the kitchen along with what looks like a partially finished pair of earrings. Music is playing through the speakers from her iPod. It's set on repeat. Her phone is on the kitchen counter, and her wallet is in her purse in the front hall closet. No signs of distress. No furniture upended."

"Thanks, Martins. I'm calling it in. I want you to hold there. I'm ten minutes out."

Kevin hit the sirens and floored it, passing vehicle after vehicle as he steamed down the highway. Roman barely registered any of it. Turning his attention to the phone, he blew out a breath and called Lieutenant Schmidt.

"Sir, Mia Reeves appears to have been abducted from her house. Front door unlocked. Phone, wallet, keys, all left behind along with her four dogs. I've got Martins on site, and I'm heading there now."

"I'll put out the APB. You sure you're steady enough to handle this?"

"Yes, sir. Absolutely."

* * *

Tony helped Mia climb into the trunk then bound her ankles together. "Don't worry, I've got the perfect spot all picked out for you. Now lie back, relax, and enjoy the trip. I'll see you soon."

The lid closed down with a sharp click, and she was in the dark. How was it possible with all her extra abilities that she'd never seen the monster inside Tony? Poor Roman. This would gut him.

Oh, God, Roman. Was he in surgery yet? But...wait...maybe he wasn't even shot. Tony had likely made up the story to get her to leave with minimal fuss and without her phone. It had worked like a charm. No one would have the slightest idea where she was.

Panic reared up again. The cloth in her mouth was now thoroughly soaked in saliva, and she felt as if she might suffocate. Her stomach churned. It terrified her to think of vomiting because with her mouth all bound up she'd choke within minutes. Closing her eyes, she forced herself to breathe in and out slowly through her nose.

The engine started, and the car rolled forward. There had to be a way to pop the trunk from the inside. Not that she'd be able to leap out and run, but just maybe she'd somehow get away. Her shoulders screamed in pain, and she rolled toward her stomach to try and relieve the pressure. When the agony lessened, she managed to roll again and position her hands by the lock on the lid.

Her straining fingers fitted into oily crevices and along the contours of the metal, but no matter what she pushed or wiggled, the trunk remained stubbornly closed. Her eyes were now accustomed to the darkness. In fact, it wasn't absolute pitch black because some light leaked in from around rivets along the side paneling. Not much, mind you, but it helped her state of mind immensely.

She rolled again and wiggled farther into the recesses of the trunk until her feet pointed straight back. Twisting and turning, she managed to lift her legs and curl them toward her body then kick out and hit the lid of the trunk. She did it over and over again until sweat ran into her eyes and her chest heaved. It was no use. There hadn't been one iota of movement or anything that suggested the lock was loosening.

The car slowed and turned, and now the road was bumpy. Her head hit the lower ceiling near the back seats. She rolled again, into the main area of the trunk and wedged her feet in the corner of the wheel well to try and provide an anchor. It helped. She lay quietly and considered.

Her fingers started tingling, and her shoulders continued to complain about the position of her arms. Mia opened and closed her fists with a mind to keeping the blood flowing. Her heart jumped into her mouth when her hand brushed against a jewelry tool in her back pocket. She'd forgotten about it, and thankfully Tony hadn't patted her down. Please let it be wire cutters, she prayed.

She hooked her index finger inside the fabric and poked around noting two prongs of metal. So either the pinchers, which wouldn't be all that useful, or the cutters. Her mind flew back to the earrings. What exactly had she been doing when she'd stopped to look out at Tony? She thought she'd finished wrapping the copper around the first crystal bead below the blue agate. Had she cut it? Yes, definitely because in her mind's eye she could now see the clippings on the table.

Excitement burst in her chest, but before she'd had a chance to wrestle the cutters out of her pocket, the car came to an abrupt stop. A door opened then slammed closed. Tony was whistling, she realized, and her hand froze at the top of her pocket. She'd run out of time.

For most of her life, she'd been surrounded by unscrupulous people. Liars, cheats, scam artists, many of them violent. Tony scared her more than all of them put together.

Stupid. Stupid. Stupid.

Tears stung her eyes. If only she'd remembered the tool sooner. Now, with her luck, he'd notice the weapon and take it away. Her one and perhaps only chance at escape was slipping away.

The trunk opened, and he reached in and stroked her cheek. "We're here, my lovely. You and I are going to have such a good time."

She lay limp and unresponsive even when he released the bonds on her ankles. With what seemed like little effort, he scooped her up and set her on the ground. His strength frightened her. She was literally at his whim and mercy, and she was darned sure he would show her no mercy.

They were parked by the foundation of an old barn. Some of the planks remained in place on the side walls, but the roof was gone. Turning her head back and forth, she couldn't see a house anywhere.

"Yes, it's nice and remote, isn't it? The property's at the end of a dead end road. I made sure no one ever comes here. Okay, let's go into the barn so I can grab something. We'll hike out. Don't forget, I still have my trusty friend with me." He pointed down to his hip where the Taser was holstered.

Nestled in the corner of the barn foundation was a shovel. Tony took it in his left hand and pushed her out through the opening in the wall. She kept her hands pressed against her back right pocket in the hopes he wouldn't notice the cutters. Realizing she needed to distract him, she made urgent sounds through the fabric in her mouth.

He shook his head and smiled depreciatingly. "Oh, I am sorry. How silly of me to forget the gag. If you promise to behave, I'll take it off. Honestly, I'm not worried about anyone hearing you because really—" He spread his arms wide. "Look around. There's no one for miles. But I won't have you spoiling our time together with screams and cries. Will you give me your word you'll conduct yourself like a lady?"

Mia met his eyes and nodded vigorously. He smiled, pleased with her response. Dropping the shovel at his feet, he reached up and gently peeled the tape away before plucking the soggy material from her mouth. She turned her head to the side and spat several times trying to clear the horrible taste from her mouth.

He shrugged and patted her shoulder. "Unpleasant, I know, but sadly necessary. Okay, we have a bit of a hike ahead of us. Best get going."

"I thought you usually kill first then move the body to bury elsewhere."

He turned his head, and his smile ratcheted up a notch as though she'd said something incredibly clever. "Ah, yes but I'm refining my process. Growing even. You notice I didn't drug you either? That was a messy business. I never really liked doing it. You may not realize it, but you mark a turning point for me. After Anita, I randomly chose my girls. You're the first one I've known and planned to kill."

"But you knew Anita."

"Very true. Anita was special though. There was no plan. The whole thing evolved organically. Some might say it was an accident, but I'd call it destiny. She showed me the way. My way. After that night, I finally knew why I was here. Up until that point, I'd thought my life pointless, a mistake even, then everything came into focus. I had a calling. And you, my lovely, are the beginning of the next phase."

"You never use a gun. How come?"

He made a scoffing noise in his throat. "Guns are for amateurs. People who can't maintain control. I find them offensive. And I'd never want to disfigure one of my girls. It would spoil everything. This is nice, us talking like this. I don't want you to get your hopes up though because it won't change anything. You and I are going to complete the experience. It has to be. And if some small part of you is thinking of running, this Taser can reach fifteen feet no problem. Plus, I'm a hundred percent sure I'm faster than you."

"Roman and his whole family are going to be devastated when they find out you're the killer."

"Yeah. I know. I've made my peace with it though. They never accepted me for who I was. Did you know they sent me to shrinks for years to make me better?" He used his fingers as air quotes on the word better.

"I'm sure they wanted you to be happy. It must have been terrible to lose your father when you were so young, especially with your mother not being around much."

"I didn't lose him," Tony snapped. "He chose to go."

"Roman told me it was a car accident."

"Yeah, right. The kind of accident that happens on a deserted road on a perfect day and ends up with my dad's car impaled on a tree. He couldn't take my mother leaving, and he killed himself. I know because I looked into it when I was older. They both left of their own accord."

"Oh, Tony, you poor little boy. I'm so sorry."

He whirled around and slapped her across the face. "Shut up. No more talking."

With her cheek on fire, Mia slipped her fingers into her back pocket again. She was too afraid of dropping the tool to try and take it out while they were walking. They'd stop at some point, she reasoned. And when they did, she'd have to find a way to cut herself free.

It seemed they walked forever. She stared at the back of his head, at the shiny wheat-blond hair, and tried to push her way into his mind. As before, it was no use. She simply couldn't get any kind of reading from him. It was as though he didn't have thoughts or feelings or memories. There was nothing except blank space.

He seemed so normal. When he was talking about killing as his life's work, it sounded reasonable, as though anyone should be able to understand. No different from someone describing becoming a lawyer or a politician. Yet surely he must look around and see no one he knew was killing people.

"Do you think murder should be legalized?" she asked.

He stopped and turned to look at her. "What an interesting question. You're turning out to be so much more than I expected. I think this new method, where I interact with my chosen one, will bring me a great deal more pleasure than I'd imagined. So, do I think murder should be legalized? Hmm…well, I don't think everyone is capable of doing what I do. It's a huge responsibility, and only those with absolute mastery over themselves should be allowed the privilege."

"Maybe the government should run some kind of program, and only those who pass the exams could be killers?" she suggested.

He tipped his head. "I don't know about that. What I do is an art. It can't be taught. Did Rembrandt need someone to teach him to paint? What about Mozart? Who coached him into becoming a genius composer?

And you?" He pointed a finger at her head. "How did you learn to read people's thoughts?"

"I always could for as long as I can remember."

"Exactly my point. Back to your main question then. I think certain exceptional individuals should not be held to the laws created for the general population of mundane people. What I do isn't wrong. It's a supremely artistic experience that only a select few will ever know. You should count yourself lucky."

When she didn't say anything, he chuckled and gestured with his head to keep walking. *Okay*, she thought as she trudged after him, *there's no reasoning with this guy.* He was way out there on the lunatic fringe.

Her mind drifted back to Roman. She saw his gorgeous dark eyes focused on her. His sexy mouth curving into a smile. He'd been so good to her, so honest and genuine, and she'd done nothing but lie to him day after day. If she'd been another kind of person who wasn't hiding from her past, she'd have fallen head over heels in love with him. Who was she kidding? She *was* in love with him.

Even under these bizarre circumstances, it felt liberating to finally admit it to herself. She loved Roman…could easily imagine waking up with him every morning. Even spending a life with him. Why had she been so frightened?

Because once he found out about my past, it would all be over anyway.

Maybe so. Maybe not though. And wouldn't it have been worth trying to figure it out? She thought about her plans to disappear, to change her identity again and build a whole new life. In the old days, she'd found it exciting and hadn't minded sprinting off and turning herself into someone new. Now, all it did was make her feel empty. Now it didn't matter because she was minutes away from dying.

No, she thought fiercely and once again brushed her hand over the tool in her pocket. *This is not my day to die.*

"We're here," he said, jolting her from her thoughts.

He dropped the shovel beside an enormous pile of fresh dirt. The hole was large. When she peeked over the edge, very deep too. A pool of water shimmered at the bottom. *Must be from yesterday's rain,* she concluded.

"This had to have taken you forever to dig," she said conversationally while her fingers closed over the handle in her pocket.

Tony slipped off the backpack and flexed his right biceps, patting it with his other hand. "Less than two hours. My body is an instrument, and I like to keep myself in excellent shape."

Backing away from the hole, she sank to the ground. "You do look very fit," she said.

Mia pulled the tool carefully from her pocket without dropping it. Managing to get it turned blade side down, she pried the two arms apart but struggled to fit it across the zip ties. She slid it farther up her hands while her wrists cramped then down again. Still no connection between the mouth of the wire cutters and the plastic.

"They won't break," he said. Her face went stiff with shock. "The zip ties. All these people on the internet love posting videos of how to get free by positioning the fastener between your hands and slamming your arms down. Trust me, those babies are industrial strength. Even I couldn't get out of them without a knife."

"I'm not...I wasn't...my shoulders are sore. I was trying to relieve the pressure."

For one terrifying moment, she thought he was going to walk over and check her hands. After shrugging as though in apology, he crouched down and unzipped the backpack. Her hands worked to hold the cutters steady on the zip ties while squeezing the handles together.

Chapter Twenty-five

With a final push of effort, Mia pressed the cutters closed and the sharp little blades sliced through the plastic in one easy snip. She slipped the tool back into her pocket and keeping her movements as small as possible massaged some life back into her screaming wrists.

Tony pulled a blanket and a bottle of water from the backpack. Straightening, he kicked sticks and stones to the side and spread the blanket out in a strange parody as if setting up a romantic picnic. He uncapped the water and drank deep, emptying half the bottle before wiping his mouth with the back of his hand.

"This spot will be perfect for us." Tony smiled over at her. "I want to show you something first."

Her heart was an independently live thing now and beat so hard against her ribs she wondered why it didn't bust right out of her chest. He came toward her, and her eyes darted everywhere seeking a weapon more substantial than jewelry cutters. The shovel remained by the hole, but if she ran for it, he'd likely tackle her to the ground or simply pull out the Taser. Same thing with the fallen branch behind him. Either way, he'd discover her hands were free, and she'd lose any advantage.

By the time she'd concluded all this, Tony was on his knees in front of her and reaching out to grasp her chin with his hand. He lowered his face to hers and revulsion swam up from her belly when she thought he intended to kiss her. Instead, he pressed his forehead to hers.

"This is going to be the best thing ever because with you I can show you all the girls who came before. Now, and for one time only, I'm going to let you look around in my head. I know you want to."

The images came so fast, so harsh, she couldn't have blocked them if she'd tried. All his victims, under him, crying, begging, while he raped and choked, raped and choked. It was like a montage from a movie except without the music soundtrack and filled with horror and cruelty and death.

"Have you ever seen anything more beautiful?" he whispered as his warm breath caressed her lips. "This was their moment, what they were born for. Now surely you must understand?"

He drew back and stared at her and finally, finally the madness shone through his eyes like a fever.

Her body was numb, and she couldn't catch her breath. Red and yellow spots danced in her vision and when her ears started tingling, she worried she might pass out entirely. She couldn't let that happen. Scrambling to her feet, she lurched away while he smiled at her.

"Good girl. You seemed so passive, I was afraid you wouldn't fight me.

Backing away toward the shovel, she kept her eyes on him. "Can you tell me one thing first? Is Roman really hurt?"

He threw back his head and laughed. "That was a good one. I swear I've never seen anyone's face go as white as yours. It was so easy to get you to leave your house. With all the excitement of finding Anita's wallet and bracelet, I bet everyone will forget to check on you. You'll probably be dead before anyone even realizes you're missing. I'm kind of hoping I'll be able to swing back to your place and say a final goodbye to the dogs."

Icy pinpricks coated her skin. "Please don't. I'll do what you want. Anything you want. Please leave them be."

"There you go. I love it when you girls beg. It makes me feel amazing." Standing tall, he tapped his chest as though he were Superman. "Okay, enough foreplay. It's time to get down to business."

She backed farther away while frantically judging the distance to the shovel. Less than three feet now. She could be there in one leap. Right beside it would be better, she thought, shuffling her feet. If she were to have any real chance, he needed to come closer. She faked a stumble and went down on her knees practically on top of the shovel. She hoped he'd see her as completely powerless in this position.

"Please, no. You don't have to do this. We can get you help," she said, making sure her voice wavered.

He rose to the bait and rushed toward her with teeth bared. Pretending to cower back, she waited until he was within range then twisted to the side, grabbed the shovel, and swung high and hard. There was an instant of shock in his eyes before the blade smashed into the side of his head. He staggered back, and she was on her feet and swinging again. His arm came up and blocked the blow. She danced away, repositioned her arm to swing again and made contact with his head for a second time.

Now he dropped like a stone. It was exactly like in the movies. Tony's eyes went glassy, his hand clutched his head, and he keeled over on one side. A fountain of blood poured over that ear and down his neck. He didn't move after that.

Mia's first instinct was to run. But to where? Even if she made it back to his car, it wasn't likely he'd conveniently left the keys in the ignition. He'd have them with him, wouldn't he? Except what if he was pretending to be unconscious and she got caught again?

Air pumped in and out of her like a piston engine. *Slow it down,* she thought. *Take a second and get yourself together.* She glanced over at Tony. He didn't appear to have moved. Okay, first she'd figure out if he really was unconscious. Keeping herself well back, she poked his leg with the handle of the shovel. Next, she tried his shoulder before finally circling around and jabbing him in the chest. There was no reaction whatsoever.

His eyes were closed, and it was impossible to tell if he was breathing. Blood continued to flow though it was more of a dribble now. Okay. She was pretty sure he wasn't going to leap up and grab her. Still, it didn't hurt to take preventative measures. She rushed over to his backpack and rooted through it.

Wet wipes, another bottle of water, two Cliff bars, a navy blue lightweight jacket. A small red velvet box inside the pack made her stomach clutch. Not brilliant. Maybe she could tie his hands with the jacket. The first side pocket held gum, but in the second she finally hit pay dirt. Zip ties.

She circled him several times trying to figure out how to get his second hand free. Studying his top arm and the way his legs were curled to the side, she had an idea. It took four ties plus the two she added for good measure, but when she was done, his left wrist was tied to his bound ankles.

Seeing him like that, everything in her released. There was no way he could get her now. In fact, she leaned down and put some muscle into it, rolling him slightly until his right hand was free. She pulled two more zip ties from the package and completed hog-tying him. For a brief moment, she understood some of the pleasure he'd derived from incapacitating all those women because joy rushed through her as she stared down at him.

Wait, was he even alive? Reaching out with her mind, she could definitely sense something, although it wasn't clear. She crouched and put a hand to chest. His heart beat under her palm, slow and steady. Okay. She hadn't killed him. Good. She wanted this bastard to pay for what he'd done, preferably in a maximum security prison for the rest of his sorry life.

But what about the Mancinis? Once they found out, would it be harder for them if Tony was dead or alive?

All at once she started to tremble. Why was she standing here thinking these inane things when only moments ago she'd been at the mercy of a vicious serial killer? She needed to get out of there and fast. Where were the blessed car keys?

Since they hadn't been in the backpack, they must be on Tony. Steeling herself, she knelt beside him one last time and pushed her hands into the back pockets of his jeans. Tears clouded her vision when she pulled out a key fob. Clutching them to her chest, she rocked back and forth. Everything really was going to be okay now.

She scrambled to her feet, turned, and ran.

* * *

Roman was on the phone with Special Agent Millar when Kevin, with his own cell phone glued to his ear, signaled him.

"We might have some news. Hang on a sec," Roman said into his cell.

Kevin angled his phone away from his mouth, directing his words to Roman. "Mia managed to escape and is apparently fine. She called nine-one-one. They're triangulating her location now and ready to dispatch emergency vehicles. It sounds like she's on Shaker's Line over near Walkerton."

"Did you hear that?" Roman asked Millar. "I'm going there now. I'll keep you posted."

They sprinted to the car. Outside the house Mia's dogs ran along the fence line barking and yipping. Roman slid behind the wheel and slammed his door. "Anything else? What are they saying?" he demanded.

"Yeah. It's Shaker's right at the end beside the forest."

"And they're sure she's okay?"

"That's the word. She's still on the line with them. They're reporting she left the killer unconscious and tied up in the woods."

"Holy shit. She caught him."

He glanced down at the speedometer. How could he be going a hundred and twenty when everything swam by the car in a weird slow-motion visage? He leaned forward as though willing them to fly while a million scenarios of Mia and the killer flashed through his mind.

"Hey, she's safe. You're not going to lose her," Kevin said.

"I won't believe it until I see her with my own eyes."

He slowed marginally when he turned onto Shaker's Line. The laneway on the property was nothing more than a muddy track. Up ahead, he saw the ambulance, and his pulse beat in time to the flashing lights. It was parked beside a brown Chevy Malibu. The back of the medical vehicle was opened wide. Leaning against the door stood Mia.

Roman pumped the brakes. The car shuddered and skidded to a stop, and he threw it into park. Leaping out, he hurtled across to her and grabbed her up in his arms. His throat was raw and his breath ragged. She felt warm and soft and so real against him.

"You're shaking," she said, patting his shoulders.

Fighting back a sob, he exhaled long and slow. "You're shaking too."

"I know. I can't seem to stop. It's okay though. I'm okay. I'm so glad you're here."

He drew back and stared down at her while his hands moved over her face. "He didn't…hurt you?"

"Not much. Some bumps and bruises. My wrists are sore. Otherwise, I'm fine."

"Where is the bastard?"

"He's in the woods. I can show you. Are you sure you should go back there?"

"You bet your life I'm going back there. I want to see this sicko with my own eyes just the way you left him. He's still alive right?" She studied his face for several seconds, and he saw grief come into her eyes. "What? Tell me."

"I thought you knew. It's Tony."

Reeling back, he reached out blindly with his arm and steadied himself on the side of the ambulance. He shook his head but couldn't think past the buzzing in his ears. Heat flashed up his neck and his vision filled with a red haze. The boy he'd grown up with. The one who'd been an integral part of his family. Tony couldn't be the killer. He swallowed down the bile in his throat.

"My cousin, Tony?"

She touched his arm. "Yes, I'm so sorry. I still can't believe I never sensed it until it was almost too late."

"I want to see him. Now. Take me there."

Kevin approached hesitantly. "Mia, I'm seriously glad to see you…um…Roman, I need a word."

"What?" Roman snapped once they were back inside the Impala.

"Schmidt's taking you off the case. He's ordered you to stay away from the crime scene."

Roman thought his head was going to explode. His fist slammed down on the console between them. "That's complete bullshit. He's my cousin. My sister was murdered. The woman I love abducted. I'm going out there, and I'm working this case."

Kevin shook his head. "No, you're not. Come on. We need this to be a clean bust. Nobody's going to slip through on some conflict of interest loophole. So you and I are going back to the station. They're sending Jensen to bring Mia in once she's cleared by medical. And before you ask, no, Schmidt doesn't want us to drive her. He'd prefer if you don't talk to her until she's been interviewed. I know it sucks but tell her you gotta go. Then I'm taking you back to Dalton. Scratch that. I'll tell her. You stay in the car."

Roman didn't fight his partner on it. He turned his head and watched Kevin walk to the ambulance and squat down in front of Mia. The EMTs had wrapped a blanket around her shoulders. Her hair was falling out of her braid and hunks of it hung down, covering part of her face. She looked at Kevin and nodded slowly. Then she lifted her head and glanced over at the Impala. Streaks of mud covered her right cheek, and even from where he sat Roman could tell she was crying.

Kevin patted her shoulder and stood again. He leaned down and must have said something else because she shook her head and pulled the blanket tight under her chin. After several beats, he turned and walked away. Mia slumped down and hid her face in her hands.

The door opened beside him, and Kevin swatted his shoulder. "Get out. I'm driving."

Roman didn't respond. He simply slid out from behind the wheel, and like a sleepwalker made his way around the front of the car. "What are the paramedics saying about her?" he asked.

"Seems to be okay physically. There's a good ding on the back of her head, scratches and bruises here and there, nothing much otherwise. They want her to have some Ativan, but she says no, she's fine. She's got the shakes, which is understandable."

A black and white cruiser approached the laneway as Kevin turned their car onto the dirt road. It stopped, and the driver's window came down.

"Hey, Jensen," Kevin said.

"Latterly, Mancini. It's a hell of a thing."

"You can say that again. Take good care of her, okay?"

"You have my word."

They drove in silence for several minutes. The radio squawked updates. Mia was now on route to Dalton. The perp had been located in the woods and was still unconscious. He appeared to be Antonio Mancini.

Kevin slid his eyes to Roman. "You doing okay?"

He shook his head and returned to staring out the window.

Soon enough they heard a medivac copter had been dispatched. Techs were already photographing the scene. EMTs suspected Tony had a skull fracture and brain injury. His pupils weren't responsive to light. They were attempting to get him out of the woods on a stretcher.

For Roman, it all seemed to be happening to someone else. They weren't talking about Tony and Mia, but two strangers. None of this in any way had to do with him or his family. He couldn't even picture his mom and dad's reaction. Was it possible any of them would ever come back from this?

He pulled out his phone. "Ma," he said when his mother answered. "I want you and Dad to meet me at the station."

Her voice was hard. "Did you get him? Did you get my baby's killer?"

"You need to come. Don't talk to anyone but me. I'll see you in ten minutes."

Kevin sighed. "Schmidt won't like it. Still I can't say I wouldn't have done the same thing."

They were on Main Street now. Everything looked the same. Absolutely normal. Like nothing had happened, and lives weren't being ripped apart. Which was true. Only his life.

Roman waited in the lobby until his parents arrived.

"Has anyone heard from Mia? Where is this man, this killer?" Molly demanded when she and Frank rushed into the station. "I want to see him with my own eyes."

"Mia is fine, thank goodness. Let's go to my office," Roman said.

Molly made an impatient sound in her throat, and Frank's expression darkened.

"If you're going to tell us bad news, spit it out, Son," Frank said.

"Ma, Dad, I don't want to do this out here. Come upstairs where we'll have some privacy."

In his office, he gestured his parents to the visitor's chairs and closed the door before walking over to stand in front of them. *Fast is best,* he thought.

"As you know Mia went missing this morning. She was kidnapped and forced to walk into the woods where a grave had already been dug. She managed to get her hands free and strike the man unconscious with a shovel. After tying him up, she ran back to the car he'd driven. Inside she found a burner cell phone. A little over an hour ago her call came in to the emergency dispatcher."

Molly's hand shot up and covered her mouth, and she stared at Roman with wide eyes.

Frank cleared his throat. "She's unharmed?"

"Yes."

"The police…they captured the man?" Molly asked.

"He's being airlifted to St. Mark's with a suspected skull fracture. This next part is hard, and I wanted to be sure you heard it from me first. It's Tony. He abducted Mia. In all likelihood, he's the serial killer."

His parents turned to stone. Roman stared from one to the other before slumping back onto the top of his desk and rubbing a hand over his eyes. He heard his mother take in a sharp breath. When he glanced over, Roman saw the flush riding high on her cheekbones. She got to her feet and stabbed a finger at him.

"It's not true. I don't know why Mia would say these things. She's not who I thought she was. Tony could never do this." She shook her head, and her eyes blazed into Roman's. "He wouldn't kill Anita. It's not him."

"You're saying Mia overpowered Tony and fractured his skull?" Frank shook his head. "How could a little girl like that get away? Maybe Mia lured Tony into the woods and made it look like he was the killer. A frame-up job. We only have her word he abducted her. We should wait and see what Tony says."

"Yes. We need to hear Tony's side," Molly agreed, crossing her arms over her chest and staring defiantly at Roman.

"It may be a while before Tony can talk, assuming he recovers at all," Roman said. "In the meantime, we'll work the case. Well, not me. Schmidt pulled me off because of the conflict of interest."

"I want to talk to your Lieutenant Schmidt," Molly said.

"Yes, we should be interviewed," Frank agreed.

Roman sighed. "I'll let the lieutenant know you're here."

Chapter Twenty-six

In the back of the police car, Mia could barely keep her eyes open. Her head throbbed, her body ached, and she was so thirsty she was having trouble swallowing. Hugging her arms around her chest, she sank into the corner by the door and closed her eyes. She wanted her dogs and her house and most of all Roman. The look on his face when she'd told him it was Tony was something she'd never forget.

She flashed to the last time she'd seen Tony at the memorial where he'd presented a solid unit with the Mancini family. He'd even released the butterflies. Afterward, he'd hugged her. In some ways, it still seemed impossible he was the killer.

Then her mind flooded with all the scenes he'd shown her. Nine girls brutalized and killed because he'd decided it was his life's work. One of them his own cousin. It was only by a miracle she'd escaped the same fate.

She straightened and shifted to the middle of the seat until she could see into the rearview mirror.

"Officer Jensen, what will happen when I get to the police station?"

His eyes met hers in the mirror. "You'll go through processing. They'll want your clothes and fingernail scraping, things like that. I imagine they'll need to go over what happened, probably multiple times."

"It sounds like I could be there for a while," she said.

"I don't think it'll be quick," he agreed.

And indeed, Officer Jensen was right. By the time she'd told her story for the third time, she was pretty much all talked out. The more she spoke about it, the less real it seemed. Like something she'd watched in a movie. Her mind was numb, and she wondered if the pounding behind her eye would ever go away.

"Thank you, Miss Reeves. You've been very cooperative. I need to step out for a minute."

She couldn't remember the detective's name. She nodded wearily and rubbed her eyes. It was the same room she'd been in when she'd first come to the police station all those weeks ago. None of this would have happened if she'd left it alone. Including Roman.

Given a choice, she'd do it all again, she decided.

It took hours that felt like days, but Mia was finally released from the police station shortly after ten p.m. A uniformed officer named Murphy drove her home. Inside, at the core of her being, she was broken. Because she was shaken so badly, she wondered how she'd ever recover. Having always considered herself tough as nails, this was a bitter pill to swallow. She hadn't seen Roman since the ambulance on Shaker's Line and imagined he must be in a state far worse than her own.

When Murphy made the final turn to the parking area, the headlights flashed over the dogs in the run behind the house. They charged at the fence, leaping and barking when she got out of the car. The house was ablaze with lights. A second police car was parked off to the side of the walkway. The officer, a woman, got out and walked over to speak to Murphy. Mia stood there uncertainly.

"We're all done here," the woman said. "You're cleared to go in."

Mia nodded and walked up the steps and into her house. She went straight through to the kitchen and opened the side door. The dogs rushed in, bumping against one another and pounced on her. Sobbing, she slid to the floor and gathered them to her. Mac half crawled onto her lap and wedged his head up between her arms so he could lick her face. Tucker, unable to contain his excitement, jumped back and forth over her legs letting out barks of frenzied delight.

"You guys, I missed you so much," she hiccupped. "I never thought I'd see you again."

It was a long time before she stopped crying. The dogs, gradually subduing, sat on her legs or pressed up against her. When she finally crawled off the floor, she locked the kitchen door, noticing the tape across the broken pane by the handle, and turned off the light. Then she walked back to the front door, checked it was locked and, as one, she and the dogs climbed the stairs and went straight to bed.

Mia's dreams took her back into the woods. Only this time she couldn't get her hands free. Or the shovel turned into a plastic lightsaber and bounced harmlessly off Tony's head. One time she reached in to get the car keys from his back pocket, and he came to life, no longer tied. He tackled her to the ground. She woke gasping for breath, shaking, sometimes crying out, with the dogs all around her whining on the bed.

Finally, at a quarter to four, she'd had enough, and after a bracing shower, she went downstairs. *If ever there was a morning for coffee,* she thought, starting a small pot, *this was the day.* Her phone was on the counter, and she stared at it for a full thirty seconds before picking it up.

Three missed calls. All from Roman. She should call him. Well, not now, obviously, since it was four in the morning, but soon. She needed him, dammit. And she'd never, in her whole life, needed anyone before.

After giving the dogs a double ration to make up for the day before, she drank coffee out on the back porch and studied the horizon waiting for sunrise and a new day to dawn.

Why was she so afraid?

* * *

It was barely after five when headlights bounced off the shed at the end of her driveway. The dogs came to attention before rushing to the fence and barking out their severe displeasure at being interrupted.

Roman parked beside her Escape, stepped out, and scanned the property. Mia didn't move, didn't make a sound, but he must have sensed her even in the half-light. Instead of following the path to the front porch, he made his way across the lawn and unlatched the gate by the kitchen.

The dogs surrounded him, welcoming him back like a long-lost brother. He crouched down, patting and stroking without taking his eyes from her. Because of the shadow of the house and the sun rising behind him, she couldn't read his expression, but she sensed the anxiety well enough. It looked like they were both on unsteady ground and feeling their way forward.

Except she knew what she was going to do. What she must do. And nothing had ever scared her as much. *No guts, no glory,* she thought and smiled to herself.

"Hi, Roman," she said. "Do you want coffee?"

He rose slowly, nudging the dogs to the side and stepping up onto the deck before kneeling down in front of her chair. His arms came around her shoulders, and his forehead pressed against hers while he hugged her so tightly she worried a rib might crack. His breath was unsteady, and she could feel the thumping of his heart against her own chest, strong and fast.

She stroked his cheek, raspy with stubble, then angled her head and kissed him softly. When his lips turned needy and demanding, she gently pushed him back until their eyes met. She could read the questions, the fatigue, and most of all the unbearable grief.

"Are we not okay?" he asked. "We have to be okay. I almost lost you yesterday, and I swear to all that's holy, I thought I'd die right there with you. I know you must be shaken, but don't turn me away. Please, God, don't shut me out."

Leaning into him again, she kissed one cheek then the other, and smoothed a hand through his hair. She shifted to the side and gained her feet.

"Remember the other day when you told me you knew Mia wasn't my name?"

He got to his feet too. Crossing both arms over his chest, he faced her with wary eyes. "Yes, I remember."

"Once I knew you knew, I was planning to run. I didn't go to the security firm like I said. I went into Dalton and got as much cash as I could along with some supplies. I also stole a couple of license plates in case I needed them for cover on toll roads. Yesterday morning, after you were called to Walkerton, I started packing."

Roman drew away several paces until his back was against the wall of the house. "Why are you telling me this?" His voice was all official cop now.

Dropping her head, she exhaled long and slow then lifted it again and met his gaze. "Because I'm not going to lie to you anymore. I suspect it will be the end of us. I hope not because I'm in love with you. It's my first time being in love, by the way. Anyway, I need you to promise something first."

"I'd like to, but I'll want to hear what you have to say before I give you my word on anything."

She nodded slowly once, twice, scanning across the yard where the dogs were sniffing around by the far line of fencing. "I guess that's fair. So, not a promise then, but I'll ask you anyway. When this plays out between us…and you decide which way to go if something happens…if I'm no longer able to take care of the dogs, please find them homes. They don't deserve to pay for my mistakes." She turned back to face him. "And not a shelter, okay? I know it's too much to expect a home for all four, but maybe you could keep the pairs intact. It would mean so much to me."

He blinked at her, clearly not having expected this. "I'll do my best," he said at last.

She paced back to the chair. Rubbing her palms down the front of her jeans, she then sat for a moment but bounced back up to her feet. "I'm nervous. This is harder than I thought."

"Start with something small," he suggested.

"Okay. My true name is Jennifer Melanie Dawson. Jenny, really. And that's actually not small, is it?"

"I don't know. It'll depend on why you're using an alias." After unfolding his arms, he hooked his thumbs in the front pocket of his jeans.

"For the reason I imagine most people do. To get away from my past. It's not the first time I've switched identities, but this name was different because I'd seen the light. Not in a come-to-Jesus kind of way…more that I wanted to start over fresh and live a good, decent life that didn't involve running scams or…well, some of the other things I did in the past."

She sighed, and all the anxiety went out of her. Sitting back down on the Muskoka chair, she took a sip of her coffee before continuing. "I wanted to settle down, run a business, and stop having to look over my shoulder. And it was great for a while. When I was younger, I always imagined I'd be bored to death living the straight life. So not true. I loved it. Loved my house, making my jewelry, and especially the dogs. Then I loved you, and it hurt so much because I knew I couldn't keep you. A cop and a criminal together? How would that ever work? The answer was, it wouldn't. Somehow though, you made me believe I had to try."

"Did you kill anyone?"

"What? No. Never. I didn't even have a gun. My specialty was theft. I'd befriend some guy, a rich one usually, of course. And with my abilities, it didn't take long to learn alarm codes, combinations to safes, things like that. Then I'd take what I wanted and move on to a new mark. I mostly stuck to cash and jewelry, though sometimes a painting would catch my interest. For a brief period of time, I had a Monet in my possession."

Other than the blinking of his eyes, Roman had been practically immobile during her confession. When she looked up at him and shrugged, he finally came to life.

"Tell me the truth. Have you targeted any of the citizens in Dalton?"

"Not a one," she said easily. "I told you, I'm living the straight life now. Well, except the license plates. Besides, I only ever went after the uber rich anyway. I'd never take from some hard-working soul just trying to get by."

He blew out a breath and shook his head, then rubbed a hand across his face. "I don't think I can take anymore. Between Tony and now you, I feel like my whole world is imploding."

"I know," she said quietly. "It's a lot. But I was terrified locked in that trunk. Later when he marched me through the woods, I promised myself if I survived I was going to do better. Be better. I'd already started down a more decent path, but this feels like the final step. If I have to go to prison, well…" She spread her hands. "I'll find a way to deal with it."

"You've put me in a hell of a position."

"I'm sorry. Don't forget though, you asked for it. You pushed and pushed and wouldn't let me go. You told me you wanted a relationship. Well, here you are. I'm all in, just like you wanted."

He stepped away from the wall and paced over to the gate and back up the stairs onto the deck. "Why couldn't you have had an abusive ex or something? That would've been so much easier to deal with."

"Because I'd never have let anyone abuse me. I already told you, I'm no damsel in distress."

"Where's your family in all of this?"

Her head tipped forward, and her hair fell over her face, hiding her eyes. "Don't know where my mom is. I imagine Pop's running cons same as always. He liked Vegas, but he could be anywhere."

Roman didn't say anything for a moment. Finally, he walked back over and sat on the second chair. "Did he hurt you?"

"Pops?" She snorted. "No. He never hurt me."

"But he got you into the life, didn't he?"

"Sure. Taught me everything he knew."

"Jenny…No, you'll always be Mia to me. Mia, it's not your fault."

"Maybe not at first when I was a little kid, but kids grow up. Learn right from wrong. For a long time, I knew I wasn't a good person." She shrugged and slid a lock of hair behind her ear. "Eventually I made the decision to go down a different path. I can't go back and change my past. Can't fix what I did. This is part of me, and you'll have to decide if you can live with it."

He exhaled. "I have a couple more questions. First, did you do any jail time?"

"I was sent to juvie once for shoplifting. Didn't much like it."

"Why'd you decide to get out of the life? In my experience, criminals don't simply wake up one day and turn in their bad guy costume."

"Yes, well, there's a story. Let's just say I got cocky. Thought I was invincible. Turns out I wasn't. One particular mark, my last one actually, somehow caught on to me. Since he was affiliated with the Russian mob, you could say I didn't fare too well. I came to in an alley all busted up and my entire stash gone. Close to a million dollars. I couldn't go to the hospital. And obviously, the police were out. It gave me a lot of time to think. Too much time. When I finally got back on my feet, I knew I was done with the cons."

"But you had no money," Roman said.

"You don't miss much, do you?" When he continued to hold her gaze, she sighed. "Okay, I didn't run any more cons, but I did hit Atlantic City and then went down to Vegas. Poker. It's a good game for me. I was careful. Moved around through all the casinos. Made sure to lose here and there and not keep raking in the big pots. After a couple of months, I had a good nest egg. I'd already started making jewelry on the side. For fun mostly. Whenever I wore one of my pieces out and about, people commented, and it gave me the idea to start Healing Crystals. That's it."

She sat back in the chair, rubbing a hand over her forehead. The dogs had returned to the deck and lay sprawled at her feet. With the sun halfway up the sky by now, shafts of light caught fire in her hair. She looked tired but resolute and didn't avert her eyes while he studied her.

"Okay," he said at last. "Thank you for telling me. I'm not sure what I'm going to do. I need time to think it over."

"I understand. Do you still want that coffee?"

"Um…no, I should probably get back."

"Can you tell me what's happening? How are your parents?"

"Not so good, as you can probably imagine. At first, they didn't believe it was Tony. But the Nashville police found a bunch of aliases and the forged documents to go with them." He winced at the words and flicked a glance over to Mia who didn't respond. "Anyway, it led them to a storage locker, and everything was there. More emerald rings. Souvenirs from the other women, mostly wallets, and purses. Another Taser along with chloroform and ketamine. He'd even printed out news stories of each disappearance and murder and was keeping a kind of bragging file. The evidence is irrefutable."

"I guess your parents will eventually come to grips with what he did, but it's so awful. Do you think they'll be okay?"

She reached across and patted his arm in sympathy. He stiffened and though it was subtle, shifted enough that the contact was broken. She understood. He wasn't doing it to hurt her, but to protect himself while he made up his mind about everything she'd told him. It did hurt though. Like a knife to the belly. Well, she'd asked for it, hadn't she?

"I honestly don't know if they'll ever recover. We're all shell-shocked."

"And Tony?" she asked hesitantly.

"At St. Mark's and still in a coma. My parents are there praying he wakes up. I don't think he's going to."

"I'm so sorry, Roman. I didn't…wasn't trying…I was terrified. I didn't have murder in my mind. I only wanted to get away. Get back to you. It's funny how clear everything becomes in a situation like that. I knew I had to tell you everything. I was so scared I wouldn't get the chance. Then you'd never know how I truly felt about you."

After a beat, he leaned forward in his chair and reached over, taking her hand in his. "Even though it feels hard right now, I'm really glad you did. I'm gonna go back to the hospital…be with my parents. I hope you understand I want to check out everything you told me. Maybe you wouldn't mind texting me names, places, and the like? Especially your last guy. The Russian."

She swallowed once but worked up a smile. "Of course. Let me know how…well, I hope you'll keep in touch."

"You might want to think about getting some security for the next week or so. Your name hasn't leaked yet, but it will. The news hounds are at the hospital, and no doubt they'll be invading Dalton today. It won't take them long to make their way out here. Call Mitch Fowler at Tightline. Tell him I gave you the referral. They'll take care of it."

"Thanks. I think I'll leave a message this morning." She rose with him and walked over to the gate. "Guess I'll see you when I see you."

Standing on tiptoes, she placed her lips against his and breathing him in, lingered for several seconds. When they drew apart, his fingers came to her face, tracing softly across her cheeks as though memorizing the bone structure. His other hand rose and cupped the back of her head before taking her mouth in a fierce, desperate kiss.

For a split second, she wondered if this was goodbye. She pushed the thought away and dove into the kiss. He tasted of coffee and cherry gum, and she pressed against his chest needing every bit of contact she could get. Her arms clasped him to her, and she slid her leg in between his, bringing him even closer. Melding them together.

Then Roman pulled back, shifted his hips, and she let her arms drop as they fell apart again.

Chapter Twenty-seven

Over the next few days, Mia didn't venture away from her house. Roman had been right about the reports and news teams. Mitch Fowler and his crew were up to the task. He refused all interview requests on her behalf and kept the media off her property. Once again, she was thankful for the remote location and the long driveway.

She hired a man to come replace the glass the police had broken on her kitchen door. When the repairman asked about her plans for the ruined greenhouse, she shook her head and said she didn't think she'd be doing anything about it in the near future.

Thankfully, she wasn't nervous in her home, but for whatever irrational reason, had yet to walk through the tiny forest at the lower end of her property. She had rose quartz and dioptase stones with her at all times, holding them in her hands, filling her pockets, stashed under her pillow. It didn't seem to help, but it was the only thing she could think to do.

She walked the fields, made jewelry, and slept when she could.

Tony Mancini passed away on Tuesday morning without regaining consciousness. Funeral and burial services took place on Friday and were for immediate family only.

Roman didn't call, but he did text every morning and every night. Always a single line asking if she was okay. Each time Mia responded with 'yes, I'm fine' or some variation on the theme, and though she inquired about him and his family, the conversation never went any further.

Mia tried to be okay with it. Roman was going through enough hell without her complications thrown into the mix. She could surely give him more time. Still, as every day went by, her hope faded. People like her didn't usually get happily ever after. There was a price to be paid for the way she'd lived, and it looked like the bill was coming due including a whole whack of interest on top.

One morning with a box in hand, she went room to room collecting everything Roman had left in the house. Layla trailed after her whining and looking downtrodden. The golden lab proceeded to lie beside the box all afternoon.

"Don't do that, girlie. It's hard enough as it is," Mia said, squatting down and rubbing Layla's ears. "We have to be prepared for the worst. He might not want us anymore, and if he doesn't, it'll be easier to send his stuff with the UPS guy."

The Emerald Ring Killer continued to fill the nightly news shows. All the back stories of his victims were dug up and examined in excruciating detail. Her own face was splashed on the screen along with her fake history. She knew it was only a matter of time before someone from the real Mia Reeves's life spoke up. She couldn't find the energy to care.

Roman and his family were often front and center, especially on the Friday after Tony's memorial. Though they probably thought they were putting on a good front, everything showed in their faces. Or at least Mia could see it. Grief, shock, disbelief. It reminded her of footage of people who had managed to flee some brutal war-torn country and now stood on the shores of a new land with nothing but the ripped and dirty clothes on their back.

Without making any conscious decision, Mia continued packing…small things here and there. Finding the linen closet disorganized, she pulled everything out and scrubbed down the shelves in the narrow cupboard, Then somehow, she managed to put together one of her shipping boxes and filled it with towels and bath salts.

The bookshelves in her work area off the kitchen gradually became bare as she filled one of the plastic containers with mementos and paperback books. Since she was mainly eating only toast and soup, she went through the drawers in the kitchen and packed away all the cooking utensils except a vegetable peeler and her knives.

On Sunday afternoon, she was sorting through the jewelry supplies and trying to decide if she should reorder some of the staple items when the driveway monitor pinged from the kitchen. The dogs scrambled up and ran to the front door. She peeked through the window and saw a small silver car make the turn to her house and park by the walkway. The sun sparkled off the windshield, so she couldn't make out the driver.

Her heart went into overdrive. By now the reporters had mostly lost interest. Mitch and his team were still under contract for another week, since a few stragglers continued to press their luck. Maybe one of them had somehow snuck through.

When the driver's door finally opened, and Brooke stepped out, Mia didn't know whether to be relieved or even more terrified. The dogs, predictably, went into a frenzy of barking at the sound of the doorbell. Mia shrank back from the window trying to decide what to do. Maybe Brooke would go away after a few minutes.

No such luck. Brooke didn't go away. Although the doorbell quieted, Mia heard the dogs running through the hall and across the tiled floor in the kitchen. Mac broke away from the pack, coming to the doorway in her workroom and staring at her as if to say *what are we going to do about this*?

"Okay, I'm coming," Mia said, trudging out after him.

"I know you're in there." Brooke's voice came through the side door.

When she stepped into the kitchen, Mia saw the blond woman, hands cupped to the sides of her face, peeking in through the glass. Brooke straightened when she noticed Mia. Their eyes met, and Mia knew she'd have to let her in.

"Sit. Now." Mia pointed to the floor at the end of the counter. The dogs, still vibrating with excitement, plopped their butts down in a ragged line.

She unlocked the deadbolt and opened the door. Brooke flew at her, arms wrapping around her hard and fast in a hug. Behind them, Mac growled low in his throat.

"It's okay. Relax," she said to the dogs.

"Oh my God, I'm so glad to see you. Why didn't you answer my calls?" Brooke asked.

"I don't know. I guess I thought you might be mad."

Brooke reared back in shock. "Mad at you?"

"Maybe. I didn't know."

"That's the stupidest thing I've ever heard. I was worried about you. And sad. Really sad at everything you went through. What happened was awful, and I'm sorry."

All of a sudden Mia's chest was too tight, and it hurt to breathe. "I know you had feelings for Tony. I'm sorry I killed him. I killed someone…" She broke off and slammed a hand over her mouth, horrified by the outburst.

Tears tracked down Brooke's cheeks, and she put her arm around Mia's shoulders and squeezed hard. "I'm going to make you a cup of tea, and we'll sit down and visit for a while. Where's your kettle?"

"You sit. I'll make the tea. I need a moment to pull myself together," Mia said.

"Okay." Brooke wiped her eyes then crouched down to the dogs. "Now who are all these handsome babies?"

"Fifi is the little white one licking your hand. Beside her is Tucker, the Dachshund. The lab mix is

Layla, and this guy here is Mac," Mia said while adding water to the kettle.

"I had a Dachshund when I was little. She was the greatest dog. Hello, Tucker. Oh, Fifi, you're something else, aren't you?" She turned her head to watch Mia. "It must be nice having them for company."

"They're my family," she said simply.

"Your house is really great." Brooke stood and slowly turned in a circle. She paused and looked at the bookshelves, the empty DVD slots in the entertainment center, and the bare mantel above the fireplace. "You have a very minimalist decorating style."

"I'm reorganizing," Mia mumbled and turned away to get mugs down from the cupboard.

"You're packing, aren't you? Oh, Mia. You can't leave. I'm barely getting to know you."

"I'm not sure what I'm going to do. What kind of tea do you like? I have mint, chamomile, lemon balm, and green."

"Lemon balm sounds nice. Can we sit out on the deck? The weather's amazing today, warm but with the perfect amount of breeze to keep it from getting sticky."

"Sure. Why don't you take the dogs and go on out."

While the tea brewed, Mia dug into her stash of frozen cookies and popped a couple in the microwave. She put together a plate with the cookies, and some strawberries and grapes, and carried it out on a tray along with the tea. She found Brooke sitting on the steps patting Tucker while Layla watched him adoringly from where she lay in the grass.

"It's so beautiful out here. Your property is lovely."

"How are you feeling about Tony and everything?"

Brooke sighed and bowed her head over Tucker. "I'm pretty messed up, to be honest. I've had a little thing for Tony for as long as I can remember. It was always there. Then to find out what he did, it makes me sick to my stomach. Did he…I mean…how…were you hurt?"

"The tea's steeped," Mia said waiting until Brooke sat before handing her the cup. "Tony didn't hurt me, not really. He scared me. I'm sorry I killed him. I didn't mean to. Or maybe I did. I don't know anymore. I was scared stiff."

"Of course you were. You had to save yourself. I'm glad he's dead. He killed my best friend and would have killed you, my soon-to-be new best friend." She took in a shaky breath. "Although you're turning out to be a lot of work, so I'm not sure about that part yet. I mean, I've called you millions of times and had to come to your house and stalk you. Most people would have given up by now, but I'm not a quitter."

The laugh erupted out of Mia before she could stop it. "I guess I should say I'm sorry?"

"You absolutely should. And then you have to promise to be a better friend from now on. I think a pinky swear will do it." Brooke held up her left hand with little finger crooked.

Mia stared down at it then shook her head. "The truth is, I don't think I'm any good at it. I didn't really have any friends growing up."

The teasing smile fell away from Brooke's face. "Oh, sweetie, I'm sorry. Everything's crappy right now, and I shouldn't make light of it. I guess humor is my way of getting through the tough stuff."

Mia swallowed. "It's fine, truly. And I understand what you mean. I can't find my balance right now either."

"Oh, look how the dogs come to comfort you," Brooke said as Mac and Fifi pushed in beside her. "They're seriously precious, aren't they?"

Now Mia smiled full out. "They never let me down."

Brooke returned to her chair and took a sip of tea. "Mm, this is really good. Refreshing. I have to admit I'm a hardcore coffee addict, but maybe I should add in some tea once in a while."

"What's happening in town? How are your summer classes going?"

"Actually, it's been pretty busy. I'm thinking of hiring another teacher. I don't suppose you have any kind of dance training?" She shrugged when Mia shook her head. "Oh, well. It was worth a try. The town is still in shock. News cameras finally left, thank goodness, but everyone's still talking about it. Molly and Frank look rough. I saw them coming out of church this morning, and they seemed really old and frail all of a sudden. Lina's gone back to Atlanta."

Mia blinked and looked out where the dogs now lay in the grass. "How's Roman doing?"

"I heard he put in his notice at the police station. He's been staying at his parents' house. I haven't seen him, but Mary from the diner said he's been in a couple of times to pick up food. You should reach out to him."

"He really gave his notice?"

"That's what everyone's saying."

"Oh…wow. That's a surprise. I can't imagine him not being a detective. Maybe he'll rethink that decision when he's had some time to regroup."

"Maybe. Still, something like this can change a person."

"You've got that right."

Chapter Twenty-eight

For the first time since she'd been abducted by Tony, Mia slept peacefully through the night and felt a million times better for it. The sunrise was all pink and red, definitely a sailor's warning, but absolutely breathtaking in the moment.

Once the bowls of morning kibble had been licked clean, she gathered the dogs and took them walking through the fields. The air was close, though infused with sweetness, and birds warbled out a symphony of joy to the coming day.

Instead of pausing at the crest of the hill, Mia continued down and turned left, cautiously stepping into the tiny forest. Chipmunks and squirrels raced across her path and up tree trucks, chattering in their incomprehensible language. Tucker, predictably enough, made for the brook and splashed back and forth through the water…his face full of doggy smiles. She breathed deeply, inhaling the damp, leafy smell and wandered, weaving between the trees, her fingertips brushing the bark of each one as she passed.

She was going to be okay. More than okay, she decided. Roman wasn't coming back. God, it hurt even thinking it, but she'd always been one for facing reality, and this was clearly the way the wind was blowing.

He was a good, law-abiding man and she was, in essence, a criminal. There was no way he'd ever be able to reconcile her past deeds with what he'd consider the bare minimum requirement of being a decent person. He might love her, but love couldn't bridge a gap so huge. And she might love him, but she couldn't change who she'd been just because she wanted to.

And did she want to?

She paused by the brook and crouched down, trailing her fingertips along the top of the water. No, even if she had a magic wand, she wouldn't erase her past. It was part of her. Perhaps a shameful part, but because of it, she was only more proud of the person she'd become. Proud she'd been strong enough to create a new life for herself. A good, solid, creative life.

That meant the only decision left to make was should she stay, or should she go?

"What do you guys think?" she asked aloud.

Mac immediately glanced over, tipping his head to the side while he studied her. Coming to the conclusion she was fine, he went back to sniffing a pile of wet leaves. Layla and Tucker didn't respond at all, simply continued chasing one another in an endless game of tag. Sweet little Fifi walked over and placed her paws on Mia's right foot, then stared up with coal black eyes. When Mia leaned down, the snowflake dog licked her hand vigorously before prancing away to join Mac.

"Looks like the majority has spoken. I guess we're staying." She glanced around and sighed. "I do love it here. As for Roman, I doubt I'll see much of him. After a while, it won't hurt, will it? Eventually, he'll just be some guy I used to know."

Even if she didn't, not for one minute, believe it, saying the words made her feel stronger.

"Okay, troops, let's go. We have some unpacking to do and jewelry to make. And we'd better get the shipments ready for the UPS guy because he'll be here in less than an hour." Rubbing a hand over her forehead, she glanced toward Layla. "Including Roman's stuff. It'll be better once we take that step."

Once at the house, she pulled the key fob from her back pocket and clicked the lock on the Escape before grabbing the three license plates she'd appropriated ten days earlier. She might as well toss them in the box with the rest of Roman's belongs.

Out of recent habit, she glanced around and noted everything appeared peaceful and unmolested in the parking area and on the front lawn. After unlocking the porch, she walked through to the front door, and once again used her key. The dogs clipped in on her heels and followed her straight over to her workroom.

The laptop was seconds into booting up when the driveway sensor pinged. She checked her watch, frowning down to see it was only eight fifteen. Too early for UPS. Layla let out a tentative whine and rushed to the front door. The hairs on the back of Mia's neck stood up like porcupine quills, and she ruthlessly pushed down the glorious burst of hope in her belly.

Blowing out a breath, she stretched tall and squared her shoulders. *The first time will be the hardest,* she thought. She made her way along the hall and opened the front door. Roman strode across the porch, aviator sunglasses covering his eyes. His frame was leaner than the last time she'd seen him. She studied him for several seconds. He needed a haircut, she realized then stepped back and gestured him in.

"Would you like a coffee? Breakfast maybe?"

He slid his sunglasses off and pushed them into a back pocket. His eyes met hers but slipped away to focus elsewhere.

"No, I'm good."

"Are you?"

He didn't answer but continued past her and into the front hall. She closed the door and leaned back against it, studying him again. Mia reached out with her mind. Roman was in tight control, and the only thing she sensed was the strain of reining in whatever emotions he was determined to contain.

"Okay," she said when he remained silent. "How are your parents?"

He sighed long and deep. "Working their way through everything but still in rough shape."

Layla, oblivious to the atmosphere or perhaps simply unconcerned by it, prostrated herself at Roman's feet. He turned his attention to the loyal lab, leaning over to stroke her back. When the reunion continued on for some time, Mia walked through to her workroom and set the license plates inside the box of Roman's belongings, carrying it back out to the front hall.

"Your timing is perfect. I was going to send this out with the delivery guy this morning, but here you are. You can take it with you and save me the step."

He straightened and raised the flap of the unsealed box, glancing in. "You're clean-slating me?"

"I'm doing what needs to be done. Why are you here, Roman? You're barely answering my questions, so you obviously didn't come to talk."

Taking the box from her first, he set it down on the floor by the door before turning to face her. He crossed his arms over his chest. "Did you know that Claudia

Creemore is wanted for questioning in an attempted burglary? There's an arrest warrant for Emily Robinson in Missouri and Danielle Frontenac in Texas too."

She shrugged carelessly, but he saw a telltale line dig in between her brows. "I can't say I knew precisely. Still, it would be odd if none of my marks put it together and reported the thefts. I figured there might be some warrants floating around out there."

"You figured there might be some warrants floating around?" he repeated slowly. "Yeah, I guess for someone like you, a little thing like an arrest warrant isn't going to put a hitch in your step."

"Look, you can either report me or take your stuff and be on your way, but I'm not going to stand here and listen to you preach your moral code."

He shook his head and tipped his face up to stare at the ceiling. "Preach my moral code?" he mumbled under his breath.

"Yeah, I get it. You're the perfect guy, and I'm nothing but a low-life. Message received loud and clear," she said very, very calmly.

His head snapped around, and bitter chocolate eyes met hers. "What did you think would happen when I looked?"

Turning her hands palm down, she lifted them toward him. "If you want to take me in, I won't resist.

There's a file on top of the fridge with the health records of the dogs, and you'll find two extra bags of dog food in the pantry."

He stared down at her hands before glancing at the dogs sitting all around them. Whirling away, he made a growling noise in his throat, then swung back toward Mia with his arm snaking out so fast she didn't even have time to flinch when his fist struck the wall beside her shoulder. Dropping her hands, she turned and glanced at the dent in the drywall.

"That had to have hurt," she commented.

"What's wrong with you?" he yelled. Mac sprang to his feet, inserting himself in between Roman's and Mia's legs. "Don't you have any normal human emotions?"

"Easy, Mac. Go on, down." She snapped her fingers and giving him a nudge with her foot, pointed to the floor. "Down. Now."

The Doberman grumbled and curled his lip at Roman but did as he was told. Layla bellied over and licked Roman's shoe, rolling her eyes up at him in distress.

"I have plenty of human emotions," she said. "I simply don't choose to show any of them to you right at this moment."

"I'm so pissed off at you. I'm...I'm...losing my shit," he hissed through a jaw clenched tighter than any vise. His arm swung wide. This time she flinched, albeit barely enough to register. "You did this to me. It's entirely your fault, and now there's nothing I can do because I fucking love you. How can I love you? I can't."

She gulped. Blood pounded in her ears. Surely he hadn't said...had he? "Roman, take it easy. You're not making sense. You've gone through so much lately. I'm going to get you a drink of water."

He grabbed her arms. When she squirmed in protest, he closed his eyes, and he exhaled in one long, steady stream, but didn't let go.

"Didn't you hear what I said?" his voice was suddenly as soft as a priest's in the confessional. "Despite your past and the arrest warrants and whatever else I don't even know about yet, I love you. I want you. And God help me, I need you."

"I think maybe you should take some time to process everything that's happened to you," she said slowly, carefully, her eyes shifting away from his. "You're not in your right mind. I heard you quit the force."

Releasing her arms, he stepped back with a sigh. "Word travels. Yeah, I quit. Hardly a surprise."

"It was to me."

"Oh, really? What kind of detective doesn't notice the cousin he grew up with is a serial killer? I couldn't go back."

She paused and brought her eyes back to his face. "You can't blame yourself."

"I'm not here to talk about that. I'm here for you."

She nodded once. "Okay. So what does that mean exactly?"

"It means I want us to be together."

Her heart soared, but still the voice in her head urged caution. "I want that too, more than I can tell you, but I don't see how. Once you've recovered from the shock of Tony, you'll keep remembering all the things I've done and the warrants. How will you be okay with that?"

"Because in my heart, I believe you're a good, decent person who was led astray from an early age. Now you've become the person you were always meant to be. The details of the past can be dealt with in time."

"And that's all? Who cares about the rest of it?" She shook her head. "You're a cop. It's going to fester and eventually tear us apart."

"You forget, I'm not on the force anymore. It's no longer my job to chase down thieves."

Her hand flew to her mouth, and she stepped back. "Did you quit for me? Please tell me that's not why."

His eyes, soft now, stayed steady on her face. "I'm not gonna lie. It was definitely part of it. But honestly, I can't stomach going back. At least not right now. It's hard to say if I'll ever want to. All I know is I'm not living my life without you. The rest I'll have to figure out."

The trembling started deep in her core and increased like an earthquake. "I don't know what to say. What to do," she said, her breath coming in gasps.

"Tell me you want me too. Tell me you can't live without me. Tell me yes."

She stared at him while the first tear rolled down her cheek. He was such a good man. Maybe a little broken in places after the events of the past few weeks, but still stronger than anyone she'd ever known.

She trusted him. Believed in him. And she loved him with all her heart.

"Of course, I want you," she hiccupped. "Absolutely and completely."

Stepping up to her, he framed her face with his hands. "Okay," he breathed before placing his lips on hers.

This kiss was tender and sweet and felt like a prayer.

"I think a reunion might be in order," she said once they drew apart.

His smile flashed as brightly as sunlight. "I could get on board with that. As it happens, I have some time right now. Come to think of it, for the foreseeable future, I have nothing but time."

Grabbing his hand, she turned to the stairs but groaned when the driveway sensor signaled from the kitchen. "Crap, I forgot about UPS. Give me five minutes. Why don't you go on up? I'll be there before you know it."

He shook his head and turned toward the front door. "I can wait. Besides, I think I'd better go out and check my car. Make sure no one stole the license plate. I hear it's been happening all over town."

She glanced at him and seeing the amusement in his eyes, slapped at his arm. "So that's how it's going to be?"

"Looks like. I love you, Mia."

"I love you too. So much. Now scat and let me get the orders sent. While you're out there, could you grab the containers from my Escape? Later, after I've had my way with you, I've got some unpacking to do."

"Funny you should mention it. I have some stuff in my car too. I guess we can unpack together?"

She shot him a smile over her shoulder. "Sounds like a plan."

"A lifetime plan," he agreed.

The End

Other Books By This Author

Valentine's Heart: **Heart Series Prequel Novella** – Available Now

What the Heart Wants: **Heart Series Book One** – Available Now

Drawing from the Heart: **Heart Series Book Two** – Available Now

Feeding the Heart: **Heart Series Book Three** – Available Now

Acknowledgements

To my husband and sister, first readers and solid support team.

To my publishing team. Kathy Case, editor extraordinaire. Your ongoing encouragement means the world to me. Robin Ludwig, for creating an absolutely beautiful cover. Carol Eastman (The Blurb Bitch) for making my book sound so fantastic if I hadn't written it, I'd want to read it, too.

About the Author

Hello there. My name is Marion Myles. I haven't always been a writer. I spent the first few decades of my life as a professional equestrian and travelled across North America training horses and competing at horse shows.

Aside from horses, I've had an enduring love affair with the written word. My reading interests run the gamut from mystery to fantasy to general fiction and even young adult. But when it comes right down to it, my heart definitely lies in the romance section.

When not riding or writing, I devote any spare moments to battling a debilitating addiction to Smarties and stalking my favourite authors on the internet. I'm proud to say there are currently no restraining orders filed against me.

I live in Southern Ontario with my beloved dachshund and my husband (also very much beloved!)

I'd love to hear from you so please drop me a line by email: marion@marionmyles.com.

Marion Myles

Printed in Great Britain
by Amazon